A proud father of 3 daughters, Simone Jackson, Kendall Jackson and LaJasmine Jackson. Oldest daughter, LaJasmine Monique Jackson was a victim of a homicide on December 1, 2019. (RIP)

Born in Pine Bluff, AR, raised in Ardmore, OK and Plain Dealing, LA, Seldon Jamaal enlisted in the United States Marine Corps on October 31, 1995. Reaching the top grade in the Marine Corps (E-9), Master Gunnery Sergeant Jackson is still serving.

Seldon became a member of IOTA PHI THETA fraternity in the fall of 2007. After receiving his Diploma from Plain Dealing High School, he continued his education, graduating from Northwood University (summa cum laude) in 2014 with a Bachelors in Business Administration. In 2019, he graduated from Florida Institute of Technology with Masters in Human Resources Management.

After years of shopping his first novel "Done with the Chase" to publishing companies, he decided to begin the process of starting his own publishing company. Founded in 2019 by Seldon, Thre3Point Press will publish his first novel on August 21, 2020.

DONE WITH THE CHASE

Dedicated to the Memory of

LaJasmine Monique Jackson

June 6, 2001   -   December 1, 2019

#LLJ

SELDON JAMAAL

This novel is a work of fiction. Names, characters, places, and incidents either are the product of the author's imagination or are used fictitiously, and any resemblance to actual persons, living or dead, business establishments, events, or locales is entirely coincidental.

Copyright © 2020 by Seldon Jackson

All rights reserved. No part of this book may be reproduced, scanned, or distributed in any printed or electronic form without permission.

ISBN: 978-1-7350572-0-0

Published by:
Thre3Point Press
1501 Arnold Avenue
Fort Worth, TX 76127

Visit our website at: www.thre3pointpress.com
Instagram: 3point_press
Facebook: Thre3pointpress
Twitter: JamaalJ07869548

Story by: Seldon Jamaal
Cover concept by Rudi_design / Seldon Jamaal
Cover design/layout by Rudy_design

Chapter 1

There are twenty seconds left in a heated rivalry game. The home team (Pine Grove Bulldogs) lead the visiting (Hidden Valley Rams) by two points. The Rams have the ball, one timeout remaining, and are within yards of their kicker's field goal range. Having the best kicker in the state, gaining a few more yards would allow the visiting team a chance to kick the game winning field goal.

It is third down and one on the home team forty yard line; and with a quarterback sneak up the middle the Rams get the first down and hurry back to the line of scrimmage to spike the ball in order to save their final timeout with eleven seconds remaining on the clock. Wanting to get in better field goal range the Rams line up for what should be their last play before a game winning field goal attempt.

With their best wide receiver and playmaker (known as Bump) lined up wide left, the Bulldogs know they will be trying to get him the ball. To counter they send Demyre (known as DJ), who is their best player and cover man to match up with him. Bump (whose known on and off the field as having a bad temper) and DJ (who has a reputation for getting into numerous altercations on and off the field); have been battling and jaw jacking the entire game. They now line up opposite each other to determine what could be a key play of the game.

The ball is snapped, and DJ is locked on his man one on one. Bump runs up field and begins a slant to the inside. DJ seeing the move to the inside know they have run this play earlier in the game and uses his instincts to jump the play. As the quarterback releases the ball, DJ has already read the play and cuts in front of Bump intercepting the ball forcing the Rams to use their final time out.

Frustrated and upset, Bump kicks and spits on DJ as he is lying on the ground after intercepting the ball. Without hesitation DJ jumps to his feet and charges him, ripping off his helmet while simultaneously picking him up and slamming him to the field.

As the players from both sides run to the fight, DJ repeatedly punches Bump in the face before being separated. As they are being held back DJ continues to scream "you don't know where you at homey! You don't know who you ran up on! That's a wrap for you once we get out these gates"! The referees and coaches from each team continue their attempt to separate the two at which time DJ's anger increases.

Noticing the escalating situation DJ's brother (Kevon) comes from the stands to calm him down. DJ, "calm down lil bro. Don't let another person control your actions!" Kevon exclaims. "I ain't trying to hear that; wait til we get in the parking lot, I'ma give it to that clown", DJ responds.

The two are finally separated and both are ejected from the game and sent to the locker room. After the melee has been controlled the referees restart the game and the Bulldogs snap and kneel the ball to run out the remaining time and secure the victory for the home team.

Once the final whistle blows the players retire to their locker rooms. Understanding his brother, Kevon realizes this situation can get dangerous. Worried for his brother safety he decides to wait outside the gate for him to exit the field.

Waiting on his brother he notices other cars pull into the parking lot. Stunned he looks closer and recognizes one of the guys in the lead car. Continuing to survey the scene the other guys begin to exit the following cars. Anxiously leaning back in his seat, it dawns on him that those guys are members of the "Chopdown Boyz".

Moments after the cars pull up, he observes, "Bump" run from the visiting locker room to the lead car and engage into conversation with a few of the guys. With prior knowledge of the ChopDown Boyz and their violent reputation, Kevon's anxiety heightens, as his primary focus becomes getting his brother out of this situation and keeping him safe.

Suddenly yelling comes from the home locker room, "it's on now, we bout to see where this coward's heart at!" DJ screams as team members and coaches follow him to the parking lot attempting to calm him down. Immediately upon seeing Bump and without any regard to his surroundings, DJ begins to run towards him. Knowing the danger of the situation Kevon grabs his brother and asks for assistance from the team members to get him to his car.

Seeing the altercation that's about to take place, security begins to clear the parking lot. Recognizing a police officer whose assisting in escorting Bump and the members of the gang away from the school, Kevon's apprehension begins to decrease.

Now in the car with his brother, DJ sees Bump riding away and yells, "He leaving, let's go! What you waiting on!" Signaling to the coaches and teammates that he will take care of DJ, Kevon listens to DJ's rant and watches the cars leave the parking lot. Once clear he drives him home.

Breaking the silence in the car on their drive home Kevon asks, "why do you always have to prove something all the time?" With a grimacing voice, DJ responds, "Everybody not a square like you." After a few seconds he continues, "I'ma see that dude, he gone get his, you betta believe it!"

Flustered Kevon attempts to convince him to let it go. "Those guys are dangerous lil bro, sometimes you have to know when to go and when to stay. You have to trust me on this one. Let it go!" Kevon exults hoping to get through to him.

Balling his hands into a fist, he becomes angry yelling "They better be worried about me. You think I'm a damn square like you? This clown better be worried about me". Comprehending that he is not getting through to his brother they embark upon silence. Driving home Kevon fears that the situation will only get worse.

Looking in DJ's direction he sighs "Bro not sure why you think I'm square, but I'll take that over being dead." Directing his eyes back on the road he continues "You may not think so, but I know how the streets work."

Catching DJ's attention, he sarcastically jests "Whatever, Not trying to hear all that." Becoming agitated Kevon abruptly replies "I try to keep you safe DJ. I know out here in these streets, *that you can't be to clean! I know being to clean can make you weak and yeah, sometimes you gotta get dirty to stay clean.*"

Glaring with a confused look DJ mocks "What the hell does that even mean? You just spitting nonsense that I ain't tryna hear right now." Shaking his head in frustration he responds "Ok DJ. You don't understand or appreciate it now but one day you will get it, I'm done talking." Throwing his arms up in disgust he counters "You think I care? I've been done listening."

Chapter 2

Pine Grove, Louisiana has slowly begun to recover from its history of violence, crime, and racism to become one of the more prosperous and diverse economies in the state. Spear heading the rise in economic stature has been the popularity of the cities high school and college sports teams. Boasting some of the best sports protégés in the state, basketball and football games have become sell out events in the city.

The popularity of these sports bolsters the local economy from the boost in revenue it receives from the sold-out games. As a result, families have begun to move into the city realizing the potential of the sports programs and how they can benefit their children and families.

Professional scouts, sports agents, and merchandising companies have also flocked to the city. All have come with hopes of recruiting, signing, or finding their next star athlete. With basketball athletes having the ability to make the leap from high school to the National Basketball Association (NBA), news reporters frequent each event seeking the opportunity to break the story of the next sports phenom.

With so much interest in these athletes, companies sponsor events and donate to the schools in the hopes of developing good relationships so that not only school officials but also coaches and families assist in their recruiting and contract signing efforts.

As a result of the success the city has garnered from its sports teams, Kevon and Demyre have become local celebrities because of their athletic abilities and accomplishments.

Brothers born in Pine Grove, Louisiana. Their African American father who was a popular two sport athlete (football and basketball) was murdered when they were both in elementary school. They were raised by their Spanish mother, Roberta, who became a part time caregiver to support her sons after her husband was murdered.

At twenty years old, Kevon is the older of the two brothers. Standing six foot four, dark skinned, and two hundred pounds with a toned shape, he has become a standout basketball player. At a young age he took pride in his appearance. He was always well dressed and well groomed.

Witty and charming he is also a lady's man but tends to focus more on his family and friendships vice putting his time and effort into the young ladies that flock to him. He accepted a basketball scholarship to the local university. This meant passing up numerous national scholarships and an opportunity to make the leap to the NBA to become a star shooting guard in his second year of college.

Now in his junior year of high school, DJ didn't follow in his brother's footsteps as a basketball star but instead excelled on the football field as well as track. Since the fifth grade he has been the fastest and most athletic kid in his class. In high school he set state and national records in the high jump as well as the one and two hundred-meter dashes.

Applying his skill to football allowed him to achieve all-state honors as cornerback, and kick returner in his freshman and sophomore years of high school while also being a standout wide receiver. The national recognition he has received as a junior has enabled him to become the bone fide star on the football team.

At one hundred ninety pounds, six feet one inch tall, a light skinned complexion with a muscular build, DJ has grown tired of sports. Choosing to spend more time with his friends and hanging out in the streets than in training has altered his demeanor.

Once a scholar in the classroom his grades have taken a decline. The shift in his grades and demeanor starts to affect his associations. Refraining from sports team events and academic activities he has begun to spend more time with his street affiliates.

Unlike his brother who caters to the casual, preppy look, DJ is normally wearing baggy sweats, a hoody, or a plain T-shirt with sneakers. Not much of a social person and always displaying an inability to show respect to women he has never been in any serious relationship but instead engages in an openly promiscuous lifestyle.

His risky and violent behavior has become obvious in his personal life and is beginning to take a toll on the direction of his future.

Unfortunately, with the success of the cities sports teams it has also created a market for corruption in the form of gambling, boosting, bribes and payoffs. For the athletes and families this market puts pressure on them and places them in the middle of the sports money grab.

Financial incentive and outright criminal activity drive this market. Gambling has taken on a much more sinister role in the last few years. Bookies, crooked city officials, and top gang members solicit, bribe and in the most extreme circumstances coerce athletes to take financial profits for "throwing or fixing" games.

Chapter 3

A couple weeks after the football game in which DJ got into an altercation with Bump, Kevon decides to track down his brother and have a conversation about how he's feeling now that he's had time to calm down.

DJ looks down at his phone and sees that Kevon is calling; feeling agitated and not wanting to talk to him he pushes the ignore button and continues cutting hair. Seconds later DJs phone rings again and he sees that it is Kevon calling a second time.

He tells his customer to give him a second as he picks up the call "What!" shocked at how he answered the phone Kevon responds "DJ, Be easy bro. Just checking up on you. Where you at? I'm trying to get up with you! I haven't seen or heard from you in over a week".

In a dismissive tone DJ says, "I'm at the barber shop, what do you want?" Noticing that his brother is still upset Kevon asks "Are you getting a cut? I'm bout to come through, I want to holla at you about something." In a rush to get back to his customer DJ says "You know I cut my own hair, so why would I be getting a cut! I'm working here now!"

Taking the phone from his ear he contemplates hanging up before getting back on the phone saying "I'll be here for a few more hours if you need a cut or want to come through", after the brief conversation DJ doesn't give Kevon a chance to respond to his last comment and quickly hangs up the phone.

With thoughts of wanting to blow up on DJ for his disrespectful attitude toward him, Kevon understands that he has to keep his emotions in check as it will only serve as a setback to their broken relationship in which he is attempting to repair.

Dealing with the crooked sports market, gangs and vindictive individuals in Pine Grove, Kevon has personal experiences of the problems his brother could end up facing. His intent is to figure out a way to make him understand that his intentions are genuine and only in his best interests.

He also intends on warning him of the trouble that is ahead of him if he continues down the road he is going. On his way to the barber shop Kevon ponders of ways to communicate to DJ the dangers of individuals that want to take advantage of him, the ones whom want to use him for what he can do for them, as well as exploit his athletic talents.

Pulling up, Kevon notices how packed it is in the barber shop. As he enters, he blurts "It must be free hair cut day up in here today." Looking up and seeing that Kevon is joking around, one of the barbers replies, "If these haircuts are free, I'm about to stop cutting right now!" Everyone in the barbershop laughs at the comments and daps up Kevon as he moves to the back of the shop toward D'Js booth.

As the only one not laughing at the comments, DJ looks up and tells Kevon "I got about four in front of you, you can wait or come back in about two hours." Frustrated at the greeting he gets from DJ, he responds "I'll wait. I don't need a cut today I'm letting it grow out. Just wanted to catch up with you before you bounced for the day". Not acknowledging his comment, DJ keeps cutting hair as Kevon takes a seat near his booth and begins to joke around with some of the customers he knows.

Over three hours later he finishes up with his last customer. As he is putting away his equipment, DJ looks over and sees Kevon still sitting and waiting. He begins to feel ashamed of the way he has been treating his big brother. Not being one to apologize or admit fault, DJ instead decides to appease Kevon by listening to what he has to say.

Being the last barber in the shop, DJ begins to close the shop and yells over to Kevon "I'm bout to ride out Kay (DJ's nickname for Kevon), what's up!" Startling him from his daze, Kevon gets up and walks over to his booth and asks, "So how long you been working here?" Letting out a sigh DJ responds, "Is this what was so important that you had to talk to me about?" after a brief silence he goes on "I been here for about two weeks!

I got kicked out of school for the fight remember. So, I had to do something." Shaking his head, Kevon replies "Why do you always run to the wrong place when things get hot? There are other places you know you can go to for peace."

Looking over seeing he is still agitated, Kevon continues "but anyway I wanted to talk to you about that fight situation. I talked with the coach and the principal and they will let you back into school and onto the team. There's a catch. You must agree to apologize to the team, write a paper on the negative outcomes of fighting, alternatives to fighting, why a person should not be fighting, and then serve a two game suspension from the football team".

Looking confused DJ yells "Apologize! Apologize for what? Didn't you see the fight?" Not knowing how to respond Kevon just looks at DJ as he continues "I don't have a damn thing to apologize for. I guess I was supposed to sit up there and let that clown spit on me and kick me? What kinda sucka shyt is that?"

Sensing DJ's anger increasing, Kevon decides to just let him vent. He then says "You right DJ, nobody saying to be a push over, but it's done and over with. You still have a chance to be something great on the football field, on the track, or both. You got a chance to do whatever you want to do --- for real lil bro, you also know you can make good grades when you want to".

Noticing that DJ is tuning him out and beginning to get upset, Kevon gestures for him to calm down and just listen as he continues "What is your move? You gone run the streets, be a trap boy or something?" Before he can respond, he goes on "I am telling you ain't nothing out there besides trouble and these dudes and chicks don't give a damn about you especially if you ain't doing something for them."

Trying to calm down, DJ says "First of all, I'm not done with that dude. I was trying to forget about it for a minute and get money but you wanna bring it up". Interrupting him, Kevon retorts "Hold on! Calm down! All I'm saying is getting back at him is not going to get you anywhere but getting back in school and on the team will benefit you."

Trying to get his attention he goes on "So screw all that other crap that people will try to shoot at you and do what's best for you --- Besides, at the end of the day if you go through with what I'm telling you, you'll be back on the team by the homecoming game. You know the scouts, and everyone will be there".

Seeing that the conversation is going in a direction that he did not intend, Kevon tries to change the subject. "You know we are playing one of the best basketball teams in the state on Friday? You coming through?" Obviously upset from the previous conversation, DJ doesn't respond. Instead, he continues to get his things together so that he can close up the shop and leave.

In an attempt to diffuse what he has started Kevon remarks "DJ you know I love you lil bro and don't want anything to happen to you. You may not believe it, but I've been out there and know what goes on. I'm coming to you because you at the crossroads right now. You can get through these next couple years and get into college and away from this place.

If not, you will get caught up with what everyone else is doing. If you choose to get caught up in the negative stuff, I guarantee you will regret it and years down the road you'll still be doing the same thing everyone else is doing in these streets." Disappointed that DJ isn't listening, he continues "Trust me everything they doing out in them streets right now they will always be doing. You have a chance to do something better. Do you really want to do be out there?"

Continuing to pack his things and close the shop, DJ is still not responding to Kevon's comments. Feeling he has gotten everything off his chest, Kevon thanks him for the time he gave him and says, "I'll be looking for you at the game".

As he leaves out the door, Kevon says "You don't have to respond, just think about what I said. If you don't listen to anything else I tell you, make sure you are always paying attention. You learn more by listening than talking. So be quick to listen and slow to talk." Walking toward the door he glances back and bellows "Also DJ, these dudes out here gone tell you what you want to hear to get you to do what they want you to do. Pay attention."

Chapter 4

"Come on Pickles, the game bout to start. Coach about to get pissed" Kevon tells Kasyn (nickname Pickles) as he is finishing up a phone conversation on his cell phone. Kasyn has been Kevon's best friend since elementary school. Kasyn is now at six foot two, one hundred and ninety-five pounds, dark skinned, with a muscular build. He has recovered from a permanent high school basketball suspension by walking on and earning a starting role on the same college basketball team Kevon plays on.

Playing basketball together growing up Kasyn was always a better basketball player than Kevon. However, after being out of the spotlight for years and unable to be recruited he is now in the shadows of Kevon. He has worked hard on his basketball game, has earned recognition as the star of the team, and the talk of the town.

In one of the biggest games of the year with NBA scouts in attendance there is not only team pressure to win a game versus one of the best teams in the state but also individual pressure for athletes to highlight why they are candidates to play at the next level.

As the game is about to tip off Kevon looks in the stands for DJ as he is usually his biggest supporter and motivation to play at a high level. Continuing to scan the crowd he does not see his brother however he catches a glimpse of Fannah and her friend Chasity who are both waving in his direction.

He grins slightly and waves back with excitement that Fannah is in the crowd but is disappointed that DJ is not in attendance. After gazing in the audience for a moment longer hoping to see DJ, he notices Kasyn running from the locker room toward the huddle and he trots behind him.

During the first half of the game Kasyn is in a zone. He has scored 22 of his team's 51 points as his team enters half time winning by a score of 51 to 49. Kevon leaves the court heading toward the locker room with his head down sulking from his disappointing first half performance.

He missed 8 out of 10 shots ending the half with only 5 points and 0 assists in a game that he was expected to be a key contributor. Seeing his low confidence, Fannah yells to Kevon as he walks toward the locker room "Keep your head up Kevon, you'll get it going, you always bounce back"! Walking behind Kevon, Kasyn hears Fannah's voice of encouragement and yells back toward her "don't worry, I got his back"!

As the coach gives his halftime speech Kevon sits at his locker and starts to think about his brother, his past, his future, his horrible first half performance and the NBA scouts. He then starts to enter a momentary state of depression. Suddenly, Fannah's voice enters his mind and his thoughts drift toward her encouraging words. He starts to hold on to her words and tune out all other distractions.

The third quarter begins and Kasyn starts by missing his first five shots and turning the ball over three times as the team quickly falls behind ten points. Kevon takes charge of the game and reels off ten points in the last few minutes to close out the third quarter on a run to tie the game 70 to 70.

Yelling uncontrollable in the stands during Kevon's ten-point run, Fannah screams "I told you! I told you! Keep going! I told you that you would bounce back!" Looking over toward Fannah and then the NBA scouts Kasyn thinks to himself that he has to do more in the final quarter of the game.

Being the shooting guard, Kevon must depend on Kasyn, who is the point guard, to get him in the game. Before the fourth quarter begins the coach lets Kasyn know that the offense will run through Kevon since he has the hot hand. Feeling he can resume his hot shooting spree from the first half and despite what the coach instructed, Kasyn comes out in the fourth quarter shooting on the first four possessions.

He misses on all four, with each shot selection being worse than the last. Noticing that their team is out of sync the visiting team takes advantage and scores on each of Kasyn's missed shots on fast break points.

Now down eight points with seven minutes left in the game the coach calls a time out. In the huddle Kevon seems irritated and says, "swing the ball Pickles, I'll hit the shot, I'm on right now". Not responding Kasyn nods his head.

As they break the huddle the coach reminds Kasyn to run the offense through Kevon. As the minutes tick away, Kasyn finally begins to run the offense through Kevon. He immediately responds by reeling off three consecutive three pointers and putting the team ahead by one point.

With a win within reach, the coach reminds the players that they are up by one point and there are only forty-five seconds remaining in the game. He instructs everyone that the team is holding the ball for one final shot. Hearing the chants for Kevon coming from the crowd, Kasyn decides to drive to the rim and seal the game.

He attempts to split two defenders and has the ball stolen with twenty seconds remaining. The visiting team goes the length of the floor and scores on a fast break taking a one-point lead with ten seconds remaining. With no timeouts Kevon quickly inbounds the ball to Kasyn. He runs the length of the court and finds an open spot in the corner.

The team leaves him open. Confident he can hit the shot Kevon begins to wave his arms and calls for Kasyn to pass the ball with gesturing that no one is guarding him. Sprinting down the floor with the ball, Kasyn is double teamed as soon as he crosses mid court.

With three seconds remaining and Kevon open in the corner waiving for the ball, Kasyn decides instead to split the double team which frees him up for a three-point shot. Pulling up and releasing as time expires, the crowd becomes silent as everyone watches the ball soar through the air toward the rim.

The ball hits the rim breaking the silence. As it rolls around the rim everyone anxiously looks on as this will decide the outcome of the game. The ball rolls off the rim and hits the court as the buzzer goes off. Looking at the missed shot and the ball hitting the court, Kevon looks at Kasyn in shock while he sits on the floor with his head buried in his hands.

Chapter 5

In the city of Pine Grove after a loss by one of its sports teams there is a somber feeling across the entire city. This Saturday had an even gloomier vibe than usual as the college basketball team lost a close game to one of the best teams in the nation the day prior.

As the sound of clippers cutting hair fills the air in the barber shop, missing was the usual laughter and jokes of the customers and barbers. Looking over at DJ, one of the barbers yells to his booth "DJ why didn't they give the ball to your brother? He was on fire in the second half! ---- he could've ended that game!"

Breaking the silence, in a dim voice DJ mumbles "I don't know, I wasn't at the game." Sensing his dismissive demeanor, the barber continues to cut his customers hair and doesn't add to the conversation.

Suddenly, the barber shop begins to rattle from loud banging noises which become increasingly louder and louder and as the noise seemingly gets closer, pulsating thumps accompany the rattling.

After a while, the rattling stops, and the pulsating fades away and moments later Terrail (nickname Trail) walks into the shop with two females tagging along. Both females are scantily dressed. The customers and barbers are taken aback as they can't take their eyes off of the ladies.

The taller of the two is wearing a tight-fitting white halter top, which shows off her slim waist. She also has on short, tight fitting, white mini shorts that hugs to her body outlining her petite curvy five-foot, nine-inch body frame. She has long hazel hair flowing down her back and a beautiful light skin complexion matched by gorgeous facial features with gorgeous, hypnotizing, light brown eyes.

Immediately catching DJ's attention is the other lady's big booty. She is dark skinned, curvy, and five feet, four inches tall. Dressing a little more conservative compared to her friend, she is wearing pink yoga pants with a fitted gray v-neck crop top. Despite her more casual look, her attire manages to reveal her eye-catching physique. She has black curly hair which highlight her juicy pink lips. Her dark brown eyes give her an innocent look as they give off a calming and gentle sensation.

Trail, who owns the barber shop is a twenty-three-year-old, six foot five, two-hundred and thirty-pound, former Pine Grove basketball and football superstar. Trail is a dark skin, heavy set guy who physically is not known as an attractive guy.

Although, his charming personality, seductive conversation and financial success allows him to keep the company of the most gorgeous ladies and some of the most successful men in the city. In recent years he has also become known as an "OG" (original gangsta) who younger guys look up to because of his status and street credibility.

Dapping up all the customers and barbers as he moves towards DJs booth, a barber shouts "Trail what in the world was all that noise outside"? Pausing for a moment surveying the barber shop he laughs "I just upgraded. That's them six, twelves beating up the block"!

Watching Trail's entrance with the women and noticing that he is dressed in designer clothing, and wearing three hundred dollar sneakers with glistening jewelry around his neck to go along with his nice watch and car, DJ stands in awe as he watches him approach his booth.

Holding his hand out for a handshake Trail jokes "What up DJ?" Looking down at his hand he jokes "How long you gone leave me hanging Bro". Snapping out of his daze DJ returns the handshake and quickly responds "My bad Terrail, been busy my G, trying to get these customers taken care of".

Noticing that DJ is somewhat nervous, Trail calms him by saying "Relax playboy, you at home. Call me Trail." Releasing the handshake, he goes on "I see you doing yo thang, I just wanted to check on ya and see how this gig working out for ya and chop it up for a minute." Nodding in acknowledgement DJ lays down his clippers and asks his customer to give him a minute. "Naw, naw playa", Trail interrupts, "Get at me when you finish up---me, and the girls will be in the lounge area".

Making his barber shop stand out from the rest, Trail added a lounge area that features a bar, a DJ, and food where special guests can go for drinks, listen to music or just wait their turn for a haircut and get something to eat while they wait.

Not wanting to keep Trail waiting DJ finishes up his last appointment and has another barber take care of his walk ins. Making his way to the lounge area the two females that are with Trail are standing by the bar area.

Not being able to control himself he begins to stare at the ladies. His attention quickly diverts to the lady in the pink yoga pants. Noticing that she isn't as excited to be there as her friend he continues to walk through the lounge. Unaware that they have noticed him staring DJ continues to gaze at the dark skin lady in the yoga pants.

Watching him stumble around the lounge area, Trail takes note of DJ's interest in the dark skin lady in the yoga pants. Catching his attention, he waves over in his direction gesturing for him to join him at his table. Still in a daze he finally notices Trail signaling him toward his table and makes his way over.

"You like that huh!" snickers Trail. Seeming unsure of what to say DJ ponders his next thought and after not having a response for the comment Trail continues "Shawty with the pink yoga pants nice...that's your style huh bruh?"

with a devious giggle he goes on "I can put you on if that's your thing".

Finally becoming comfortable, DJ counters "Yeah man, that's nice work right there...that is what I need in my life." Grinning and shaking his head in agreeance, he snickers "Well say no more my guy, I got you! I'mma tell you like this though, don't be tryna fall in love with this broad, she a jump off ya feel me".

He walks over and whispers in the lady wearing the pink yoga pants ear and points over to DJ. Frowning before he completes his request, she leans away from Trail. Looking back at DJ he gestures to give him a minute as he walks over and talks with the lady in the white shorts. Shortly after the conversation, she leans over and whispers to her friend in the pink yoga pants.

Receptive to her comments she looks toward DJ, makes eye contact, and waves in his direction. Feeling a little awkward he returns the wave as Trail returns to the table. "You in there lil homey." Dapping him up, he sits and bursts "but on sum real shyt though I heard about what happened at your game the other day---I want to straighten that out for you!" Confused about the sudden change of topic DJ quips, "You really showing some luv big homey. Is it really like this? I mean everyone wants something right? Why you looking out for me?"

Seeing where he is going with the conversation, Trail cuts him off, "You a real dude and real recognize real, ya feel me? Plus, you from my hood...I surround myself with real dudes like you and in turn I step it up to show you I am a real dude you can rock with --- shhhh, we take care of each other no matter what and no matter who bro! This all real lil homey, I don't do the fake and fraud type stuff, I know your boyz already told you about me, all real, all day with me, bro".

Reclined in his chair, Trail raises his arms toward DJ as to gesture whether he's going to be down with him or not. Feeling good about the situation DJ looks around the room, at the nice establishment, at the girls and then at Trail with a sense of comfort and support.

Moments later he ascends from his chair without notice and walks over to greet a seated Trail. Holding out his hand in acceptance Trail reciprocates the greeting by rising from his chair and by-passing the handshake as they both embrace in a mutual hug.

Several minutes into the hug Trail pulls away and jokes "Let us not be getting all soft up in here G." Slapping him on the chest he remarks "We in there. Whatever you need I got you. I'm about to go put you on ole girl. Oh, and just so you know, the barbershop a safe zone. I got security cameras all over this place.

Smirking he cracks "So if you trying to do some oochie coochie stuff, or something like that, you may want to take her somewhere else." Laughing he taps him on the shoulder continuing "I'll go send her your way."

Chapter 6

As Kevon drives Kasyn home after the game they embark upon an awkward silence in which both await the other to express what they are thinking. Feeling guilty, Kasyn peeks over at Kevon trying to figure out what he can say to try and explain his actions at the end of the game without seeming insincere.

Reluctantly, Kasyn murmurs "Are you just not going to talk on what happened?" Pausing he gets no response and continues "Fam I was trying to look out for you man---you bounced back in that game and I didn't want you to mess it up by risking the chance to miss the game winning shot."

Looking over at him in a puzzled gaze, he finally responds "DUDE! That makes absolutely no sense at all!", "the scouts were out there and I needed to show that I'm clutch...make or miss I needed to show that I wasn't afraid to take THE shot!" after a slight frustrated hesitation, he takes a deep breath "Plus I was on! I was on dude! YOU of all people know I don't miss when I'm on like that!"

Seeing his frustration being elevated by the conversation Kasyn decides to change the subject. With a smirk, he retorts "Soooo, I see you had a fan rooting you on tonight huh? What's up with her? I didn't know you all were kicking it." Sensing he wouldn't get a response; he looks out the window as they continue to drive. Understanding the anger Kevon is exhibiting he suppresses the urge to probe for an answer.

With guilt overcoming him, Kasyn decides to break the silence and carry on a conversation alone. Hoping that something he says will elicit a response he taps on his shoulder bellowing "KV! We been rocking since the first grade; you know I wouldn't mess you over big dawg. You know I've always had your back."

Trying to catch eye contact he goes on "I'm not going to let a basketball game come in between our friendship. We like brothers and you know that."....but on some real talk, I heard that Bump, the dude your brother got into it with at the football game, is down with Prince and you know how that dude get down".

Calming down with the thought of his brother's safety being at risk he looks over and ask, "Wait. What did you just say?" Relieved that he has attention he responds, "You know we been tight since we were little boys and you know I wouldn't try to play you." Disturbed he interrupts "No. I'm not talking about none of that. What did you just say about my brother?"

Taken aback he replies, "Well from what I hear them Chop Down Boyz want it with DJ." Hesitant after noticing Kevon's reaction of alarm he pauses before proceeding "Bump was on the hook to win that homecoming game,

but your brother came on the scene and got in the way"
Shaking his head he goes on, "You need to put DJ on game
so he can work it off or they gone be coming for him."

Curious he questions "So Chop Down coming for my
brother? How do you know that Pickles?" Stunned he
evasively replies "Are you even listening to me. I just told
you this is what I heard. The streets be talking." With the
trust unraveling Kevon calmly responds "So that's what you
heard huh Pickles? So where were you when all that went
down after the homecoming game?"

Feeling cornered he snaps "What you trying to say KV?
I'm here trying to help you out. I don't know what you on
but if you got something you want to say just say it. I don't
have anything to hide." Playing it cool, he decides to mask
his true sentiments in an attempt to find out what is going
on.

Choosing to focus on what Kasyn has disclosed he
counters "My brother does not have anything to do with
none of this and I'm definitely not about to put him on
game. I know how this work and you can forget it."
Nodding in agreeance he replies, "I hear you, but you
already know how the game go, once you in, you in."
Attempting to convince him he continues "I keep telling
you I'm on your side, you know what I been through for
you and that's why I'm trying to tell you how to get out of
this."

Becoming angry he quips "What are you talking about!"
After a slight hesitation he goes on "Don't start trying to
throw stuff up in my face! We all knew what it was when we
got into it and now, I'm out! I been out!" His voice getting
louder "You know why I came to this school. I had
scholarships to the Big Universities! I could have gone
straight to the NBA. You know that!

Banging his hands on the steering wheel he affirms "I paid
for my part in what happened and I'm done with the game
and my brother not about to get tied up in something he
doesn't have anything to do with." Reclining in his seat and
taking on a more serene mood he mutters "Alright KV, I
got you. I'll leave it alone. I'm just trying to put you on and
let you know what is going on that's all. Just trying to help,
that's it. So, I'll fall back."

After a tense silence Kasyn decides to vent. "KV, since
you don't want to talk about what your brother has gotten
into let's talk about the basketball game...I will tell you like
this, you not the only one who can ball and you not the only
one scouts can come and see, you might want to get your
head out of the clouds. Just because you got females
coming to see you ball and everyone on your nuts that don't
make you special! Here I am trying to be a friend and bring
you the word from the streets about your brother and you
think it is ok to pop off on me?"

Not moved by his antics Kevon listens on as Kasyn
continues to rant "Think about it, I don't have anything to
gain by telling you what's going down. I have had your back

from jump, but you seem to have forgotten all of that. Since you are one to always use quotes remember the one that says those who forget their past are doomed to repeat it"!

Finally fed up with his tantrum Kevon responds, "Are you finished?" because I'll tell you like I've said a million times, I know exactly what I did and I'm well aware of my past. I'm at a damn school I didn't want to be at. Jealous dudes taking jabs at me behind my back every time they get a chance, and I get new friends damn near every day who are just trying to be cool with me because of what they think they can get! I was born at night but not last night. I know what it is."

Taking a deep breath he goes on "So if you think all of this is something that makes me think that I am special then you are the one who needs to get your head out of the clouds." Breathing heavily, he asks "So what the hell do you want from me PICKLES, huh! You not the only one who sacrificed! I'm out, you hear me, and I won't let DJ get jammed up. You got me bent and if you was a real friend you would respect that."

After a moment he responds "I didn't know you had all that on your mind. My bad, and like I said you can count on me and I'll leave it like that". Reaching his hand out to shake his hand as they pull up to Kasyn's apartment Kevon hesitantly returns the gesture. "It's all good. We have been cool to long to let something like this mess up our friendship. I'll holla at you at practice".

Chapter 7

Looking over toward Trail and the ladies DJ notices that they are engaging in conversation. After a brief moment they look over in his direction at which time he begins to feel an angst that he has never encountered. He can't bring himself to comprehend what this feeling means and how to deal with it.

He feels his heart beating faster and his mind suddenly begins to race as he starts to consider numerous lines and openings that he will say to the lady in the pink yoga pants when he gets a chance to talk to her. Wanting to impress her his emotions begin to run wild and he feels himself beginning to sweat.

Being only familiar with "ratchet" females and groupies who throw themselves at him because of his popularity in sports as well as his notoriety on the streets, DJ has never had to impress a female with intellect nor mentally engage in a conversation in order to win a woman's affection. In his experience, females were the initiator and aggressor. There was very little effort that he needed to exert in order to win them over.

He feels the difference. In the past, he never felt the need or had to pursue a female. Never had to court, date, put in time or even show respect. For him, the women he had been accustomed to felt coveted being in his presence and in turn fought for his affection and attention.

With all his past relationships with women destitute of value and fulfillment he subconsciously lost respect and appreciation for women. Not knowing up until now what he was missing in a desire to have love, fulfillment, and value in a mate.

Before even meeting her, he begins to feel a strong connection. High expectations of this meeting begin to overwhelm him. He becomes nervous wondering if she will have the same mental, emotional, and physical connection as he is feeling for her.

As he fumbles around to catch his composure the lady in the pink yoga pants catches eye contact that makes him anxious all over again. As she approaches, he hears Trail's voice in the background "I'll holla at you DJ! Stop by the court and kick it one day. We hang out and ball out there, it's a good time." Throwing up the peace sign he quips "Just shoot me a text."

Before he can respond, the lady in the pink yoga pants is now standing in front of him with her hand extended. He throws the peace sign back to Trail without verbally responding which prompts Trail and the lady he is with to giggle at how nervous DJ seems as they exit the lounge area of the barber shop.

"I'm Chasity, how are you?" The lady in the pink yoga pants says with her hand still extended. Seeing that he is visibly nervous she continues "Hi, your name is DJ, right?" After another pause DJ comes to himself and finally returns her handshake. "Ahhhh. My bad. I apologize. I am good and my friends call me DJ, but name is Demyre".

With a giggle she replies, "Great so is it okay if I call you DJ?" breaking the ice with her pleasant conversation they both laugh as he gives her a head nod approving her request. "Okay so this has to be the longest handshake in history" she says smiling. Looking down at their still clinched hands he quickly releases and apologizes for the prolonged handshake.

In a sincere tone she says, "you don't seem like the person I thought you were". Taking a step back he goes on the defensive, "So what does that supposed to mean?" Cautious of hitting a nerve apologetically she continues "No, no, I don't mean anything bad by it."

Smiling she goes on "I just heard a lot of things about you and I expected you to maybe be a little aggressive, rude or not have any manners". Becoming more relaxed he nods and acknowledges her response. "So, I can say the same for you. From these few minutes of talking you aren't what I expected either".

Taken aback she smiles "So what exactly did you expect Mr. DJ?" Seeming to come out of his shell he counters "are we being real, or do you just want me to say what you want to hear?" Folding her arms, she cringes her face gesturing for him to finish his comment.

"Well you asked for it so here it goes. But before I start, I will say you are stunning, but those yoga pants are a little fitting and telling Victoria's secret you know."

Seeing a smile on her face he becomes comfortable and continues. "Because you are running around shape showing, I thought you would be dry, shallow, have no morals, lack communication skills, unintelligent, with no sense of humor. You know just a pretty face with a nice waist, but in your case a nice booty too."

In amazement she shakes her head before answering "I appreciate your honesty. You guys are so typical, but I get it, kinda like if you dress like a cop don't get upset when people think you are the police right? Like if you dress sexy, we have to assume guys think we open for business. Is that what you mean DJ?"

Rolling her eyes, she continues "If that's what you think you are wrong Mr. I was being facetious. I don't get that foolishness and furthermore I really don't like to dress like this in public and as a matter of fact I need to go change."

Seeing that the conversation is not going the way he wants it to go DJ quickly changes the subject and before making a bad impression he decides to be slightly aggressive and asks "So do you want to hang out today?"

Hesitantly she says "sure, I guess, why not, but I do have to change, so if you can take me by my apartment it will not take me long and we can go from there". Excited from her response he tells her to give him a second as he rushes back into the barber shop to close his booth.

With his booth closed he hurries back into the lounge to escort her to his car. Opening the passenger door so that she can enter she gives him a look of admiration before she enters the vehicle. Feeling excitement and butterflies that he's never experienced he closes her door and goes to the driver side as they drive to her apartment.

Before he is able to ask her address, she begins to type her address into her phone and says, "If you are like me, I need GPS to get me wherever I am going." She then raises the volume on her phone so that he can hear the directions. Suddenly her phone gives direction prompts, and he pulls off and drives towards her apartment.

While they are driving Chasity suddenly blurts "So I'm confused; tell me how a mild mannered, smart, light skin dude from Pine Grove who is also a sports phenom get a rep for being a gangsta? Because I am not seeing it." Caught off guard by the question he responds "I don't tell people what to think, they chose their own thoughts. I just do me." Looking over at him with a look of disbelief, "really, is that the best you can do?"

Feeling that she is genuinely interested in who he is as a person he starts to open up "seriously though, this athlete, superstar life ain't what it's made out to be. Mentally, physically, and emotionally it breaks you down you know? It's like everyone expects you to do this or do that or be this or be that and if you don't live up to their expectations then you become a disappointment."

Feeling himself able to easily talk to her he continues "Like for real, how do you live up to being the best every day all day? It's like in the streets everyone's the same. You know like it's just an easier life. No one really judging, we just all out there kicking it, having fun, and enjoying life with no expectations, no responsibilities."

Giving him a look of empathy, she nods in agreement as he continues. "Everyone always wants something from me; it's like go to practice, get good grades, you are the man so we depend on you to win the game, you have to win the race; on and on you know and in the end no one asks or cares about what I want. Anyway, I know you didn't want to hear all that but that's my story. So now that you have my life story tell me something about you?"

With a chuckle she proceeds "I think my story is a tad bit longer and a little more complicated and depressing than yours." After hearing no objection from him she proceeds; "I know some people see me as just a good looking female with a fat booty or that I am sexy, fine, blah, blah, blah but because I am friendly and I have guy friends for some reason I always get the label of being a too flirty, or I get hated on and all of the other derogatory things that come with getting attention."

With a more serious look she continues "but truth be told I'm pretty much a virgin and have never been in a relationship. So it gets really frustrating and it is hurtful for people to think of me like that and talk behind my back with such negativity when the only thing I want is to be happy and the people around me to be happy."

Seeing her about to tear up he grabs her hand to comfort her. His mind now thinking back to what Trail said about her he now begins to wonder if she is just running game or has Trail just not taken the time to get to know her. Now massaging her hand to make her feel better he requests her permission to ask a question and with a warm look she acknowledges and motions for him to continue.

"So, I totally understand how you feel about why people perceive you in such a negative manner but why wear clothes like you have on now in public if it's not something you normally do? I mean it definitely fits you right in every way possible but maybe that does play a part in why you have the haters and negativity."

Waiting to see her reaction he goes on "I mean it's like they say. First impressions are lasting ones and like we talked about earlier…she interrupts, "ok, I know, yes I know where you are going with this and here is the answer to your question. Some people are not who they seem, and I am sure you have noticed, Trail loves to stunt, and my girl has been cool with him for some years." Hesitating as she looks down "I have also known him for some time, so my thing is I want to make sure my girl safe you know."

Beginning to sniffle she proceeds "When Trail has a party or something going on, he seems to always contact my friend and I know how that can go sometimes." Gasping "So today he called her up saying he wanted some girls to come hangs out with him, like on some music video type stuff."

Her voice becoming solemn "She likes that kinda stuff, So I told her if she wanted to go that I would go with her. You know you can warn people about people and situations but if they aren't listening to what you are telling them then the only thing you can do is just make sure you do what you can to make sure they are safe."

After another pause, he looks over as he notices the somberness in her voice and sees that she is beginning to tear up. Concerned about the sudden change in demeanor he asks "Are you okay? If this is something that bothers you, you don't have to talk about it. We can talk about something else." Looking up with a grin she sniffles "Thank you. You are sweet. I'll be ok".

They arrive at her apartment and seeming to be in a better mood she says "So it will only take me about 20 to 25 minutes, and I'll be ready. Do you want to come up?" Looking at himself he responds "I live right up the road, so let me go shower and change so that I can get this hair off me from being in the barber shop all day and I'll be right back. Is that okay with you?"

Giving him the thumbs up sign, she trots to her apartment. Remembering that he never got her phone number and has no way to contact her upon his return he yells her name. "Chasity!" looking startled she turns around as he jogs up to her. Thinking in her head that it is much too early for a kiss she waits for him to meet her to find out what's wrong.

"So, you know that I don't have your number, so I wouldn't be able to let you know when I am on the way back." Laughing out loud she asks for his phone and types her number in. Receiving his phone back with her number he meekly says "Thank you, I will text you when I am on the way back" watching her shake her head in agreement he turns and jogs back to his car.

Chapter 8

Sitting in his apartment Trail looks at his phone for several hours before finally picking it up. Taking a deep breath, he dials and anxiously listens as the phone rings. He hopes that he receives no answer. After several rings he anticipates leaving a message. Before the voicemail activates, he hears someone on the other end answer "Hello." The voice immediately puts him in a state of distress.

Without hesitating he responds, "This Trail, how is it going big homey." Sounding a bit agitated the receiver of the call comments "I hope you have some good news for me!" Always exuding confidence despite how he may actually feel Trail responds, "Do I ever let you down?" With a nervous hesitation he proceeds "You just have to give me some time on this one because we have new players to deal with...but I have it under control."

With a shrewd sigh he yells "Look! I don't know and don't care what you have under control, but I'll tell you right now, DO NOT take my kindness for weakness!" Understanding he means business Trail attempts to calm the situation "Prince, relax big homey! You can count on me. I got it all under control".

Having had the opportunity to calm down Prince asks, "Did Bump screw this up or are you trying to get over on me?" In a serene tone Trail answers back, "It was neither of us. This new kid they got over in Pine Grove named DJ screwed this one up. Dude is a problem on the field. He is Kevon brother...you remember KV."

After a pause he mumbles, "So Kevon huh? That was him at the basketball game with DJ the other day." Thinking to himself before going on "Hmmm okay. So, I guess this puts Kevon back in the mix along with his brother." Coughing into the phone after puffing a cigar he mocks "Send a kite to him and his brother and let them know they are both on GO and that I don't need any misunderstandings in our affairs." Relieved from the way the conversation is turning out he readily agrees.

Now in a relaxed state Prince goes on "I'll take you at your word because you been putting in work BUT if there happens to be anymore screw ups there will be examples made. I hope I'm very clear on that." His voice becoming louder he says "Only two choice. One we can all eat good at the table together or two somebody can be permanently removed from the table --- period."

Before he has a chance to respond he quickly changes the tone of the conversation quipping "So speaking of that basketball game we were talking about earlier, I don't know what or how you did it but that was good. You made it look close and for a minute I thought you were going to screw that one up too, but you came through".

Noticing that there is now a lull in the conversation Trail sneaks in the opportunity to pacify his mentor, stating "I already talked to the kid DJ at the barber shop you set me up with...I put him on with a gig there in order to earn his trust by putting money in his pocket and showing love."

Feeling proud of his accomplishment he proceeds "I think we got him. So, when we need him to come through for us, he won't mind helping out but as for his brother Kevon I am not sure about that guy. He seemed to be really done after he agreed and completed his final gig."

Waiting for a response and after not receiving one he goes on "I know we get more for the high school games so I'll make sure to see what the lines are for these upcoming games so that we can get what we lost back off that first game."

Interrupting Prince counters "Hold on I am thinking!" Afraid that he may have said something wrong Trail corrects himself and confirms "Prince! I can get the money back!"

With an agitated look he yells "BOY! I said hold on! Do it look like I'm hurting for money?" After gathering his thoughts, he continues "First of all, I was talking about that basketball game. It looked like we were about to win, and I thought you screwed it up and then Kasyn came through and saved it in the end." Giggling he cracks "Or better yet he blew it."

Once again thinking to himself before going on "Let me put you on game. The money is power. We use it to our advantage. When we get these super stars involved, they stuck. So, after that they move how we tell them to move you understand? So yes, you are going to get my money back but the big picture for us is having something on these dudes, so they work for us."

Blowing out smoke from the cigar he goes on "What just happened works for us. We gone make DJ think he screwed us in that game and Bump already thinks he messed up. So, if this DJ kid is as good as you say he is then we need him on our team. KV know how we get." Agitated he says, "Unfortunately we had a talk with him, and he doesn't want to cooperate."

Shocked at the turn in the conversation Trail's mind begins to wonder. Looking at the game from a new perspective, he begins to notice the power, greed, deception and lies that occur behind the scenes to make this work.

Snapping out of his daze he hears Prince "Did you hear what I just said?" Embarrassed that he got caught in a daze he quickly responds, "I caught most of it but can you repeat it so I can make sure we on the same page?"

Starting to get agitated he proceeds "Keep doing what you are doing with this kid and make sure there is no interference from Kevon and if so let me know! I will handle him myself. Any questions?" Before hanging up he sternly responds, "None at all! I'm on it!"

Chapter 9

Prince is a forty-five-year-old bi-racial, half white and half Hispanic, business entrepreneur. He is the owner of apartment complexes, automobile dealerships, as well as clubs in the Pine Grove and Hidden Valley areas. In addition to those business ventures he also is part owner of a sports management company.

Prince was raised by his father who has served as a State elected political official for the last 20 years. Immersed in the political world has afforded Prince to develop ties to the states most influential political leaders.

With his retirement from politics pending, his father has used his position to pave the way for other family members to win positions as government and city officials. Residing in one of the most affluent areas in Pine Grove he has always lived amongst judges, lawyers, doctors, business owners and some of the most high-profile citizens in the city.

Constantly instilling in him the value of networking and the importance of powerful affiliations, Prince's father ensured he benefitted from residing in such a prestigious environment. To strengthen those ties whenever possible he made it a priority that Prince attended community events and activities.

Prince's mother comes from a different background than that of his dad. She is Hispanic and comes from one of the most poverty-stricken areas of Hidden Valley. Not allowing her environment to dictate her financial condition she learned to use her family's notoriety in gang activity, drug trafficking, and street prestige to align herself with businesses and city officials.

Her feisty, intellectual, and classy demeanor allowed her to catch the attention of Prince's father. After dating for a few months, she unexpectedly became pregnant with Prince. Not wanting children to interfere with her goals they decided that Prince's father would take custody of him once he was born.

Continuing her path to achieve her goals she became one of the most highly touted social activists for the poor communities. Her liaison became invaluable to city officials and businesses. By earning the trust and confidence of the residents she attained the ability to convey to the individuals of these communities that the projects and opportunities that these officials and businesses offered were in their best interest. This not only helped in winning votes and election campaigns for city officials but also helped businesses overcome roadblocks in land development projects and other business ventures.

Her ties to the drug traffickers and gang members who were some of the most financially successful individuals in the area, albeit its illegal financial successes, were beneficial to city officials. Through these alliances and with her help city officials were able to make deals and arrangements for the drug traffickers and gang members in exchange for significant financial contributions to their political campaigns.

Serving as such a valuable conduit in the area and having such damaging inside knowledge of the inner workings of city and government affairs, allowed her to become one of the most powerful people in the area.

After years of having notoriety as one of the most powerful people in the area she became guilty in choosing her career over her child. Receiving word that her son fathered a daughter and refused to acknowledge her she sought out the child's mother.

With word from her affiliates she located her granddaughter. The mother who was a local prostitute and drug addict had no means or desire to raise her child. Utilizing her ties to social services the grandmother facilitated the process that transitioned custody of the child to her.

Contacting Prince to take the paternity test she received confirmation that he was the father. Refusing to believe his mother and bitter that she was not in his life he turned his back on her and the child.

With greed and pain hardening him, Prince submerged himself into politics, corruption and becoming rich and powerful. Leaning on his father's teaching he began to understand what powerful alliances could allow him to achieve.

Taking advantage of this valuable knowledge he began to build powerful networks and fearless coalitions. Combining the connections that his mother and father had established made him the most powerful person in the area.

Chapter 10

Sending a short text "I'm on my way", DJ jogs to his vehicle from his apartment and begins to drive toward Chasity's apartment. While driving he wonders to himself why is he having these feelings for a girl who Trail just told him was a hoe and not to fall for her. He tries to convince himself that he needs to take control of his feelings because Trail has earned his trust and wouldn't tell him anything that wouldn't be in his best interest.

Feeling himself become anxious all over again he pulls up to her apartment. Attempting to hide his excitement he notices her eagerly waiting outside for him to arrive. She's now wearing a sleeveless but conservative white blouse top with fitted blue jeans that define her shape. On her feet are decorative sandals that show off her manicured toes and her hair pulled back in a bun. Immediately he loses his thoughts of controlling his feelings and begins to succumb to a realization that she is the lady he was meant to be with.

Giggling as he pulls up, she is waving towards him as if he doesn't see her. Lost in his emotions he sits in his car as she walks over and waits for him to open the door so that she can enter. After moments of waiting she realizes that he is not going to come over at which time she takes it upon herself to open the passenger door and enter his vehicle. Now in a giddy mood she jokes "I guess chivalry is dead?"

Feeling embarrassed because he recognizes his error of not opening her door, he searches for the words to apologize.

Looking over and seeing that he is remorseful she continues "It's ok! Don't worry about it. I'm a big girl. However, you did lose some cool points." Comforted by her warm attitude he responds, "I promise to make it up to you." Pausing as he looks over at her "I'm just not used to someone like you. I just didn't expect you to be as great as you are...I mean I can't really explain it and actually I can't even believe that I am actually talking to you about my feelings."

Pausing for a moment he notices her start to blush as he continues "I admit that initially when I saw you I could not get over how sexy and beautiful you were", looking in her direction he smirks and adds "the nice booty was also a plus"...she gasps and playfully hits him on his arm as he continues "seriously though you are easy to talk to, funny, smart and just a cool chick".

He pauses and again looks over in her direction to gauge her facial expression and after noticing that she is now blushing he goes on "I have to apologize, I started talking and forgot to compliment you, because you look amazing and smell wonderful." Speechless she continues to blush and manages to whisper, "Thank you, I'm glad that you noticed and that means a lot coming from you."

As they begin their drive toward the Grounds, she thinks to herself that he is not the thug that he has been portrayed as and is actually a very caring, well spoken, gentleman. Already physically attracted to him her mind wanders off with thoughts of him being the perfect partner for her and how wonderful it would be if they were in a relationship.

Pulling up to the parking lot of the Grounds he parks and quickly runs over to her side and opens her door. Snickering she looks up at him and exits. "So, I guess you are bringing chivalry back from the dead" she jokes as they walk toward the entertainment area.

While walking they make jokes about DJ's awkward demeanor at the barber shop when they met and after a moment Chasity looks around and quips "this place is dead today!" Softly grabbing her hand, he pulls her along. Taken aback by the confidence he is exuding she begins to feel a comfort in him that takes her by surprise and doesn't resist and allows him to lead her.

Taking in her surroundings she observes an area of the Grounds she never knew existed. They pass through an opening with perfectly cut shrubs and flowers on each side of the walkway. Lost in the beauty of her surrounding, a sudden smell of euphoria in the air becomes apparent.

Soon they embark upon a crisp flowing river located in between the pathway they are on and rows of perfectly planted gardens on the opposite side. Astounded by the scenery she looks toward the end of the path and takes notice of a breathtaking view.

Before she can comment they end up at a bench positioned under a calming waterfall. Assisting her as she sits on the bench, he joins her, and they enter an exhilarating silence.

Speechless she stares at DJ with a fondness that he senses while holding her hands. "How did you know about this place" she bellows. Gazing into the waterfalls while now caressing her hand he responds "life can deal you a bad hand at times you know? And even though a house can be beautiful on the outside, it can be on flames about to burn down on the inside!"

Looking confused she loosens her grip from his hand as he continues "My mom would bring me here when I was younger after my dad beat her. This place is my release; it is the PEACE when we need to get away from everything. She came to get away; you know, just to find some peace."

Seeing that he is beginning to tear up she tightens her grip on his hands and moves closer to console him. Not knowing what to say she rubs his back as he continues in a whimpering voice "Nobody really knows me or even takes the time to understand what I go through. Out here you have to always watch your back and prove yourself."

Tensing up he continues "I'm a smart dude but what are good grades going to do for me in the streets? Plus, I'm light skin so I have to go extra hard or someone will try me. Then I could be just walking down the street and I get slammed to the sidewalk by the police...just harassed because I'm wearing my sweats or my hoodie and I look like I'm a trouble maker or someone who fits a description.

Watching his temperament change she stops rubbing his back but continues to listen with empathy. "It's like I can't win. That's why I'm not feeling football anymore because everyone is in it for the wrong reasons these days. People think because I don't talk on it that I don't know what's going on." Shaking his head in angst "I help win championships. Good for me but do you know how many crooks in on the money grab? And I get a scholarship?"

Shaking his head he continues "The same scholarships that I would get by putting myself through long hard practices in the extreme heat and cold, getting my body broken up and putting my life on the line on that football field...they give those same kinda scholarships to kids for academics and for other sports like CURLING or golf." Shaking his head in disgust "And they don't have to do half the stuff I do or have half the risk. So why play football? I mean I can just get a scholarship for being black and not have to deal with all this."

Becoming agitated his voice gets louder "But tell me what sport brings in the majority of the money! Out of all those scholarships we know the one that tears you down the most! But everyone wants to tell me not to throw away my opportunity! I have a gift! I'm a minority right...I can make good grades...so why put myself through this football crap when I can just take one of those scholarships?"

Feeling vulnerable he pulls away from her and puts his head in his hands. Moving closer to him she feels helpless while also feeling a deep connection with him and decides to confide in him in the hopes of making him feel better.

Wrapping her hands around his arm she says softly "Demyre, you aren't the only one that has had to deal with terrible situations." Looking up at her in disbelief he drops his head back into his hands.

"Seriously! There are things I've been through that are extremely difficult to deal with and much harder to talk about." After a slight hesitation she blurts "I was raped!" Taking his head out of his hands he looks up at her as her usually confident poise is replaced by fear.

Seeing her distraught state DJ moves closer and puts his arm around her as the tears began to flow. "I didn't know what to do" she cries "We were all partying and having a good time and things went dark. I blacked out and the next thing I remember I was naked. He was on top of me, inside of me, moaning and groaning. I couldn't get him off."

Now profusely crying she goes on, "I remember I kept trying to tell him to stop but I was blacking in and out of consciousness. When I finally came to, I was naked in the bed alone with blood and cum in between my legs---it hurt!" Sinking her head into DJ's shoulders she continues crying "I was a virgin! I always thought my honeymoon would be my first time."

Shocked at what she has told him he holds her tighter and is overcome by an overwhelming urge to protect her. Rocking her in his arms he professes "I got you Chasity! What happened to you was not right but as long as I am alive, I can promise you it won't happen again!" Soothing her hurt she is comforted by his words and holds him tighter as he wipes away her tears.

Chapter 11

Working out in the gym with the basketball team during the last workout of the week, team members exchange stories of who they are hooking up with over the weekend. Sitting off to himself Kevon's mind wanders away from the conversations to thoughts of Fannah.

Known for being a ladies' man, Kevon has always felt obligated to keep up that persona. An image that he now understands has hindered him from pursuing Fannah and the feelings that he has always had for her.

With his mind still wandering he replays her cheers at his games and her words of encouragement. Understanding that she may be transferring schools after the semester he musters up the courage to look for her and let her know how he feels about her.

After showering and gathering his belongings, he daps his teammates up. Heading toward the exit Kasyn yells over to him, "You going to hook up with that Fannah chick huh?" Taken off guard by his comment he pretends he didn't hear what he said and throws him the deuces while walking out of the locker room. Strapping on his backpack he walks toward the campus and to his surprise he spots her standing across from the gymnasium.

Caught off guard he rethinks his plan. After a few moments he convinces himself to make his move. With the opportunity he has been waiting for he walks over to her and once he arrives, he stumbles through dozens of opening lines before asking her, "Who are you waiting on"?

Seeming a bit overtaken, she pauses for a while and then responds, "you are kinda nosy aren't you?" they both laugh breaking the awkwardness of the moment and she then says, "I'm waiting on my ride to come and pick me up so I can go home."

Happy that he is showing interest in her she continues "I am glad you stopped to keep me company while I wait though". Not knowing what to expect, he breathes a sigh of relief from the inviting conversation she greets him with. Trying to take advantage of the situation he tells her, "I can take you home...I mean it is on the way to where I was going anyway...if you want?"

Seemingly shocked by his comment she quips "how did you know my home was along the way? Speechless he stares at her with a blank look. Giggling she goes on "I'm messing with you. And yes, I accept your offer. It will give us a chance to talk to one another one on one!"

Staggered by her comment he takes her hand and escorts her to his car. Upon getting to his car he opens the passenger side door for her to enter, "such a gentleman" she jests. He closes her door and then enters the car himself as they drive to her apartment.

Breaking the silence, he asks "I didn't know you were into basketball?" looking over at him she gives a devious grin. "What is that look for?" Smiling she responds, "There's a lot of things that you don't know about me."

As he exhibits a look of confusion she continues "What is my name?" Before he can answer she goes on "Do you normally approach females and have them all up in your car before even asking their name?"

Feeling ashamed he nervously responds "Fannah right? I mean all this time that is the name I've known you as." Laughing hysterically, she retorts "I'm giving you a hard time Kevon, you are so cute when you are nervous."

Smirking she goes on "And yes my name is Fannah, but for you, you can call me Fan. That is what my family, friends, and people I like call me. So, you would have to guess which of those categories you fall in."

As they continue the drive, she gives him another sneaky grin as to which he responds, "what did I do wrong now?" Initially she says, "nothing is wrong" but after a brief silence she asks him "do you have a special female in your life?" after a startled look he replies, "now you are being nosy!"

Noticing her sense of humor, he becomes more comfortable. Giving her a smirk he responds "My Mom!" seeming offended she remarks "no silly, you know what I mean, is there anyone you are intimate with?" with a bashful grin he replies "I'm not a virgin". In an agitate voice she responds, "Okay Kevon now you are doing too much".

Getting serious he says "I'm joking, I have friends but I'm not exclusive with anyone. I've always reserved that space in my life for that special someone. What about you? Are you with anyone?"

As he looks at her, she seems to be stunned by his statement but doesn't respond. As he waits for a response, she then says, "there's my apartment, you can pull into that parking spot and I can make it from there."

Feeling disappointed, he pulls up to the apartment and they gaze into each other's eyes. She grabs his hand and says "you still didn't answer my question but I will answer yours anyway", she pauses, looks down as to stop herself from tearing up, she then looks back into his eyes and says, "No, I'm not with anyone and haven't been intimate or messed around with anyone since the day I first saw you".

Comforted by his surprised reaction she continues "From the moment I saw you in passing I felt a connection like you are the one for me without even knowing you. I mean I don't believe in love at first site but if there ever was, I think that moment when I first saw you is what it would feel like."

He begins to speak as she puts her fingers to his lips as to shush him. She then says "If you have been waiting on that special one and that special one could be me, then I think you need to give us some serious consideration over the next few weeks because my mind has been made up about you since the day I first saw you".

Sitting speechless she says in a quiet whisper, "thanks for the ride and I'll be looking forward to hearing from you." She goes into her purse and writes her phone number on a piece of paper, folds it, and as she opens his hand, she places the folded paper in his hand and closes it. She gives him a sincere look, kisses him on the cheek and exits his car.

Holding the door open before closing it she looks back inside the car and stares into his eyes before saying "Kevon, for the record, I'm not really into basketball. I only started coming to the games because I like a certain basketball player." Noticing that he is shocked and speechless she slowly closes the door and waves toward him as she walks into her apartment.

Chapter 12

Friends since middle school Chasity and Fannah have always been inseparable. Chasity who is a little older and an only child sees Fannah as her little sister vice just best friends. Upon graduating high school, they decided to attend the same college.

Chasity

A very sociable person, Chasity has gained an unwanted reputation as being flirtatious. Being beautiful, dark skin, curvy combined with her friendly and flirtatious personality constantly makes her desired by guys whom she encounters.

Raised by a single father, her mother suspiciously died of an overdose of cocaine. She was the only child and grew up in what is considered the hood of Pine Grove. Despite her environment her father ensured she was sheltered from the negativity that plagued her community.

As a consequence of being raised by her father who was protective and loving she developed a false perception of men by assuming all men were as protective, loyal and caring as her father.

The qualities of always being protected and the ability to trust that her father provided did not prepare her for the harsh realities of the real world. Instead it created a naïve nature that allowed others to take advantage of her.

Her inaccurate assumption of guys not only caused her to gain the unwanted flirtatious reputation because she was so unassuming, but it has also made her susceptible to the games and manipulation tactics from guys she assumed were respectful gentlemen.

Developing a better understanding of people and how they interact has allowed her to have the ability to adapt and place herself in more positive situations. However, having to deal with all of her experiences in addition to growing up without a mom has begun to shape her character and created trust issues in relationships.

Despite the negative impact of her experiences she also continues to exhibit the positive attributes learned from her dad. Being honest and trustworthy has become her gift and curse. As a result, those qualities enable her to become a loyal person as well as protective individual to those whom she is close with.

Fannah

Fannah was raised in the more affluent area of Pine Grove by her Grandmother. Because her father disowned her at birth and her mother did not have the means to financially support a child she initially was going to be given up for adoption. Upon getting word that her granddaughter was going to be given up for adoption Fannah's grandmother convinced her mother to give her custodial rights.

Fannah's grandmother had gained wealth and was able to establish a successful career. Her prosperity was enabled by her personal sacrifice of custodial rights to her child when she was young.

Over the years her grandmother had always carried that guilt which had now forced her to take advantage of the opportunity to right her wrongs by giving her granddaughter the life she was not able to give to her child.

Growing up Fannah was given everything she desired by her Grandmother and never wanted for anything. Despite being spoiled and always afforded the better things in life there was a void she constantly was burdened with that was caused by not growing up with a mother and having her father disown her.

Fannah who was given her nickname "Fan" by her grandmother has always been complemented with model like features because of her beauty. Considered tall for a lady at five foot, nine inches her petite frame, long hazel hair and hypnotizing light brown eyes makes her the fantasy of every guy she comes in contact with.

She is bi-racial (white and Hispanic) with a light skin complexion. Despite her beauty and the constant compliments that come her way she has always been oblivious to her physical beauty.

Continuously bestowed with compliments she has become numb to them in turn seeking the elusive compassion, caring and genuinely loving qualities that she never received from her mother and father growing up but has sought her entire life.

FANNAH & CHASITY

FLASHBACK START It is lunch at a middle school and two little boys are in the midst of a heated argument. The disagreement is escalating to what may become a physical altercation. One boy claims that Fannah is his girlfriend while the other makes the same assertion. At the height of the argument Fannah is asked to come and resolve the disagreement.

Confused as to what is taking place Fannah stands in silence as they both scream for an answer. Running over to her defense Chasity reprimands the two boys and yells "she does not have a boyfriend! Why are you all putting her in the middle of all this! You both were supposed to be her friend!" Pulling her away from the melee she quips "Those guys were trying to put you on blast. You can't get caught in the middle of stuff like that!" **FLASHBACK OVER**

From that point forward Fannah and Chasity were inseparable. Chasity's father provided an example of a great male figure in the household in which Fannah admired and longed for.

In turn Fannah brought into Chasity's life someone whom she could serve as a protector. The genuine love and care that she receives from Fannah allows her the comfort to be herself, making the bond they have for one another strong.

The loyalty between the two created an unbreakable friendship. Despite the friendship and loyalty, they shared throughout the years, Chasity's flirtatious personality has caused Fannah to question her intentions when it came to guys who she was interested in.

Besides Fannah's insecurities as it concerns Chasity's flirtatious ways, Chasity has been a devoted friend. She gives her last to Fannah, she makes herself available to her for any breakup or emotional situation she deals with and even confrontationally. Anyone that says anything negative about Fannah, Chasity addresses the situation whether Fannah wants to acknowledge it or not.

Although she has earned Fannah's respect and friendship Chasity continues to find herself apologizing for flirting. She constantly attempts to reassure her that there are no ulterior motives in her interactions with guys that she is interested in. It has always been her personality to be friendly even though it is perceived as flirting.

Over the years, Chasity has become more aware of how her personality can be misconstrued as being flirtatious. Understanding how the perception of her actions effects Fannah she continuously apologizes. Not wanting it to become an issue she constantly self reflects and attempts to alter any interaction that she feels her friend would question.

Valuing Chasity's friendship and appreciating her efforts to have more consideration for how her actions affect her,

Fannah has made a conscious effort not to assume anything negative when Chasity flirts with a guy whom she is interested in.

Taking a new approach to her failed relationships she seeks to place the onus on herself. She makes a concerted effort not to blame Chasity and anything she says or does for her failed relationships

Instead she decides to think of it as her having a poor choice in guys. By taking responsibility for her failed relationships and not wanting to place blame on Chasity, she has become very selective of the guys in which she introduces or talks to Chasity about.

Chapter 13

DJ wakes up in a good mood but is also feeling guilty about the way he has been treating Kevon during the past couple weeks. Not attending Kevon's last basketball game only adds to his guilt.

DJ knows his brother looks forward to him coming to his games, so he is usually in attendance. With all of the guilt piling up he decides to try and meet up with Kevon to make-up for his actions.

Looking out the door and noticing that it is a beautiful day he calls Kevon to see if he wants to go to the local basketball court to play ball. Picking up the phone he dials Kevon's number with the hopes that he hasn't planned anything for the day.

After calling several times he gets no answer and decides to put on his clothes and walk across the neighborhood to Kevon's apartment.

DJ puts on his basketball gear and leaves out the house. He takes a short walk to his brother's place who moved only three blocks over into an apartment after graduating high school.

Once he arrives at the apartment, he knocks on the door twice and follows it with a beat in rhythm and repeats that pattern as he dances. He Continues the beating pattern on the door because he knows his brother will recognize their special knock.

After a few minutes with still no answer, he goes to the window and taps on it as he yells "KV!" It's me DJ, stop playing with yourself in there and come open the door!"

Awakened from his sleep Kevon hears the loud noise and tries to avoid it. Not wanting to be bothered he rolls over with the thought that DJ will go away after he gets no answer. Not giving up DJ continues to yell "KV!", I see your car out here! I know you are in there! GET UP!"

Shocked when he recognizes DJ's voice at the door Kevon wakes from his sleep with curiosity. Dragging himself from bed he staggers to the door.

Upon opening the door, they give each other a grip and a pound after which Kevon says, "why you here at 9 in the morning banging on my door like you the police?" In a playful mood he counters "It's a Saturday man, you know the park is poppin off right about now." Knowing Kevon won't turn down an opportunity to play basketball he asks, "Let's go hoop Bro?"

Baffled by his sudden interest in basketball and change in attitude he jokes, "Are you kidding me right now? You know you not a baller. You not about that b-ball life, so what you really got going?"

With a devious grin DJ replies, "kick rocks, bus boy. It's not like you Lebron or somebody. Don't let them scouts pump your head up." After a slight pause, DJ continues "I'll break your ankles on the court, and besides that, it is sun dress and short shorts type weather. Plus, we all know the ladies can't get enough of me so go grab your gear and let's be out".

Shaking his head Kevon walks into the bathroom and washes his face attempting to get his thoughts together. Sluggish from being awaken from his sleep, he cautiously replies, "You must got something up, coming over here this early talking bout some ball----I need to get some games in anyway so I'll roll, just give me a minute".

Always keeping b-ball gear accessible, Kevon goes to his room and changes clothes. Grabbing his bag, he walks toward the front door. Looking in the kitchen noticing DJ going through his refrigerator he blurts, "What you doing? You was talking all that big noise about the court, I'm ready and you trying to eat. You want to hit the court or eat?"

Snatching a Gatorade before exiting the refrigerator he walks to the door flinching at Kevon as if he were going to hit him, "You thought I was gonna jump or something?" he murmurs as they leave the apartment in route to the park.

As they journey to the park Kevon starts to feel as if DJ may be coming around. Sensing a good vibe, he starts to pry about DJ's personal life. "So, what has been up with you? Haven't heard from you much since you got suspended from school and started working at the barber shop."

Snatching the basketball from him he answers "Shhh, I been out here trying to make ends meet! You know how it is." Laughing to himself he adds "Or maybe you don't". In a condescending voice he goes on, "Everybody ain't got it like you supastar!"

With a confused look Kevon responds, "Now you know I work super hard for what I get, don't even play it like that." Pausing after being startled by his comment he asserts, "The only way I'm making it is because of my part time job. You know what happens when you assume? You make an ASS out of U and ME." Smiling he continues "I hope you don't think this scholarship money putting bands in my pocket."

Seeming calm despite the direction of the conversation DJ responds "I can't tell, you got the apartment laid out, got a brand-new whip and stay fresh. Meanwhile I'm still at the crib with mom dukes."

Frustrated by the conversation Kevon tries to give his brother some inspiration as he suggests "Hard work. That's what I keep trying to tell you. I get that stuff by working hard and not blowing money on dumb stuff. You don't see me running around here with two hundred-dollar shoes and four and five hundred-dollar chains and jewelry that I can't afford!"

Stealing the basketball away he persists "I can get you on with me at my job and if you get back into school you know you can get a scholarship in football." Pausing he looks over to see if he is paying attention before continuing "You are a beast out there and you know it!"

Starting to get frustrated himself, DJ looks at his brother for a while before saying "I'm cool, I tried it that way, that don't work for me. Shrugging his shoulders, he continues "And on the cool I really don't even like football like that so Imma keep cutting hair and get me a side hustle".

Feeling as though he's been punched in the gut he replies "What! You got to be kidding me! What are you talking about a side hustle?" Waiting for a response he notices Fan and her friends approaching them as they walk down the sidewalk in their direction.

Not wanting his soft side to show in front of his brother, Kevon decides to hide his feelings for Fannah and instead of making his way toward her he chooses to just smile and wave in her direction as they pass.

Seeing Chasity in the group DJ becomes visually excited to see her. He runs over to the group of girls and embraces Chasity with a hug before jogging back over to Kevon.

As he makes his way back to Kevon he yells back at the group of girls "Hey! What are you all getting into tonight"? Looking back at them Chasity replies, "Nothing tonight but we having a party at our place after the homecoming game."

As Fan grabs Chasity by the arm and turns her around feeling embarrassed, she continues "You all are invited, and we better see you all there!" Catching eye contact as they walk in opposite directions Chasity and DJ stare at one another with a warm gaze of affection.

Noticing the great mood that DJ has been in all day it suddenly dawns on him after seeing his brother's interaction with Chasity what is taking place. Playfully pushing DJ, Kevon jokes "So that's why you are in such a good mood huh?"

In an attempt to avoid his question and keep the conversation off of the subject they were on prior to the females passing DJ asks, "Why you didn't try to holla at the yellow bone, mixed chick back there?" Nudging him with the basketball he goes on "Because I know you don't deal with the dark skinned sistas!"

In a guarded tone he remarks "You talking about Fan?" Looking surprised he laughs "Ahhhh, so she Fan to you huh" His laugh now calming he continues "so you know her too?" With a look of curiosity, he counters "Too? What do you mean TOO! How do you know her?"

Finding the look on his face humorous and seeing that he has touched on a possible sensitive subject he scoffs "I saw lil mama at the barber shop the other day looking straight ratchet!" Quickly responding "Ratchet! C'mon now, you just seen her. I don't know where you get that from. She not in the streets like that."

Laughing DJ states "I knew you were feeling her. Seems like she got your nose wide open playboy." Trying to hold in his laughter he goes on "I'm just telling you what I saw lova boy. She was with my guy Trail and came through half naked showing it all."

Brushing off DJ's laughter Kevon's mind quickly shifts to their original conversation after he hears the name Trail. Now concerned about the people his brother is hanging around he warns "DJ you getting mixed up with the wrong people lil bro."

After a slight pause he looks over at Kevon without a response. Annoyed with the lack of feedback he mocks "I hear you DJ." Catching his attention DJ gives him a confused reaction.

Still without a response he goes on "No answer is an answer. So, I get it DJ." Unfazed by the remark he looks toward the park urging "It's getting up in the day we have to make it to the park before it gets packed".

As they pick up their pace to make it to the park Kevon becomes concerned about DJ's relationship with Trail and starts to worry about the other things that he may be involved in.

Feeling the time is now to tell DJ about his bad past experiences, Kevon decides to open up to his brother. In the hopes that by him hearing his story it will help him understand the consequences of dealing with Trail and the street life.

He begins to speak but before he can get anything out DJ yells "KV, there's the park it's not too packed, I see Trail in there already. I know we can get a few games in now...hurry up. Vamanos!" Frustrated at the blown opportunity he looks on as DJ runs over to the park and slowly follows.

Chapter 14

Leaving their final class on a Friday afternoon, Fannah and Chasity walk toward the parking lot of the school's campus before Chasity blurts "What's up with you and going to all these basketball games this year girl?"

Surprised at the abrupt question, Fannah quips, "I like basketball. Is there something wrong with that?" shrugging her shoulders Chasity scoffs, "I guess not, but as long as I've known you I don't ever remember you liking basketball...plus you was cheering kinda loud for the one guy on the team."

Evasively she answers, "Why are you so worried about who I am cheering for? Why can't I just be cheering for our team?" Before she can respond she, continues "Anyway while you are all up in my business, what's up with you and the dude from the barber shop? I saw how he ran over and gave you that big hug in front of everyone the other day."

"He does not even seem like your type --- and just so you know I have never been with him just in case you trying to get my leftovers again?" jokes Fan. Laughing along, she responds, "Don't hate on me because the guys you date can't resist this bubble booty". Starting to get irritated she attempts to change the conversation and says, "Anyway, what's going on this weekend?"

As they drive towards their apartment Chasity states, "You know there's nothing new going on around this place. If it's not the football or basketball game, same old skating rink, and maybe something at the Grounds every now and then."

Seemingly thinking of something she continues, "How about we start planning for our party here after the homecoming game?" In amazement, she exhorts, "why here and why did you even put that out there the other day that we would have a party at our place?"

Rolling her eyes she continues "Why not the skating rink or a different location?" interrupting she answers "Girl it cost money to rent those places, plus we can get our drink on and won't have to drive anywhere. Our apartment is easy to get to!"

Thinking for a minute, Fan says, "Well you know I don't know that many people. "Hold up", interrupts Chasity, "you have got to be one of the most popular girls in the school. Everyone knows you. Why are you being like that? It will be fun." As she pauses for a moment, she shakes her head in agreeance.

As they arrive at their apartment, Fannah notices that Chasity is acting quite different and in an unusually good mood. Curious she asks "Okay so I see you're beating around the bush talking about this party and all this other stuff. How about we talk about why you are bouncing around, cracking jokes and in such a good mood?" Raising her eyebrows in anticipation she shouts, "Let's hear it".

Noticeably glowing with her thoughts of DJ she responds, "What are you talking about girl?" With a coy stare she retorts "C'mon now Chasity. It is all over your face. So just spit it out."

Excitedly she responds "Okay, Okay, I think I found the one! I did not know what to expect but this guy isn't what you'd think he'd be AT ALL! He is caring, kind, generous, intelligent, and of course so sexy. So, to answer your question earlier. Yes, he is my type."

Shocked by her response Fan says, "Are we talking about the same guy from the barber shop?" With more excitement than before she shouts "YES! Demyre! And trust me don't go by how he dresses and that hard image he gives off. This guy is a dream come true for me."

Ecstatic about the mood that she is in and that she seemingly has found someone to give her that type of feeling the girls embrace in a mutually celebratory hug.

After they hug, they begin making plans for the party. Still in a good mood Chasity stares at Fannah with a puzzled look. Wondering why she's looking at her in such a manner, Fannah asks, "What's wrong? Why are you looking like that?"

After a moment Chasity says, "Okay now Fan I let you in on what's going on with me and you are seriously going to hold back? Looking confused she goes on "What's up? I thought you were my best friend and we shared everything?"

Contemplating whether or not to talk with Chasity about Kevon she jokes "We share a lot, but we don't share guys." Laughing along she cracks "Your type of guys aren't on my level." Giggling to herself she goes on "Stop playing and just tell me so I can stop asking."

Still not receiving an answer she goes on "Seriously, you like the new guy on the basketball team, don't you?" With a deceptive look Fan blushes and snaps "No"!

Starting to become flustered, Fannah asks, "What's up with the party? Are we going to send out fliers or what?" Finding it funny that Fannah is getting agitated she pushes harder for a reaction by asking, "If you like him so much why are you still hanging out with Trail?"

Keeping her composure, Fan responds, "Me and Trail are just friends! Now are we going to get the party together or what!!!" Sensing she has hit a nerve Chasity backs off of the conversation and says, "I have friends who can make us fliers, When everyone gets the word that we are having a party they'll come anyway."

Turning to a more stern tone Chasity comments "In all seriousness, I don't think you should continue to hang out with Trail. Especially if you are interested in the basketball player guy...who you aren't telling me about." Listening and thinking to herself that she is jealous of her relationship with Trail Fan doesn't respond.

Understanding their past, Chasity attempts to reassure Fannah that she has no interest in Trail as she continues "I'm just looking out for you because I care. When I tell you, I've found my guy in Demyre, I'm really good Fan. I just really think if you like a guy there shouldn't be other guys in the picture."

Now in a somber state she goes on "I don't understand why you think I have it out to talk to any guy you've ever dated and out of all people, Trail! Seriously! It hurts that you and everyone think of me in that way --- just because I'm not a mean person and I speak to everyone people assume that I am flirtatious or thotty."

Starting to become emotional she continues "I value our friendship too much to do something like that to you." Hoping to get through she goes on "I'm not the best person to take dating advice from but I'm pretty sure that if you keep hanging around a guy he is going to think it's something more than it is."

Now frustrated with Chasity's comments Fan decides to interject "We were just hanging out with him at the barber shop and you didn't have any issues with that did you?"

Feeling that she isn't getting through Chasity counters, "We were both there together Fan, and we were able to look out for one another. That's the difference, but when you are always out with him one on one who knows what can happen and not only that..." Fan cuts Chasity off mid-sentence and in a flustered tone shrieks. "I know what I'm doing Chasity, OK!"

With a sense of obligation, Chasity makes up her mind to tell her friend what happened to her and why she feels the way she does. Attempting to build up the courage to relive her most tragic experience she contemplates how she will react to what she has to say.

After debating with herself on whether to share her story she looks at Fannah who is now becoming more flustered by the minute. Eventually, she comes to the decision that because Fan is so upset, anything she says at this point will fall on deaf ears.

Feeling guilty about not having the courage to share her experience she attempts to console herself. Telling herself that once Fannah cools off she will be more receptive to hearing her out and that there will be other days to let her know.

Breaking from her thoughts Chasity walks toward her bedroom and as she passes Fannah she says, "I know you are probably upset with me, but you know I just want the best for you." Understanding Fan is still upset and without a response she continues "You know I love you Girl. I am going to bed...Good Night."

Chapter 15

Walking toward the basketball court the two brothers navigate through rimmed up cars and trucks blaring a variety of music. The known D-boys have trap music blasting. The crunk music is played by the thugs and in other areas twerk music can be heard as scantily dressed girls provocatively dance and twerk to the songs.

As they get closer to the court there are different groups of guys drinking, eating, smoking, and hanging out. Lagging behind DJ, Kevon pauses as someone yells "KV" from one of the cars. Scanning the area, he recognizes the face and walks over greeting "What up Pickles. What you doing here?" Ducking his head into one of the cars he says "Hold on KV. Give me a sec."

With DJ getting out of view he responds "I'mma head over to the court. I'll catch up with you." Spotting Trail in the bleachers he notices that he is waiving DJ to come over. Making his way over to the bleachers he looks on as DJ daps up Trail. Suddenly one of the guys sitting with Trail asks "who is that guy? Pointing toward Kevon."

Trail looks over in astonishment, "Oh snap! My man you don't know who that is?" In response to his guy's comment. "That's that guy KEVON, KV, the B-Ball phenom!" Rising from his seat on the bleachers, he reaches toward him giving him dap. After catching eye contact, he glares at him with a piercing cold stare.

Now nervous, Kevon reluctantly returns the gesture and faintly says, "What up Trail". Looking surprised by their familiarity of one another DJ asks, "You all know each other?"

With his head down Kevon gives a slight nod while Trail eagerly replies, "Big Bro ain't tell you? We go way back, but since he hit that superstar level, he don't holla at us street dudes no mo." Visibly frustrated Kevon looks toward the court and doesn't respond.

Kevon begins to drift toward the court looking at the teams play in games that are competitive and physical. He then hears DJ and Trail conversing in the background. As he's watching the games, he catches himself replaying his past over and over in his head only to snap out of his daze with an unusual anxiety that heightens his awareness to his surroundings.

Walking back toward DJ and Trail he makes up his mind to walk back home and has the intention of convincing DJ to leave with him. Now on the phone Trail tells DJ "Fam, I got up next on the court. Y'all can walk on over so when that game finish up we can get on".

Walking behind DJ on the sidelines of the court Kevon says "I'm not feeling good about this situation Bro. We need to be out!" Seeing the dejected expression on DJ's face after making his comment confirms to him, he has no chance of persuading him to leave. He gives up his argument and slowly walks behind him down the sideline.

Making it to half court and waiting on the game to end, DJ turns and has a look of disdain as he stares at his older brother. After a few seconds he snarls "What's up with you dude?" Caught off guard by the abrupt comment Kevon just looks back at him without responding.

DJ continues "You been acting like a lil bytch since we got here! You acting all funny with my dude Trail like he done did you something." Shaking his head in disgust. "Like Trail said you act like you better than us street niggas."

Now upset himself Kevon responds "What the hell are you talking about? Not one day in life have I not looked out for you...RIGHT? Now you coming at me super stupid for some other dude who don't care if you live or die?"

Before DJ can respond Trail walks up with two other guys and seeing the argument asks, "Is everything ok?" DJ nor Kevon speak as they are both visibly upset. Nudging both brothers in a playful manner Trail says "Y'all need to calm down or get some poom or something." Trail Giggles as he grabs a basketball, "We up my G's, time to ball."

Walking onto the court one of the players from the other team chides "game to 12, no 2's, straight up" as he checks the ball to Kevon. Still upset from his earlier conversation with his brother Kevon zones into the game.

Virtually unstoppable on the basketball court when he is upset, Kevon has locked into the game. He immediately takes control and hits the first ten points before Trail makes the last two shots to end the game. "Easy work!" DJ mocks at the other teams as he is also still upset and venting from his earlier altercation with his brother.

Waiting for the next team to get ready a voice comes from the crowd "Enjoy that win. Game Over for you clowns now!" Looking for the person who made the comment they all look around the park when suddenly the guy guaranteeing victory steps onto the court with his four players. Frozen in their tracks DJ and Kevon look at the team as if they've seen a ghost.

"We gone ball or are you clowns gone sit there wasting time?" When reality sinks in DJ charges toward the guy making the comments when suddenly he is stopped by Trail and pulled to the side.

"Let it play out lil homey." Breathing excessively hard DJ says, "But that is..." Cutting him off "I know exactly who that is. Trust me lil homey. Let him think he getting his off, we gone have the last laugh...trust me."

Standing on the court paranoid, Kevon looks over at DJ and Trail as they are having a conversation. He then turns and looks at the guy talking trash. Sensing danger he begins to walk off the court when Trail sees him and yells, "KV, we need you man. Come on! Let's just finish this game?"

In a dissenting tone Kevon can hear DJ saying, "Let him go. We don't need him anyway." The sound of his brother's voice combined with the danger he feels that is imminent prompts him to turn around and walk back toward the court to finish the game.

"Ball up Chump!" the guy from the other team says as he throws the ball at Kevon. Busy looking over at DJ and Trail, Kevon isn't paying attention as the ball hits him in the chest. Startled, he picks up the ball and passes it in to get the game started.

DJ immediately throws the ball back to Kevon and runs over to set a pick on the guy who is trash talking. Not seeing the pick coming, Kevon runs the guy hard into the pick as DJ leans into it blindsiding him, knocking him off his feet and to the ground.

Now freed up, Kevon comes off the pick and hits an uncontested jump shot. Feeling the tension escalating Kevon looks over at the guy getting up off the ground. Nodding his head and clapping his hands with a deceitful grin on his face, the guy who is trash talking makes it back to his feet and dusts himself off.

The next play Trail inbounds the ball to DJ who sees the guy who is trash talking under the rim and decides to try to dunk on him. Driving to the basket DJ elevates attempting to catch the guy who has been trash talking off guard as he is guarding Kevon and his back is turned. Attempting to warn him, one of his teammates yells "BUMP! Turn around you bout to get banged on".

Turning around at the last minute just in time to see DJ soar over him and complete the dunk, as he falls to the ground. Lying Embarrassed and upset he instantaneously rolls over on the ground. As DJ is landing, Bump sweeps his legs from underneath him causing him to take a scary, hard fall on his back.

In a temporary trance after hearing the name Bump, Kevon's mind wanders back to DJ's homecoming football game. It hits him like a ton of bricks that this IS the same guy whom his brother got into an altercation with during that game.

Coming out of his daze, Kevon observes DJ laying on the court in pain and instantly runs over to his aid. Engulfed in pain DJ manages to slowly get to his feet.

Once to his feet he unexpectedly bolts over to Bump, throwing and connecting a punch to his jaw. Immediately after the punch to the jaw, Bump swings back inciting an all-out brawl over the entire park.

Kevon runs over and pulls DJ away from the mayhem as he was being jumped. A guy from Trails crew runs over and lands a flush punch to the face of one of the guys who was jumping DJ. The punched knocked the guy out cold as the fights intensify. Managing to pull away from Kevon's grasp DJ chases after Bump who is now running toward his bag.

Suddenly POW! – POW! – POW! Gunshots ring out over the park causing everyone to dive on the ground in an attempt to avoid being shot. As DJ and Kevon lay on the ground they look over at Bump and notice that he is lying on the court covered in blood.

Once the gun fire stops, everyone begins to run from the court in a panicked state. In a frenzy, Kevon runs over and picks up a startled DJ off the ground as they run from the court.

Out of breath after sprinting over two miles from the court the brothers start walking. Angry and in pain DJ yells "You not gone even squad up when I'm getting jumped? What kinda shyt you on dude! I'mma tell you like this. I don't ever want to see, talk to or hear from you ever again dude! That's on my life."

Hurt from his brother's comments, Kevon doesn't respond and keeps walking. Turning down an opposite road DJ hobbles in a different direction. Stopping on the sidewalk Kevon looks at his brother and in a sorrowful tone says "You got it all wrong. You making a mistake."

Continuing to walk he blurts "Did I stutter. You heard what I said. I'm done with you dude. LEAVE ME ALONE! And I mean that." Looking on unable to move and without any other words to say in return Kevon watches DJ walk down the sidewalk until he is out of view.

Chapter 16

Dialing her phone number Kevon waits as the phone rings. Answering "Hello" she waits for a response. In a somber voice he counters "Fan. Are you busy? Sensing the bleak tone in his voice she continues "No. Not really." With no response she becomes worried as she asks, "Are you ok?"

Retreating to silence she begins to realize that something is wrong. "Where are you Kevon? Just tell me where you are, and I will come to you!"

Feeling comfort in her concern he murmurs "I'm at the Park in the Grounds." Confused of his whereabouts Fan begins to get dressed and decides she will get directions once she is on the way.

Now dressed she scurries out the door of her apartment still on the phone. "Kevon are you still there? I'm on my way to the Grounds to meet up with you, but you have to tell me where the park is once I get there."

Feeling a little better from the anticipation of her being there with him he responds, "Yes. I'm here. I'm not going anywhere." Getting into her car Fan responds "Ok. As soon as I get there, I will give you a call. Talk to you in a minute."

Pulling up to the Grounds she gets out of her car and looks around for signs or the existence of a Park to no avail. Worried that Kevon may have been confused given his state she starts to ask people standing around if they are aware or knew where a Park was in the area.

With no one having knowledge of a Park in the Grounds Fan decides to call and upon answering she says "Hey! I'm here at the Grounds but I do not see a Park." After a slight hesitation she goes on "Are you sure you are here at the Grounds?"

With a comical sigh Kevon says, "Look to the far left of the stage, where the tree line begins to form." Looking in that direction she responds "Ok? I don't see anything but trees." Sounding more audible he goes on "There's a small trail where the concrete ends. If you continue to follow that it will lead you here."

Finding the trail, Fan begins to follow it, while asking herself why Kevon didn't come out to meet her. Continuing down the trail, she passes through an opening and notices shrubs and beautiful flowers on both sides of the passage. In awe of her surroundings Fan is overtaken by the beauty of the flowing river. Engulfed by the aura of the park she inadvertently overlooks Kevon who is slumped over sitting on a bench that she passes by.

Still on the phone Kevon says "Fan, are you there? You should be here by now." Now with her focus back on him after hearing his voice on the phone, she notices that she passed him. Looking back, she sees him sitting on the bench. Instead of responding in the phone she hangs up and runs over to him and greets him with a warm hug.

Slowly pulling away from their embrace she places her hand on his face and begins to wipe away his tears and now looking into his blood shot red eyes and his face covered in dried tears she realizes why he chose this isolated location and wasn't able to meet her in the Grounds.

Clearly distraught, Fan sits close and wraps her arms around Kevon. She holds him tight as they sit in silence. Becoming emotional herself and unable to come up with the right words to console him Fan continues to wipe away his tears.

Now drooped in her bosom while she holds and comforts him, he gazes into the river. Without notice he murmurs, "Bump was killed in broad daylight. Things are too crazy. I don't know what's next! I don't know who is next." In shock of what Kevon just revealed Fan remains silent and continues to console him.

"My brother just doesn't get it. I have been through everything he is starting to go through. I've wanted nothing more than just to protect him so that he doesn't have to go through what I've been through. These people out here are only out for themselves and what they can get."

Bewildered he jests "I don't know why he doesn't listen to me." Pausing to control himself from breaking down he goes on. "He actually thinks I'm weak or that I'm not hard enough to respect." Looking out into the river Kevon proceeds "He know I've always had his back. I shouldn't have to talk about the stuff I have done or put in work for him to listen to what I try to tell him."

Sitting on the bench Fan continues to hold and comfort him while telling him that everything will be ok. With tears now forming in his eyes he says, "Pickles saved me and won't let me live it down...he sacrificed his basketball career, almost totally lost basketball forever, looking out for me."

Reassuring him that he shouldn't feel bad Fan responds "Kevon! I remember when all that happened. I think you are taking the blame for something you should not be holding yourself accountable for."

Somewhat taken aback that she is knowledgeable of the situation Kevon explains, "But the thing is I was new to what was going on and all I knew was that we were supposed to lose. I was so caught up in the game and what I wanted that I made up my mind that we were going to win."

Taking a deep sigh, Kevon continues "Pickles knew what would happen if we did not go along with the agreement. So, he took it upon himself to keep the ball away from me and ensure we lost on his own." Interrupting she interjects, "Come on now, don't do that to yourself boo. Everyone knew what they were getting into. That was not on you."

Raising up from her grasp he sits upright on the bench and puts his head in his hands. Now distraught he quips "I could've been Bump! That could've been me laying in my own pool of blood. Now my brother is caught up in the same game and he's turned his back on me when I'm the one trying to help."

Empathizing with him she slides closer to him and whispers "I think I know you pretty well and I am pretty sure you didn't have anything to do with Bump's shooting, right?" Shaking his head in agreeance she then goes on "I didn't think so...and I do understand everything you are going through but I'm here with you. You don't have to go through any of this alone."

Slowly grabbing his hand from his head and placing it around her waist. She wraps her arm around him and kisses him on the cheek. Taking a moment, she proceeds "You just have to give your brother time. I know him and Chasity are pretty close now. I will talk with Fan and ask her to keep an eye on him and give him some advice about the things he's getting himself into."

Continuing to listen to her lifts his mood. Feeling comforted he asks, "Can I tell you something that will stay between us?" She nods as he goes on "I didn't want to go to this college. When everything happened with me, Pickles, and that game, we ended up getting paid off."

Hesitating for a moment he continues "Pickles took the wrap for the entire thing in return they gave him a suspension from playing high school sports. I made an agreement that I'd sign on and take the scholarship to this school."

Shaking his head in disgust he goes on "I had all kind of scholarships to the big schools. Schools I really wanted to go to and that wanted me. I was even projected as a top pick in the NBA. I had to give it all up to come here."

Puzzled she responds "So why did you take the money? Or why didn't you just give it back?" Smirking he says "Fan...these boosters, agents, colleges and sponsors are all tied together. It's all about the money with them. I needed the money to take care of my brother and mom. They knew it so; I had a choice but not really."

Grabbing her hand, he holds on as he proceeds "Regardless if we take it, give it back or not they can use the fact that an agreement was made to ruin our basketball careers. They take advantage of us because they know for us basketball and sports are our way to make it out."

Stunned she says "I had no idea. I apologize that you've had to deal with all of that. I have known you for some time and I'll never judge. I'll always be here for you and now I understand what you've been holding in all this time. I know it can be hard and I'm glad you chose to share with me and let me in."

Relieved from her sympathetic response he replies *"Puedo hacer otra pregunta?"* Looking at him in amazement she counters "Sure but I didn't know you knew how to speak Spanish." Giggling he retorts "*Si, mi Madre es Mexicana.* Do you remember when I drove you home the other day?"

She nods in agreeance anticipating the direction of the conversation as he goes on "So I've thought about it a lot and if nothing else this day confirms that you are the only woman I want in my life FROM NOW UNTIL FOREVER. That is only if your offer still stands. I am ready. I want us to be together"

Excited from his request she yells, "YES! YES!" Pausing she giggles "From now until forever is a very long time." She jumps into his arms and kisses him on the lips.

Pushing away after the abrupt kiss they embark on an awkward moment. Now gazing at one another they slowly lean in for a mutual kiss. They hold one another as they listen and gaze at the water from the waterfall ripple down the stream.

Chapter 17

Preparing for the homecoming basketball game Kevon and Kasyn sit at their lockers which are side by side. Looking over at Kasyn, Kevon asks if he had heard what happened at the basketball courts.

With a stoic look Kasyn doesn't make eye contact as his eyes are lowered toward the direction of his shoes and he's seemingly overly engaged in tying his sneakers.

Hoping instead of gaffing him off that Kasyn just didn't hear him initially, Kevon reaches over and taps him and repeats his question "Pickles! Did you hear about what happened at the basketball courts?"

Raising from his locker he walks over toward the other players before responding "It's game time PlayBoi! Coach getting ready for the pre-game speech."

Shocked at his response, Kevon slowly walks over to the middle of the locker room where all the players are huddled and awaiting the speech from the coach. Looking over at Kasyn, he attempts to reassure himself the reason he isn't responding is because this is a big game and he's trying to remain focused.

The coach enters and positions himself in the middle of the players. Without hesitation he begins his speech which gets the excited. Now in a frenzy they begin to chant and jump up and down while clapping their hands together. Glancing over toward Kasyn, Kevon observes that he is emotionless during all of the commotion taking place in the locker room.

Deciding to shift his focus on the game Kevon's mind wanders to the last game. Understanding that he didn't have his best game he convinces himself that this is a second chance for redemption. With the pre-game speech now complete the team runs out of the locker room onto the court.

Scanning the crowd Kevon sees a screaming Fannah waiving and blowing kisses toward him. Comforted with her presence he grins while waving in her direction. He continues to search the crowd for DJ. Realizing that he is not in the stands, he is again disappointed. Rehashing in his mind the last interaction with his brother after the incident at the basketball courts causes him to have a momentary meltdown. Looking back up at the stands and seeing Fan cheer him on he fights through the setback and trots onto the court.

As the game begins the home team wins the tip off and Kevon cuts to the corner of the 3-point line. Understanding the chemistry that he has developed with Kasyn he awaits and receives the pass from his friend and without hesitation nails the game's first 3-point shot. With a tenacious sense of urgency by the home team they erupt for a season high 30 points in the first quarter.

Having scored 20 of those points Kevon runs over to dap up Kasyn. Nonchalantly he returns the gesture. Sensing the coldness of the returned gesture Kevon now starts to have an uneasy feeling about his friend's disposition but decides not to address it during the game.

With a 10 point lead the home team starts the second quarter on the same hot streak it ended the first quarter on. Kasyn who is now on pace for a career night in assists starts to also drive to the basket and score with ease. The defense starts to give him room to drive because of his ball distribution in addition to the hot shooting streak that Kevon is on.

The home team crowd is now erupting in a frenzied ruckus based of the stellar play of their home team versus their heated rivals. Seizing the spotlight Kevon and Kasyn continue their career night pace ending the first half with a 54 to 40 halftime lead.

Walking toward the locker room Kevon looks up at Fan and blows her a kiss as she is frantically jumping up and down cheering along with the rest of the crowd.

Relaxing in his locker area Kevon listens while the coach gives his halftime speech. During the talk, the coach relays his enthusiasm to the team while also cautioning his team to not become complacent.

With the speech now complete and the team preparing to go back onto the court Kevon looks around for Kasyn and finally sees him in an isolated corner of the locker room talking on the phone.

Walking back on the court early to take some extra free throw shots he yells over to Kasyn and lets him know that half time is almost over. Responding to his comment he gives him the thumbs up as he continues his phone conversation.

Breaking the huddle to start the second half Kasyn pulls Kevon to the side and tells him that since they have a good lead that they should take it easy and not keep pushing the pace.

Confused at the comment Kevon reminds him of the coach's half time speech of not becoming complacent. Without giving a response Kasyn walks onto the court.

As the second half starts Kevon runs to his usual spot on the 3-point line and is wide open. The visiting team has switched to a tight zone defense to prevent Kasyn from penetrating to the rim which he had success doing in the first half.

Wide open, Kevon waves for him to pass the ball. Forgoing the pass Pickles starts the half by driving into the crowded zone defense and turns the ball over.

Continuing to drive to the rim on the next 3 possessions, Kasyn turns the ball over twice. After the two turnovers he drives and pulls up forcing and missing on a highly contested shot.

Now on a 10-0 run the visiting team dwindles the lead to 4 points with the score now 54-50. Looking over to the coach Kevon throws his hands in the air in frustration.

With the crowd now starting to boo the home team the coach paces the sideline. Watching the next two plays, Kasyn continues to attempt to penetrate to the rim. He again turns the ball over twice, resulting in two easy fast break attempts which allows the visiting team to tie the game.

Calling a timeout, the coach looks at Kasyn and asks "What are you thinking out there? Stick to the game plan." With a dejected stare he does not respond but instead walks away from the huddle and stands to himself.

In the huddle the coach now talks to Kevon and tells him he is running the point guard position and that Kasyn is out of the game. The coach then asks Kevon if he can he handle playing the position and watches him shake his head in agreeance. Now reenergized the team huddles and gives a chant prior to walking back onto the floor.

With the game now tied at 54 Kevon comes down the court and distributes the ball as directed by the coach. Working as planned the home team reels off 6 consecutive scoring plays. Deciding to run the press, Kevon leads the way as the aggressive defense creates turnovers that are converted into 4 additional points.

Stretching the lead back to 10 the crowd gets back into the game and begins to cheer and root their team on. Kevon dribbles the ball at the top of the key for the final seconds of the third quarter. Looking at the defense he notices the zone open up at the top of the key.

Because he has been distributing the ball and hasn't taken any shots in the quarter the visiting team now anticipates a pass. This leaves Kevon wide open on the 3-point line and without hesitation he elevates to take the shot as time expires in the quarter. Watching the shot go in sends the crowd to their feet. Ecstatic they began to cheer loudly with the home team now leading 67-54.

Dribbling the ball up court to start the last quarter Kevon gets the ball stolen. In a trance he doesn't chase behind the defender who easily scores on the fast break play. With his face now looking as if he's seen a ghost the coach yells "get your head in the game."

Patting him on the back in a supporting gesture his teammates let him know its ok. Seemingly distracted and not in the game Kevon becomes hesitant on making passes.

Visibly distracted his loss of awareness begins to affect the team. Unable to get his mind back into the game, he causes the team to commit shot clock violation and turnovers on the next two possessions.

With the visiting team on an 8-0 run the coach calls a time out. Slowly walking over to the sideline Kevon braces for the wrath of his coach. Screaming at the newly assigned point guard the coach says "I thought you said you could handle this position! You are embarrassing yourself and this team out there Kevon!"

Pausing for a minute and seeing the look in Kevon's eyes that he isn't into the game the coach looks back at Kasyn who is sitting on the bench and continues "Kevon take yourself a breather."

Waiving toward Kasyn to join the huddle the coach explains "I need you to finish out this game for us. Are you ready now?" Nodding his head, the coach puts Kasyn back into the game at the point guard position and sits Kevon.

Sitting on the bench with a towel draped over his head Kevon looks into the stands. Staring to ensure he isn't mistaken he observes Fannah sitting next to Trail having a conversation. Smirking in his direction Trail nudges Fannah and points to Kevon as he continues to stare at the two.

Seeing that she has his attention she waives and shrugs her shoulders. Reading her lips, he makes out that she is asking what is wrong and you need to get your mind back into the game.

Not responding to her gesture, he reclines back in his seat as his mind begins to race. Wondering why she is sitting with Trail? How do they know each other? And what is he even doing at the game?

With all of these things racing through his mind combined with his altercation with his brother and the strange way that Pickles has been acting he begins to experience a level of panic that becomes visible by the trembling of his hands. He attempts to contain his state of anxiety as he focuses his attention to the game.

Holding on to a five-point lead with 6 minutes remaining in the game Kasyn begins by distributing the ball as instructed by the coach. However, with Kevon, (who is the team's best shooter), on the bench they enter a cold streak and after missing on each of their next 4 possessions and not getting the rebound their lead dwindles.

On the defensive end they begin breaking down and allow four scores for another 8-0 run putting them in a 3-point deficit. With the score now 70-67 with three minutes remaining in the game the team begins to lose their energy.

Looking over at his teammates and feeling guilty Kevon's anxiety explodes enabling him to continue to sit in his seat and watch. He storms over to the coach and ask if he could go back in the game.

Prior to him responding he looks onto the court as Kasyn pulls up and misses a 3-point attempt on a 3 on 1 fast break. The home team secures the rebound with less than two minutes remaining in the game. Frustrated the coach uses their final time out.

Looking over at Kevon the coach sees that killer instinct back in his eyes while they are in the huddle and tells him he is back in the game at the shooting guard position. Before breaking the huddle, the coach reiterates to rotate the ball and look for the open shot.

Getting the inbound pass Kasyn dribbles at the top of the key letting the shot clock wind down. Frustrated that he is not rotating the ball Kevon yells for Kevon to pass the ball. Continuing to dribble Kasyn drives into the lane and forces a contested shot that is blocked and rebounded by the visiting team.

With 50 seconds left in the game and no time outs remaining the coach tells his team not to foul. At the top of the key the visiting team is now dribbling and winding the shot clock down when Kevon makes a dash toward the ball handler and steals the ball.

Seeing Kevon steal the ball Kasyn streaks down the floor. Beating everyone down the court he calls for the ball. Seeing him wide open Kevon heaves the pass down court. Kasyn catches the pass and slows up giving the defender enough time to make a play on the ball. Making it to the rim he is fouled while attempting and missing the layup.

Lining up for two free throws and a chance to decrease the visiting teams lead to one point he makes the first shot. With only a two-point deficit and 35 seconds remaining Kasyn misses his second attempt and the visiting team rebounds with no timeouts remaining.

Without hesitation Kevon runs up and presses the ball handler causing a bad pass leading to a turnover. With no time outs, the time ticking and the home team down by 2 points the coach instructs the team to drive to the hole in the hopes of tying the game or drawing a foul.

Kasyn receives the pass after the steal and drives to the rim and gets his shot rejected with 5 seconds remaining. Sprinting and retrieving the loose ball Kevon steps back to the three-point line vice going for the easy two pointer. Setting his feet, he releases the shot just as the time expires on the clock.

With everyone out of their seat watching the ball soar through the air the gymnasium becomes quiet. The shot goes in, popping the bottom of the net without seeming to touch the rim. The next sound is cheers and the fans rush the floor to celebrate the 71-70 victory.

Laying on the floor after the win the fans and teammates jump on and pat Kevon rigorously celebrating the victory and their best player's heroic efforts. Getting to his feet he looks toward the stands and no longer sees Fannah or Trail.

He looks toward the locker room and sees Kasyn making an exit without speaking to any of their teammates nor staying on the court to celebrate with them and the fans.

Wanting to escape from all the off the court drama, he decides to focus on the win. Hugging teammates and fans, he immerses himself into the celebration.

Chapter 18

Startled by a knock at the door, not expecting anyone, Chasity walks over to answer. Wondering who it could be she opens the door and sees DJ standing in a seemingly confused state.

Concerned about him she grabs his arm and pulls him inside. Assuming that something is bothering him, she escorts him to the sofa and sits next to him. As he remains silent, she asks "what's going on? You don't look like your normal self." He stares at the ceiling without responding to her comments.

In an attempt to let it be known that she is not pressuring him to converse she holds his hand and caresses it while letting him know that she is here for him.

Aware that something is on his mind and he is in no mood to talk she decides to take the opportunity to share her feelings with him. Continuing to hold his hand she says "I'm actually glad you came by and maybe this isn't the right time to tell you however it has been on my mind and I wanted you to know."

Pausing to gauge his interest in what she has to say she notices that her comment gets a reaction from him. He turns his attention from the ceiling and looks into her eyes as she nervously continues, "so ever since our time together at the park I really connected with you in a way that I've never connected with a guy or anyone before."

Smiling she holds his hand tight and proceeds "Thinking about everything we talked about I realized that you are what I've been looking for and even though it seems like it may be soon I know that I'm in love with you Demyre."

Speechless from her comment he looks into her eyes and sees the sincerity as she pours out her feeling to him and without notice tightly embraces her with both arms.

Releasing his grasp, he looks back into her eyes while holding her hands and responds "You know how I feel about you. We are in this together Chass." At a slight loss for words he goes on "You know my story and to be honest, I can't really say I know what love is."

Seeing the dejection in her face he goes on "Don't get me wrong babe. I know I really care about you and like I told you the other day I got you." Staring her in the eyes "I don't think I said that right. I am not trying to disappoint you. I just don't think I have ever been in love, but with you I do find myself thinking about you before I think about anything else."

She sits in silence not knowing how to respond to his comment as he continues "My dad beat my mom and she stayed with him. Did she love him? Because if that's love I don't want that with you. I want to protect you, hold you, support you and make you happy. The only way I would ever put my hands on you is to make you happy."

With tears in her eyes she thrusts herself into his arms and embraces him while crying "that is love Demyre! That is the love that I have wanted all my life!"

As they lie on the sofa enjoying one another's company Fannah walks through the door. Raising up they both acknowledge her entrance as she walks to her bedroom. As a courtesy Chasity tries to stop her before she gets to her room so that she can introduce her to DJ.

Stopping in her tracks remembering her promise to Kevon that she would talk with Chasity so that she can keep an eye on DJ she walks back to the two of them. Stunned by her change in attitude Chasity turns and says, "Fan this is DeMyre."

Reaching to shake his hand she asks, "So you are Kevon's brother?" Hearing the name and knowing that it sounds familiar, Chasity sits and thinks for a moment before blurting "KEVON! The basketball player. That's your brother?"

Starting to get irritated he looks at Chasity and says "That's one of my issues. At this point I don't even want to talk about him." In a dismissive tone "If you want to call that dude my brother then ok yeah, we have the same parents."

With his mood shifting into a gloomy state he snaps "I came over here to be with you and take my mind off that clown. The dude foul and never has my back. My guy Trail had to step up and get my back. But he my brother. Trail feel more like a brother at this point."

Taking a deep breath, he proceeds "This dude Bump got bodied in the park the other day and before it happened, we were right there and literally brawling on the basketball court. My guy Trail was right there with me throwing blows, but do you think that guy had my back?"

Getting louder he goes on "As a matter fact even before that fight I got into it at the homecoming football game and do you think he even acted like he wanted to help me? Shaking his head "Nah. He playing peacemaker."

Walking over to the table and taking a seat Fannah embarks upon a somber disposition while Chasity looks at both of them in confusion and finally remarks "I'm lost. Someone got killed at the park?" In a more serene mood now that he's dumped weight off his shoulders DJ nods toward Chasity confirming her inquiry.

Engaging back into the conversation Fannah becomes flustered by DJ's negative perception of Kevon and says "DJ, you do know that Kevon was trying to get you out of harm's way, right? He only wants the best for you."

Glancing in her direction Chasity counters "so you knew about the shooting too?" Nodding with confirmation to her question Fannah responds "Yes. Kevon told me about it."

Now smirking from her comment DJ says "Ahhhh so that's where this coming from. You see what I mean? Dude running his mouth to any and everybody. He know he dead wrong so he trying to run around the city and soak up some pity."

Flustered he continues "Who does that? He try to tell his side of the story to make it seem like he was bout that action or something." Perturbed with how DJ is dissecting her comments Fannah waves her arms in a halting manner "Hold on! No! It's not like that DJ.

Kevon and I are together, and he shares everything with me just as I do with him. He broke down and is really hurt about everything that happened so I promised him that I would try to get to you and let you know that he only means well for you." With an empty expression on his face after hearing her explanation DJ sinks into silent thought.

Trying to soak in all of the information and decipher everything that is taking place Chasity's mind races, from Demyre hanging out with Trail, to the shooting that got someone killed, Fannah still hanging out with Trail despite her warnings and finally to the history she's had with him.

She starts to feel a sinking feeling in her stomach getting a picture of the evil person that Trail is and how he has manipulated and continues to manipulate everyone he comes in contact with.

Breaking the silence Chasity yells "HEY! Don't you all see what's going on?" Alarmed by her outburst Fannah and DJ stare at Chasity without responding.

Having their attention, she goes on "Trail is the issue!" Annoyed by her comment Fannah replies "Really Chass. You're going to start this crap again?"

Hoping that DJ is heeding her warning she chooses to ignore Fannah's comment and looks over toward him and asks, "When that guy got killed at the park was Trail there?"

Surprised at her accusation DJ gets up from the couch walking toward the door to leave while countering "What does him being there have to do with anything? Have you been listening to what I've been saying? Trail is one of the few dudes who got my back."

Tears now starting to form in her eyes she becomes emotional while whimpering "DJ, you just met this guy not long ago. What do you really know about him? Can't you all see that trouble follows this guy?"

Getting up from the table in disgust Fannah walks toward her room while saying "Chass this was supposed to be about DJ and Kevon and even the guy who got killed on the court but as usual you let your jealousy come into play and have to make it all about Chasity. Always have to be the center of attention. I'm over it. I'm going to bed."

Turning the knob on the door to exit the apartment DJ says "I can't believe you Chas. We just had the best moment of my life and now this?"

Now with her head in her hands, visibly broken down and crying profusely, without looking at either of the two as they leave the room she yells "IT WAS TRAIL WHO RAPED ME!"

Chapter 19

The phone in the apartment rings as Chasity rushes to answer thinking that it may be DJ. "Is Fan there?" Not recognizing the voice, she asks "May I ask whose calling?" Recognizing her voice, he sighs "Chasity! This Trail...Why are you playing like you don't know my voice?"

Now in a more chipper tone he goes on "So tell me what you wearing sexy?" Feeling disrespected she slams the phone down and yells "FAN, TELEPHONE!" returning to her room feeling disgusted.

Infatuated with Fannah, Trail always makes an effort to show her attention. Valuing his friendship and the respect he shows her she finds pleasure in hanging out with him.

Not giving up hope that he can win her affection he continues to shower her with gifts and show her how much he cares. Seeing no harm in what they share she has come to trust him and appreciate the friendship they share.

Lying in bed Fannah rolls over after she hears Chasity tell her she has a phone call. Not wanting to get out of bed she asks, "Who is it?"

Not receiving a response, she rolls out of bed and walks out to the dining room to see that the phone is laying on the table and that Chasity is nowhere in sight. A little confused she picks the phone up "Hello."

Having patiently waited for her to come to the phone he answers, "What's up with ya girl?" Still waking up from her sleep she yawns "Is this Trail? Why didn't you just call me on my cell phone?"

Not sure if Chasity may have complained to her about his out of line comment from earlier, he cautiously cracks "You know you don't like to answer your cell...So what's up with you? Do you have anything planned today"?

Starting to fully awaken from her sleep she responds "I was going to ask Chasity did she want to go to the skating rink to hang out but I also heard there was an event on The Grounds that I wanted to go to."

Knowing that she couldn't afford tickets to go to the event and that Trail always had money, she decided to cleverly mention it to him. Understanding that he never turns down her requests and would do anything for her she felt confident he would agree to take her.

After a slight hesitation he responds, "What event are they having on The Grounds today?" In a relieved voice she replies, "There's a step show there and also a car show with local bands performing later this evening."

Not wanting to sound selfish she asks "So what about you? Are you doing anything today"? Seeing this as an invitation he responds "No, I don't have any plans, but I would like to take you to The Grounds today, so how about it"?

She immediately replies "Yes, that would be perfect. I think Chasity is upset with me anyway so I'm sure she won't mind me leaving her alone."

Giddy she pushes "So do you mind being here in a couple of hours to get me? I'm already dressed." Grasping at the opportunity he puts the phone down and runs into his closet and begins to get dressed.

"Are you there? Hello! --- Hello!" she bellows in a disappointed voice. Now feeling that she put herself out there she starts to feel guilty that she was so assertive in her request.

Minutes later he picks up the phone and answers "I'm on my way now", as he runs out of the door of his apartment and down the stairs to his car.

Somewhat flustered as well as relieved she says, "You could've said hold on or something...You had me talking to myself on the phone." Entering his car, "Calm down Ms. Overdramatic, I didn't want to keep you waiting so I threw on some clothes while we were on the phone and now, I'm on the way." A little out of breath from running to the car he pants "So a simple thank you would be nice".

Now less embarrassed she jests "Technically, we weren't on the phone because you weren't talking so can you just get here please? It's getting late".

Happy to hear the anticipation in her voice he replies "Alright, alright, I'll pull up in a few. You do know there are speed limits; are you trying to have me get a ticket or something".

Arriving at her apartment he pulls up into the parking lot. Sitting in his car he texts her and then blows the horn. Running down the stairs from her apartment she rants "What is your problem? You couldn't come up to the apartment and knock on the door?"

As he sees her running, he meets her before she gets to the car and embraces her with a hug, "Calm down ma', you know how I joke around" he whispers in her ear.

"Whatever TERRAIL, let's just go!" As they drive toward The Grounds, he decides to pry into her personal life asking, "So what's up with this new guy who has your nose wide open?" Evasively she retorts "Excuse me?" After an awkward silence, an agitated Fan asks, "Who are you talking about?"

Pushing on him in a playful way "Why do people always choose to mind everyone's business but their own." With a smirk he responds "Really! You're going to act brand new now huh? It's cool your secret is safe with me".

They arrive at The Grounds and he pays for their entry fees. As they walk around Trail spots Kasyn watching the step show and escorts Fannah over to where he's sitting.

After they dap each other up, Kasyn leans over and gives her a hug before asking, "So are you still coming to the homecoming game?" Jokingly she responds "Hello to you too! And yes, I plan on coming".

Trail tells her she can start walking over to the stage and he will catch up to her as him and Kasyn have a brief conversation. After talking with Kevon, Trail jogs over to one of the vendors to make a purchase. Placing the item in a bag he jogs over to catch up to Fannah.

Out of breath when he finally reaches her, she cracks "Seriously? You are out of breath from that short distance? You may need to hit the gym or something."

Laughing along he pants "Here I am getting something for you and you wanna joke on me." Pulling the item out of the bag he hands it to her. Looking at it with astonishment she gasps "What is this for?" Placing it in her hand he says, "This is for you."

At a loss for words she stares at the 3P medallion in amazement. After a moment he picks it up from her hand and places it around her neck stating, "It looks good on you."

Feeling fulfilled by her astonished reaction he decides to change the subject asserting "I know we went to the game the other day, but I didn't know you were into basketball like that?" Still surprised from the gift she quips "You never asked."

As they reach the stage, she takes a deep breath and exults "Trail thank you for this gift, but I have something I want to tell you."

Pausing to gather her thoughts she continues "There is a guy on the basketball team that I do like and we decided to give the dating thing a chance." Giving her a puzzled look, he says, "So have you told him about us?"

She immediately screams "What? There's nothing to tell. We aren't together, TERRAIL! We are just friends and always have been just that. Why do you continue to try and make things so complicated?"

With a serious expression he looks her in the eyes "Fan, let's be real. You know I want you and always have. So please tell me what is so complicated about that?"

Surprised at the conversation she answers "We have a great friendship. That's what this is. I know you care about me and I care about you but only as friends." Not happy with her statement Trail gets quiet.

Holding her hand, he resumes "So is this the dude you were cheering for at the game we were at the other day? And what does this dude have that I don't have? What can he do for you or give you that I can't?"

Breaking eye contact she begins to take interest in the step show hoping that the conversation they are having will go away. Disappointed he looks on at the show along with her.

Feeling her pull her hand from his palm to clap for the show he turns and asks "So Fan. Don't you think this guy that you're into will have a problem with another guy hanging out with his ole lady? You know he saw us at his game. How do you think he feels about that?"

Getting unnerved she says "First of all I'm not his property, and second I am grown and I can hang around whoever I want to, ok...So there's nothing wrong with us hanging out as just friends and last I'm done talking about this"!

Seeing that she is agitated he decides to change the subject. Gently pulling on her arm and calling her name she pulls away. He continues his attempt to calm her down as he asks, "So is there anything I can do that will make you change your mind about being with me as more than friends?"

After a long pause she turns to him and says "Look! I'm fine with being just friends and like I told you before I'm with Kevon, we are trying to make it work."

Pausing she turns her attention from the step show toward him and asks "What's going on with you and DJ? I heard you have been hanging around him and you all have been into some issues.

Giving her a blank stare, he becomes silent. Pushing him she goes on "So now you become quiet?" Giving him a stern stare, she asserts "His brother is worried about him?"

Seeing that she is concerned, he reaches for her arm and calmly affirms "DJ good. His big bro don't have anything to worry about. You can let him know I got him."

Still seeming unnerved he playfully pushes her and asks "What else? Is there something else bothering you?" Turning toward him, she says, "I am fine with that, but I need you to answer a question for me honestly." Becoming a little uneasy he notices her serious disposition.

Maintaining his cool he calmly responds, "What's up? What else you got? You know I always keep it 100 with you." Looking him in the eyes she asks, "So Chasity says that you raped her...Is it true?"

Caught off guard he gulps before gaining his composure and with a confident tone he responds "Really Fan! You know your girl got a reputation and you know me. Do you think I'd do something like that?" Without responding she turns her attention back to the stage.

Chapter 20

Laying across her bed on the day of the party Chasity reflects on DJ's distant reaction to her statement about her rape. Thinking of how Fan responded to it and the shooting at the park. Allowing it to all consume her thoughts she sinks into a depressed state, curling up in her bed staring at the ceiling.

Barging into her room unannounced breaking the silence Fannah jovially jumps on her bed plopping next to her and says "Get up! We have to get ready for this party! You are the one who wanted to do it in the first place. So, don't think you are going to have me setting up everything."

Still not having discussed Chasity's remarks, Fannah feels guilty that she hasn't consoled her friend. Feeling that she may have made the comment out of anger and resentment she decides to avoid the conversation. Hoping that time will cause the topic to blow over and that having the party will put her in a better mood.

Finally convincing her to get up Chasity slowly walks toward the bathroom to shower and get ready. Going back into the kitchen Fannah begins to decorate and make arrangements for the party. Hearing the shower come on and knowing that she is now up and did not get back into bed she yells "Is DJ coming to the party?"

Hearing DJ's name shifts her mind back into a somber mood. Not hearing a response, she continues "Kevon will be here so I think it would be good for him to come over also so they can see each other. Hopefully, we can help them come together you know." Still not responding Chasity finishes up her shower and begins to get dressed.

While putting up streamers Fannah spots Chasity slowly walking out of her room. Understanding that she may not be in a good mood she quips "Cheer up girl! How can you be sad when there is about to be a party?" Looking up to gauge whether the attempt at encouraging her is working she goes on "Being sad and party doesn't even go together."

Unpacking the groceries that they brought for the party Chasity pauses before blurting "Why don't we just cancel or postpone this party?" Giving a confused look in return Fannah shrugs her shoulders and shakes her head in disagreement.

Continuing to unpack groceries she goes on "It's just so much going on right now. I feel like moving forward with this is not a good idea". Suddenly a knock at the door startles them both. Fannah darts toward the door while reassuring her that everything will be ok.

Gazing toward the door Chasity observes a group of ladies eagerly coming inside as Fannah greets each guest. After entering the ladies walk toward Chasity and she also greets them while attempting to show enthusiasm for the event.

Once the last lady enters Fannah closes the door and retorts to the guests "Since you ladies are here early you all can roll up your sleeves and help us set up."

Laughing, the ladies gladly oblige and begin to assist in setting up. Fan pulls out her phone and walks over to the stereo system. After strolling through her phone, she begins to giggle. Seeming excited she links her phones blue tooth to the speaker system and turns up the volume.

Without notice music blares from the speakers causing the ladies to jump around in hysteria before dancing along with the song. Feeling the positive energy from everyone Chasity starts to sing along with the music and eventually joins in with the ladies as they continue to dance and twerk.

As they finish up with the decorating and setting up one of the girls pulls out a bottle of liquor and says, "it's time to get this party started."

Enthused with the idea of drinking Fannah responds with two thumbs up and skips over to the cabinet and pulls out shot glasses. Placing the glasses on the counter the lady begins to fill them up with Vodka.

Standing off to the side Chasity declines when offered a glass. Once all the glasses are filled, they hold them in the air. Before taking the shot Fannah looks over at Chasity and asks, "Are you sure you don't want to join us?"

Observing Chasity rigorously shake her head "NO" she turns her attention back to the ladies who bring their glasses in together as Fannah chants "*Salud!*" The other ladies echo her chant and they tap glasses and take their shots.

They follow with three additional shots. Moving toward the kitchen Chasity distances herself from the girls. Worried they are drinking too much too early she fixes her a plate and cautiously looks on while eating.

The group of ladies continue to drink while party goers begin to trickle in to party. Some were bringing in more alcohol as Chasity greets everyone at the door.

Noticing Kevon at the door Chasity invites him in. Greeting her with a hug he asks "Where's your girl? I've been trying to call her all afternoon."

Pointing over toward Fannah she responds, "her phone is hooked up to the stereo, playing music, so that may be why you haven't been able to get through." With a look of relief, he laughs "Ohhh! Ok. I see. She got the party started for real with no D.J. huh." Thanking her for the information he walks toward Fannah.

Walking up to the group Kevon speaks to the ladies prior to giving Fannah a hug and kiss on the cheek. The ladies who are now somewhat inebriated begin to tease her by cat calling and mocking her.

Laughing it off Kevon asks, "Fan can I speak with you for a few minutes alone?" Reluctantly she complies walking toward her bedroom to escape the noise.

Following her into her bedroom he closes the door after they enter. Noticing her necklace, he comments "That's a nice medallion you have. When did you get that?" Visibly irritated she scoffs "Really? Is that what you want to talk about?"

Staggered by her reaction he says, "No. That is not want I wanted to talk about." Reaching for her hand he continues "I just wanted to know what happened to you at the game the other night?"

With a puzzled look she responds "I was there? What are you talking about?" Sensing her becoming irritated he attempts to calm the situation by changing the tone of the conversation.

He counters "Well you used to stick around after the game to talk to me and let me take you home." Snatching her hand out of his grasp she spouts "Kevon did you really just drag me in here to ask me that?"

Looking at her in shock based on her sudden irrational behavior he asks, "Does your attitude toward me have anything to do with the guy you were with at the game?" Staring at him in anger she asserts "Trail is just a friend and I don't understand what he has to do with any of this."

Her voice getting louder she yells "I don't tell you who you can and can't be friends with so why are you trying to control me Kevon?"

In a bewildered state he backs toward the door attempting to figure out why she is reacting the way she is. Recognizing she has had a few drinks he decides to walk away and let her calm down. As he walks toward the door to leave, she says "Maybe you aren't ready for a relationship because of your jealousy."

Before he can respond they hear yelling coming from the living room. Opening the door DJ is in the middle of the apartment yelling and drinking directly from a liquor bottle. Attempting to calm the situation Chasity tries to convince him to put the liquor bottle down and come into her room so they can talk in private.

Putting the bottle on the counter he turns and sees Kevon coming out of Fannah's room. Turning his attention back toward Chasity he yells "Y'all didn't tell me that this lame was going to be here! Because I definitely wouldn't have come had I known."

With a look of disgust Kevon walks toward the door to leave. Seeing the disappointment in his face Chasity pleads for Kevon to stay and for everyone to calm down.

Hearing her plea DJ becomes enraged before yelling "So first you want to let Trail hit and now you want to drop the drawls for this lame too? I should've listened to Trail when he told me you wasn't nothing but a ho."

Immediately after his comments Chasity drops to the floor in tears. With everyone's attention now on DJ he continues "Why are you all looking at me? She's the ho and this dude is a clown."

Shocked and embarrassed Chasity lay curled on the floor crying. Walking over to check on her, Kevon looks toward DJ and responds, "Dude you might have something against me but you dead wrong for going in on her like that."

After his comments DJ walks out of the apartment and brushes against Kevon as he passes by him. Without breaking eye contact he replies, "Do it look like I give a damn about a ho or a ho ass lame like you?"

Looking back toward Fannah he continues "You need to be worried about why your little girlfriend bussing it open for Trail while you all up in my business."

After DJ slams the door on the way out of the apartment Kevon remains behind in a transfixed state. Helping Chasity off the floor and to the couch he looks over at Fannah whose jaw is dropped as she stands speechless. Placing a pillow under Chasity's head he gets up to leave. Looking at the stunned party goers he opens to the door to leave. Before exiting he looks back at Fannah with a look of disappointment.

Chapter 21

With the conversation he had with Fannah the day before still on his mind Trail leaves his apartment. He makes up his mind to drive over to her apartment. His plan is to convince her that Chasity is lying about the accusation she made and that she is attempting to ruin their friendship.

Understanding the trust that Fannah has for him Trail begins to giggle to himself. He is now contemplating different ideas of how to use Fannah's trust in him to turn her against Chasity.

Walking toward his car he notices a black stretch Maybach pull into the parking space in front of his apartment. Unfamiliar with the vehicle, Trail darts back into his apartment.

Living in a bad area of the city he understands that seeing expensive vehicles like this drive through could mean trouble. Peeking through his window blinds he observes two tall heavy-set guys exit the vehicle. Concentrating on the individuals he finally recognizes them as Chop Down gang members.

The men open the back door and let another passenger out of the vehicle and point toward Trail's apartment. Concerned for his safety he goes to his bed and raises up the mattress where he has two loaded guns stashed. Quickly choosing the .45 he shoves it in the rear of his pants.

Trail cautiously walks over to answer a knock on the door. He now has one hand on the doorknob and the other in the back of his pants grasping his .45. Snatching the door open without asking who was there, his intention is to begin shooting once he makes eye contact.

Once the door flings open and before he can pull out his gun, he sees Prince standing in the entrance of his apartment laughing. Relieved he takes his hand off his gun and invites Prince and his two friends inside.

With his heartbeat still racing he manages to calmly ask the guests if they want anything to drink or eat. Declining the offer, the men walk over to his couch and seat themselves.

Reclining on the sofa and placing his feet on the coffee table Prince's expression turns more serious as he asks, "So what happened at the park the other day?" Fumbling in the kitchen before walking toward the living room area where the men are Trail gives a look as if he doesn't understand the question.

Taking his feet off the table, Trail sits erect on the couch with his arms on his legs. His hands rubbing his face he falls into a deep thought before asserting "Apparently you don't remember our last conversation. Shyt don't move on these streets unless I say so!"

Seeming unfazed Trail takes a seat and continues to listen. Calmed by his confident demeanor, Prince reclines back into the sofa. Expecting his presence to rattle Trail, he starts to think that Trail may not have been involved.

Looking directly into Prince's eyes Trail responds "I told you back then that I wasn't sure about Kevon big homey. I was out there when it happened. The boy Bump got into it with Kevon's brother and next thing I knew somebody started clapping and then Bump dropped with blood splattering everywhere."

Shrugging he goes on "And you know how them people get out here, so everyone dipped before twelve rolled up."

Pausing to gauge how Prince is receiving his information he goes on "DJ is on lock like I was telling you. He down with the team fa sho." Sitting up once again Prince replies "Lil homey listen, whoever making these moves ain't good for business."

Tapping his fists on the arm of the recliner he proceeds "Bump was up next. He was in line for major sponsorship and endorsement deals...this is bigger than making money off the line or even wins and losses. If things don't go how I want them to go nobody eat and a lot of people will stop breathing."

Glancing at the two men he walked in with Prince turns his attention back toward Trail and continues "I put you in position to make sure everything goes how I plan it. People need to also be aware that if it doesn't go as planned there are consequences."

Eagerly Trail counters "what I was also going to tell you about this whole situation is word around town was that Bump was talking to the Feds. They say he was scared for his life when they lost that homecoming game."

Hoping to relieve him he goes on "They say that he was going to start rolling over on everyone. So, Bump got what was coming to him...Not one time have I let you down and like I've always said you can count on me."

Again, looking at the guys that are with him and turning his attention back toward Trail giggling he replies "Bump was my guy. If he got outta line someone was supposed to come to me to find out how to take care of the situation."

Sliding back in his seat now seeming uneasy Trail listens on as Prince proceeds "I've been doing this for a while. People said the same thing about Kevon. People gone talk, DAMMIT that's just how it go. As long as I know who doing the talking and who they talking to then everyone safe."

Tapping his fingers on the table he looks up continuing "Do you know what happened to Kevon and his brother's dad?" Looking confused Trail shakes his head with confirmation that he is unaware. Laughing out loud Prince again looks toward the men with him as they also laugh.

Looking at the three men laugh Trail understands that Prince's intent was not to reveal what happened to Kevon and DJ's dad but instead instill fear. Despite the frightening threat Trail attempts to mask his fear.

Taking a moment to gather himself Trail then boldly asserts "The homecoming game is DONE big homey. It is supposed to be one of the biggest games this year based on what happened at the last game. This time we have DJ on our side and he's the biggest star in town right now."

With his bold proclamation the men stop laughing and look on as Trail shows no fear in his responses or to the subliminal threats aimed at him. Grasping at the opportunity as he now becomes more confident seeing that the men aren't as aggressive he continues "I know you lost Bump but I can assure you that DJ will bring in way more than Bump ever would have."

Scooting to the edge of his seat now displaying a devious grin he goes on "I know I've only been in this game for a few years but I know a little something and what I have found is that drama sells."

Rubbing his hands together he continues "Yes Bump got killed but that can make the story of DJ legendary. You know, young black dude from the streets make it out of the ghetto where other known super stars were gunned down. Plus, it doesn't hurt for his street cred that this is the same guy he was beefing with."

Sending the guys that are with him back to the car Prince stands up and walks toward the door. He waits for the men to exit the apartment and closes the door behind them at which time he turns to Trail and says "You know I could've called you but I had to come over here personally and look in your eyes."

Remaining confident Trail looks him in the eyes attentively listening. Walking closer to him Prince calmly says, "This is what is going to happen...Pine Grove is favored in the homecoming game."

Nodding in agreeance he proceeds "So the boy DJ WILL make sure he does what he needs to, so they lose. Pay him off for it and make sure someone is around when you are making the arrangement."

Finishing the conversation, he turns and walks toward the door. Before exiting he faces and sternly stares at Trail before saying "When I say nothing happens in this city without me knowing remember I mean it."

Squarely staring him in the eyes he goes on "Cops, City officials, Drug Dealers, Prostitutes or not even a business comes here without me knowing." Smiling he turns to walk out before commenting "And by the way I hope that .45 you got tucked in your back wasn't supposed to be for me."

Watching Prince exit his apartment and walk back to his vehicle Trail begins to relax while closing the door. Peeping out of the window blinds he looks at them pull away.

Spooked by Prince's visit he goes to his kitchen and retrieves his prepaid phone.

Making a call and receiving an answer he says "Dude! I think Prince on to us. Dude just came to my spot with two hittas." With the person on the other end heavily breathing with no response after hearing Trails news he continues "I think we are going to have to take him out sooner than later!"

Chapter 22

Waking up on the floor not knowing where he is DJ panics and looks around to assess his whereabouts. Recognizing his bed and television he calms down knowing that he is in the confines of his room. He looks at himself and realizes he passed out fully clothed and attempts to sit up.

Feeling a throbbing and nauseous sensation he quickly grabs his head and lies back on the floor. Thinking to himself "This is the worst hangover ever." Then he vows to never drink again.

Laying on the floor he attempts to rehash the events of the previous night with the hopes that he wasn't involved in anything that he will regret.

His memory brings him to the incident when Chasity told him that Trail raped her. After that new, he remembers driving around all night feeling like his heart had been shattered. The next memory is him waking up in his car sitting in the parking lot of the barber shop.

Reliving the hurt his mind flashes back entering the barber shop's lounge area and drinking non-stop to ease the pain. While drinking he remembers receiving a text from Chasity asking to please respond to her to let her know he is ok.

With the details of his drunken stupor becoming clearer he descends into a destitute state. He recalls being at Chasity's party, disrespecting her and embarrassing her in front of her friends along with everyone else at the party.

Rolling over on the floor disgusted with himself more thoughts of that incident resurface. He thinks back at the look on Fannah's face when he called her out in front of everyone just to make his brother mad.

Seeking to gather some clarity out of the situation and make himself feel better he finds comfort in his loyalty to Trail. Remembering that he has been there for him and kept his word on his pledge to take care of the situation with Bump.

Sobering up he's able to get off the floor and take a seat on his bed but feels his head still pulsating. As his nausea begins to subside, he staggers up to his feet. Suffering from a pounding headache he holds his head as he walks into the kitchen.

Going through his cabinets he locates two BC tablets. Immediately tossing them into his mouth he follows them with a glass of water hoping to cure his headache.

As he places the glass on the counter, he notices his phone lying face up. Slowly turning his attention to the phone, he reads the last message which is from Chasity which says "DJ! Please call or text me and let me know that you are ok."

After reading the text over and over, guilt begins to sink in. Again, thinking back to how he treated Chasity at the party overcomes all other thoughts.

Realizing that despite everything he did and said to her she still loved him enough to care if he was ok. Now sick from an emotional let-down he drops his head on the counter. Now banging his head, he stops to pick up the phone. Rereading her text messages, he sits in silence.

He realizes that not only did he humiliate Chasity and Fannah but himself as well. Understanding his actions, he knows he has to make an attempt to apologize. Rehearsing his apology several times in his head he picks up his phone and dials Chasity's number hoping that she will answer.

After a couple rings it goes directly to voice mail. Not leaving a message he immediately dials her number again hoping that his persistence will pay off and eventually she'll answer.

This time his call goes directly to voice mail. Noticing the difference, he knows that she has either turned her phone off or as soon as she sees his number, she automatically declines the call.

Starting to feel desperate with the thought that his actions have ruined the best thing that has ever happened to him he paces the apartment thinking of ways to make things right. Mind racing, he thinks back on Trail's words when he warned not to fall in love with her - she just a jump off.

Wondering to himself, why does Trail think so negative of such a wonderful person? Why did he let Trail's opinion of her ruin what they had? Was Trail jealous because she didn't want him? Was it true that Trail actually raped her? What is Chasity thinking now? What is she doing and why was I such an idiot!?

With all of the thoughts swarming his mind coming to a head he grabs his keys and heads out of his apartment with the purpose of going to Chasity's place to beg and plead with her face to face until she accepts his apology.

Arriving at Chasity's apartment he second guesses himself but manages to get out and walk towards her place despite his inhibitions. At the same spot he stood just hours previously, intoxicated, and full of hate and discontent he is back only this time with an entirely different mind-set.

Knocking on the door he patiently waits. With no answer he looks over to see if anyone comes to the blinds and peeps out of the window. With no movement in the blinds he dials her number after waiting a few more minutes.

Her phone once again goes directly to voice mail prompting him to knock on the door a little harder in frustration. With still no answer he paces back and forth in front of the door before taking a seat on the step-in front of her apartment.

Sitting on the steps looking at his phone he calls Chasity number again. Anticipating it going directly to voice mail again he waits. Once the voicemail picks up, he doesn't hang up but leaves a voice mail saying "Chasity I love you! I don't know what I was thinking last night. Being drunk, being disrespectful, being an idiot. None of it is an excuse"

Looking back at the door hoping she answers he continues "Please forgive me. You deserve better than the way I treated you. I am willing to do whatever it takes to make it up to you and..." before he can complete his message the voicemail ends. Looking at the phone a few more minutes he gets up to walk toward his car and make the drive back home.

Once inside his car he continues to replay the previous night events in his head. Focusing on Fannah's comments she made about Kevon and how he only wanted the best for him.

His mind then goes to the park and how Kevon anticipated the violence before it happened and wanted to get him out of harm's way. Bouncing back to his football game he remembers that Kevon was right by his side keeping him in the car and making sure he got home safely.

Fast forwarding he thinks back to the previous night. Realizing that Kevon was trying to calm him down and prevent him from disrespecting Chasity. He's hurt from his revelations that he has been so disrespectful to two of the people who care about him the most. Starting to feel horrible about how he's treated his brother he reaches for his phone again and dials Kevon's number only to hear it go directly to voice mail.

Hanging up without leaving a message he sits in his car tightly squeezing the steering wheel. Before cranking up the vehicle he reclines into his seat. Piercing into the windshield he reflects on his life. Beginning to come to grips that for each decision he makes it has a result that he chose.

Cranking up the car he pulls away. Opening the blinds, Chasity watches as he drives away. Listening to his voicemail, she tears up. Closing the blinds after seeing his car travel out of eyesight she pounces back across her bed sinking her face back into her tear drenched pillow.

Chapter 23

Everyone has left the party. Chasity has fallen asleep in her room while Fannah sits on the sofa alone. Unable to sleep Fannah changes into her pajamas and continues to drink. With each drink she becomes more upset with everything that has happened.

She starts to think that Chasity and Kevon are jealous of her relationship with Trail. Continuing into her thoughts she feels that they are attempting to ruin their friendship because they are envious of what they have. As tears begin to form, she decides to call Trail in the middle of the night.

Answering the phone Trail immediately hears the anguish in her voice and asks, "What's wrong?" Keeping herself together she says "I'm ok, I just need to talk. Can I come over for a minute?"

Without hesitation he responds "Definitely!" Pausing for a moment he puts down the phone before picking back up and goes on "I'm not at the crib now but give me about 30 minutes and by the time you make it over I will be there."

Reassured by his support and availability she replies "Ok! I'll put on some shoes and I'll be over in about 30 minutes." Hanging up the phone she takes another shot of liquor before putting on her shoes. She splashes water on her face before grabbing her keys to head out of her apartment.

Fan arrives at Trail's apartment just as he is getting out of his vehicle. Recognizing Fan's car, he walks over to greet and walk with her to his apartment. Seeing her stumble out of the car he runs over to assist her.

Smelling the alcohol coming from her pores he jokes "That must have been a great party you all had." Not responding she puts her arms around him and commences with the walk toward his apartment.

Getting into the apartment he escorts her to the couch and takes off her slippers to make her more comfortable. Relaxed on the couch she props her feet on the coffee table.

Crossing her feet, she begins to ramble "I'm not sure why everyone is so jealous of our friendship. I constantly have to defend what we have to people like Chasity and Kevon who are supposed to have my back and just be happy for me." They are just jealous."

Listening and nodding in agreeance he asks, "Do you want something to drink or eat?" Accepting his offer, she replies "Yes. Can you get me a bottle of water please?"

Retrieving a bottle of water out of the refrigerator and opening it for her he stops to make him a drink before coming to join her in the living room.

Trail sits on the sofa next to Fan and hands her an opened bottle of water. He continues to agree with her comments as he replies "I already told you about Chasity but after you got upset with me for saying anything I decided to let you find out for yourself."

Rubbing on her leg he goes on "And for Kevon I've heard stories that he's the jealous type and I didn't understand what you saw in him anyway. I knew things would work out." After a slight pause he asks, "So where is the medallion I got for you?"

Drinking the water, Fan reclines deeper into the couch while whispering "I left it in my car. I can't keep wearing it." Speech beginning to slur she continues "I need to give that necklace back. I can't keep it."

Starting to feel uneasy she murmurs "Water usually hydrates me and makes me feel better. For some reason I'm getting really tired now."

Dozing in and out of consciousness she manages to profess her love for Kevon saying "I think Kevon is the only man I ever loved and ever want to love. I don't know why he doesn't trust me."

Continuing to rub on her leg he moves closer to her as she dozes in and out of consciousness. Despite being woozy she comes to long enough to recognize his advances and pushes his hand away. Not wanting to give him the wrong idea she reiterates that they are just friends and she doesn't look at him like that.

Laughing as he slides closer to her, Trail says "Come on now Fan. We both grown so there's no reason to be shy about what we have." Stunned by his neglect for her denial of his advances she attempts to scoot away. Using the force, she can muster to push his hands off her. Grabbing her hand, he says "Fan we are always hanging out together, everyone notices the attraction between us."

Starting to become frightened she tries to stand up but becomes dizzy and plops back onto the couch. Watching Trail slide closer Fa reiterates "Trail we are just friends! I don't look at you like that."

Steadily sliding closer he responds "I understand. You are playing hard to get. Coming over in the middle of the night after drinking all day and wearing what you wearing and looking like you looking. C'mon Fan you don't have to spell it out for me, but I'll play along with your hard to get game."

Becoming woozy again her speech is slurred as she stutters "Stoooppp! I love Kevon. We are just friends. What are you doinnnn" before she is able to finish her sentence she blacks out.

Noticing that she has slumped over Trail picks her up and carries her to his room. He then lays her across the bed and takes her shirt off while kissing on her neck and moving down to her belly.

Now at her waist he pulls down her pajama pants and starts to remove her panties. Stammering to a slight

consciousness and in a haze, she murmurs
"Stop...Stop...Please stop!"

Noticing that she is awake he attempts to calm her by
holding her arms down and straddling her. Laughing as he
is on top of her, he jokes "So this is the play hard to get
game that you want huh?"

Afraid she vehemently attempts to push him away with the
limited energy that she can muster but after a slight struggle
she passes out again.

Seeing that she is no longer resisting he proceeds to
remove her panties and bra. Once undressed he quickly
takes off his pants and boxers and inserts himself into her.

Initially stroking slowly his pace quickens as he begins to
reach his climax. Fiercely stroking her unconscious body, he
kisses and sucks on her neck and breasts.

Now ejaculating his pace begins to slow down. While
cumming, he doesn't pull out but instead chooses to release
inside of her. After he finishes, he kisses her on the lips and
then walks over to the restroom and washes himself off and
changes into pajamas.

Walking back over to the bed he raises her legs. Pulling the
covers from under her body he lowers her legs onto the bed
and pulls the cover over her. He then jumps in bed beside
her and pulls the covers over the both of them.

Lying beside her naked body in bed he cuddles and kisses on her as she lay unconscious. With a sense of accomplishment, he smiles uncontrollably and thinks to himself that he has finally gotten the girl he has always wanted.

As Trail looks over at Fan lying in his bed, he is confident that what has happened will change how she feels about Kevon. Wanting to savor the moment he lifts the cover and admires her body.

Feeling his breathe on her back as he holds her, she momentarily regains consciousness. Now afraid, shocked, and confused she tries to yell for help but all that comes out is a moan.

Hearing her moan Trail seeks to comfort her and moves closer holding her tighter. Experiencing extreme fear, she uses all her might to push him off her and scream for help.

All that she can muster are additional moans. Attempting to break free of his arms that are draped around her. Fan pulls, struggles, and continues to moan. Panicked, fatigued and without the energy to continue to scream for help, tears fall down her face until she again loses consciousness.

Chapter 24

After getting dressed following an early morning basketball practice Kevon daps all his teammates as usual before leaving to drive home. He walks around the locker room looking to find Kaysn to see if he needs a ride home.

With no success in his attempt to find him he proceeds to leave. Before he gets to the door Kasyn runs from the shower. Trying to get his attention he yells "Kevon. Hold on bruh. Can I get that ride to the crib?" Giving Kaysn a thumbs up, Kevon responds "I got you. I'll be in the car waiting."

Sitting in his car Kevon finds himself captivated watching the cars cruise down the main street. Bouncing from side to side an old school Cadillac Deville scrapes the ground.

Now rolling in three-wheel motion all the pedestrians are watching in fascination. Unable to take his eyes off the vehicle Kevon continues to watch as the car travels down the road.

Hitting the switches and slamming the car back on all four wheels the driver laughs and throws the deuce sign to everyone who is now on the sidewalks watching in amazement. Seeming to recognize the driver and the car Kevon looks closer.

Getting the opportunity he was waiting on, the driver turns and looks in his direction. Avoiding direct eye contact Kevon suddenly puts it together. Recognizing the car from DJ's football game he realizes that the driver is Prince.

The sudden thump on his car window jars Kevon out of his daze. With his nose pressed up against the passenger window Kasyn mutters "Open the door man".

Laughing to himself Kevon unlocks the doors and motions for him to get in. Opening the door and climbing inside he jests "You locked up in this thang like you the president. Somebody got you shook huh."

Laughing along he replies "My bad man. I thought the door was open." Driving off Kevon points toward the main strip at the Cadillac De Ville that is still in sight hitting switches back and forth.

Continuing to point he asks, "You know who that is?" Nodding, Kaysn responds "That's Prince man. Who don't know who that is?" Feeling slighted, Kaysn replies "that's the same car that pulled up with the Chop Down Boyz when DJ got into it with Bump. Quiet after his comment, Kasyn looks down at his phone hoping to avoid the conversation.

Sensing the tension about the topic Kevon is undeterred. He realizes Kasyn is attempting to change the subject in order to avoid the topic. Concerned for his brother he continues "Do you think Trail is also involved with those dudes?"

Clamming up, Kaysn peeps out of the corner of his eye to gauge whether or not Kevon is looking at him. Detecting that he is looking at him, Kasyn does not respond and instead, peers out of the passenger window.

Beginning to get agitated but remaining calm, Kevon exclaims "Dude you haven't made a comment about what happened at the park. Plus, your play on the court has been questionable. I've seen you ball out. Now you're muting yourself when I try to talk to you about Prince and Trail! What's really going on?"

Turning to face him after his incendiary remarks Kasyn gives a seething stare while still not giving a response. Staring back, they look at one another eye to eye and Kevon sees that he has hit a nerve but still continues "So since you not gone respond to any of my other questions tell me this. Are you still in the GAME?"

Breaking eye contact, Kaysn turns back toward the passenger window. With a frustrated sigh Kevon proceeds "Really man. After everything we been through with all that you still risking it all for what? Money?"

Finally breaking his silence, Kaysn responds "No! I'm not into all that anymore but what's up with all these questions? I am not the enemy and if I had something going on you know I would have been told you."

Unsatisfied with his comment Kevon responds "It's a lot of suspect stuff going on in the city and it seems like everyone know what's going on except for me. So yes, I'm going to ask questions."

Throwing his hands in the air he counters "Suspect stuff! Are you serious? Nobody talking to nobody if that's what you think. You of all people know better than that.. You just have to be out there to know. You can't be jelly because we out here and you decided to call it quits." Shaking his head, he turns his attention to the road.

Arriving at Kasyn's place Kevon grabs his arm before he exits and says "Bro we can't keep letting this go. We have to get over this." Kaysn takes his hand off the car door handle, looks back at Kevon, and responds "Get over what?"

Giving an astonished look Kevon replies "C'mon now dude. You gone play that with me? We been down since grade school. You should know by now that I can feel when something ain't right."

Shifting back into the passenger seat Kevon releases Kaysn's arm saying "We've never talked about it. It really seems like you keep holding what happened in high school over my head."

Facing him Kasyn says "How am I holding anything over your head?" Getting his thoughts together Kevon begins to answer before Kasyn interrupts "You know I was that guy in high school. I brought you in. I took you with me to the courts. I took you with me to the basketball camps."

Voice starting to crack he shrieks "I paid for your way into the camps with me. I put money in your pockets. I was the star on the team. I told the coach to bring you to Varsity and give you some run. I did all that and what did you do when you got a chance?"

Now flustered he pauses to calm himself. Not prepared for the response he received, Kaysn becomes saddened. Not knowing what to say he holds his head down. Looking over and noticing the guilt his friend is emitting Kevon begins to feel bad for his harsh comments.

Wanting to repair the damage he's caused from his statement Kevon exclaims "Look man. On the real I've never blamed you for how everything went down. At the end of the day Prince was in charge. He paid us to lose that game and we all had to do what we had to do to survive. Right."

Listening to Kasyn's version of the incident jolts Kevon's memory. His mind now flashes back to the incident in high school. Recalling that Trail tells him that he needed to do what he needed to win that game.

Hoping to have made amends for his previous comments Kasyn asks "You good bro?" Snapping out of his flashback Kevon responds "Dawg. You just said Prince paid us to lose that game...I talked to Trail the day before that game and he told me that I needed to do whatever was necessary to win that game."

Jerking his head around now facing one another in a stunned voice, Kaysn blurts "What!" Kevon repeats his statement "The day before that game Trail told me I needed to do whatever was necessary to make sure we won that game." Slowly sitting back in his seat, Kaysn rubs on his chin without responding.

Thinking over their conversation Kasyn feels relieved that they actually discussed this issue and says "I'm set on this man and honestly I was pissed at you when it happened but I see you had to do what you had to do like I did."

Sucking his teeth, Kaysn continues "Back then when everything went down, I just thought you should've stepped up and took the charge. Because I told you what the move was, and you didn't go with it, but I get it now. It's all good."

As they both enter a brief silence Kevon deviously laughs "Man all this time to find out that Trail was the one who played both of us." With a sigh of relief Kevon extends his hand. Returning the gesture Kasyn grabs his hand and with a vigorous hand shake they break into laughter.

Exiting the car Kasyn looks back at Kevon hearing the laughter quickly flee his voice. Ducking his head back inside he observes his now stoic look and asks "What's wrong now fam? I thought we just hashed out all of the issues we had." Forcing a grin, he says "Man it was that party the other day. My girl been acting different for some reason."

Sitting back down in the car, Kaysn bellows "Tell me you not talking about Fannah dude!" Without answering Kevon shamefully nods. With a condescending tone, Kaysn goes on "Leave that chick alone bro. I always see that chick with Trail. I don't know what she telling you but if the broad was really about you, she wouldn't always be housed up with that dude."

Kaysn gets out of the car but looks back before closing the door, he exclaims "She not worth it! If that's what you worried about you got an easy fix for that. Cut that chick off."

Watching him close the door and walk away Kevon mulls over Kaysn's words and begins to compare them with what DJ has said. Replaying the image of Fannah at the game with Trail he shakes his head. Laughing to himself he cranks up the car thinking "WOW! It all makes sense. I can't believe I fell for it all."

Chapter 25

DJ pulls up to the barber shop. He sits in his car in the parking lot talking on his cell phone. After a few moments he exits the vehicle and walks toward the shop to get his day started. Looking around something feels strange as it is an unusually quiet day for the area of town that the barber shop is located.

Pausing for a moment DJ continues to walk before stopping in his tracks. A glare temporarily obstructs his view. Blinking his eyes to regain focus he turns toward the glare long enough to see the muzzle flash. POW! POW! POW! POW! POW! Five shots later he lay on the ground in a pool of blood.

Running to his aid Kevon grabs DJ off the ground and holds him in his arms while yelling for someone to help. Out the corner of his eye he observes a familiar face running from the scene. Turning his attention back to DJ he tries to calm him. He begins to beg "Please stay with me. DJ, BREATHE."

With blood spewing from his mouth DJ starts to shake uncontrollably. Continuing to yell for help Kevon continues to hold his brother in his arms until he stops moving.

Shaking DJ, Kevon again yells "Stay with me." Once he realizes that DJ is no longer breathing Kevon looks around and begins to yell at the top of his lungs for someone to call 911.

Waking up in a cold sweat Kevon looks around the room. Heavily breathing he feverishly pants "It was just a dream! It was just a dream!" Jumping out of bed he runs to the bathroom looking in the mirror as to check for blood on his pajamas. Reassured that it was just a dream he turns on the water faucet and splashes water onto his face.

Up early and unable to go back to sleep he turns on the television and tries to watch the basketball game that he recorded the night before. While attempting to watch the game his mind reverts to the shooting incident that occurred on the court. Replaying the conversation, he had with Kasyn about DJ being in trouble with the ChopDown Boyz he becomes concerned.

Now knowing that Prince is also associated with the Chop Down Boyz Kevon's concern increases. With the added knowledge that Bump was affiliated with the ChowDown Boyz and is now dead after having an altercation with DJ, his concern turns to fear for his brother's safety.

His mind now racing he starts to have flashbacks of his dream with Trail running from the scene. Now shifting to what occurred at the court he envisions Trail in the middle of the melee. Kevon tries to calm his thoughts, but his efforts are in vain. No longer able to fight against the thoughts, his mind begins to spiral recalling Kasyn's warning of how Trail was always with Fan. His mind now replays see Trail with Fan at his last game.

With everything running through his head at once the fear he had for his brother's safety begins to change into anger toward Trail.

Still attempting to watch the game his thoughts divert to Trail and his sudden friendship with DJ. Unable to sit still or sleep he makes up his mind to confront Trail. Turning the T.V. off Kevon leaves his apartment in the early hours of the morning with the intent of not coming back until he takes care of Trail.

Driving toward Trails apartment Kevon second guesses himself understanding that Trail stays strapped and isn't afraid of violent confrontation. Pulling over to the side of the road he then thinks of DJ. He understands how the association with Trail can ruin his career.

Pounding on the steering wheel in frustration Kevon's thoughts drift to the Chop Down Boyz. He has visions of their violence. He imagines them in cahoots with Trail and doing harm to DJ. The thoughts subside his reservations and fear. He puts the car in drive and heads to Trail's apartment.

Pulling into the parking lot before getting out Kevon reaches underneath his seat and grabs a gun. Comforted with his protection in hand he bolts out of his vehicle and inserts the gun into the back of his pants. Walking toward Trail's apartment he abruptly stops in his tracks.

Turning back toward the parking lot Kevon does a double take at a vehicle that looks like the one Fan drives. Taken aback he moves closer to the vehicle to confirm his suspicion. Spotting a 3P medallion in the windshield of the car his suspicions are validated.

Puzzled as to why her car would be in the parking lot of Trails apartment at this time of morning, Kevon walks back to his car confused. Getting inside his car he grabs his phone and dials Fan's cell phone number. The call goes directly to voice mail.

Becoming even more suspicious he doesn't leave a message and decides to call Chasity hoping that she's able to give him reassurance that Fan is home.

Dialing Chasity's number, he waits as it rings while attempting to reassure himself that maybe her car was just left here as a safety precaution. He's certain someone drove her home because she was drinking.

Finally answering the phone, Chasity catches him off guard as his mind is consumed with thoughts of Fan. He wondered if she is with Trail or if he is just jumping to conclusions.

Agitated that she is getting no answer Chasity squeals "Hello, hello!" jolted out of his daze Kevon responds "Chasity! This is Kevon. Is Fan home?" Surprised that he called her phone she replies, "Hold on, let me go and check."

Walking toward Fannah's room she notices that the door is open. Entering she calls "Fan! Are you in here?", with no response she looks inside the bathroom. Getting back on the phone she answers, "Kevon she is not here." Not hearing the news he wanted, he asks "Do you know how long she's been gone?"

Starting to become concerned herself Chasity responds "Ummmm, looks like she has been gone all night because her bed is still made. Is something wrong? Have you tried calling her cell phone?"

Becoming emotional Kevon quips "I called her before I called you, but her phone goes straight to voice mail. I thought I saw her car and just wanted to make sure I wasn't tripping." Pausing he looks over at her car and goes on "I'll keep trying her phone. Thanks."

Walking back to his car Kevon contemplates whether to confront Fan and Trail, or just drive home. Starting to feel stupid for putting his trust in Fan, he replays what DJ said at the party.

Feeling even more down on himself Kevon's mind goes back to his basketball game. He recalls Fan and Trail being there together and leaving without speaking to him. Opening the door of his car he slowly enters while thinking to himself "I am so stupid! What in the hell was I thinking!"

Convincing himself to not let his emotions get the best of him he decides not to confront them. In a dejected state he attempts to pacify himself spouting "She already made her decision. I just have to live with it. I can't make her love me."

With the thoughts of Fan and Trail now flooding his mind the initial reason for his trip is flushed away by feelings of heartbreak.

Cranking up the car Kevon begins his drive home. He is unable to understand why Fan has hurt him. He thinks of how she confessed her love for him. He wonders how something can feel so sincere but be such a lie. Banging on the steering wheel he shouts, "How could I be so stupid!"

Chapter 26

DJ sits on his bed looking at his phone. He thinks about the last couple days and the hurt he has caused in the lives of people that care about him. DJ slams his phone on the bed.

Rolling over to retrieve the phone, he calls Chasity. Her phone again going directly to voicemail he dials Kevon's number. Not expecting an answer, he gets the voicemail. Without leaving a message he hangs up.

Fed up DJ gathers the energy to get dressed. Again, picking up the phone he dials. Receiving an answer on the other end he says, "What's going on big homey...I need to holla at you...nothing serious, but I wanted to get out of the crib for a minute."

Receptive to his request Trail responds "I'm here. I got company but come on over. My address is Dogwood Complex Building 8, and I am in apartment 26. I got some drank we can sip on and chill." Comforted by his warm welcome he replies "Fa sho. I'll be over in a few."

Without hesitation DJ enthusiastically jogs to his car and drives to Trail's apartment. He begins to feel better about his situation. Finally, he arrives. He gets out of his car and starts to walk toward Trail's place before pausing. Looking at the parking lot he notices a car that looks like the one Fannah drives.

Slowing down in an attempt to verify the vehicle DJ starts to wonder if it could be true that Fan and Trail are more than just friends. After a few moments he continues his trek and refocuses on getting a moment to relax and vent about everything he is dealing with.

Making it to the apartment DJ taps on the door. Moments later Trail eagerly swings open the door. Dressed in his pajamas they shake hands and embrace each other as he pulls DJ inside.

In an unusually happy mood, Trail puts his fingers to his lips as to shush DJ before whispering "We gotta keep it down. My company still knocked out - if you know what I mean." Directing him to take a seat he goes on "Imma get us something to drink so make yourself at home."

Taking a seat on the couch DJ looks across the room and recognizes a pair of female shoes that he recalls seeing at Fannah and Chasity's apartment the night of the party. Thinking back to Fannah's car in the parking he starts to get a clear picture.

After confirmation of his thoughts DJ begins to absolve himself of the guilt he felt. He is no longer remorseful for spewing accusations in front of everyone at the party toward Fannah for sleeping with Trail.

Bringing him a drink Trail sits down on the chair next to DJ while opening his drink and reclining in his seat. Taking a sip of his drink Trail looks up at DJ and quips "It's been a minute since we had a chance to chop it up...that incident at the court was crazy right?" Nodding in agreeance DJ sinks into the couch and takes a big gulp of his drink.

Continuing to drink Trail goes on "Told you I got your back lil homey. Nobody messing with the fam and still walking around to talk about it." Looking at him with a sense of appreciation DJ raises his drink toward Trail.

Leaning in toward Trail he reciprocates the gesture as they clash drinks and chant cheers before taking a gulp and enjoying a laugh together.

Laughter subsiding Trail asks "So how did that party turn out last night? I heard that there were a lot of people over there turning up." Just having cleared his mind of the events from the party DJ now feels himself becoming engulfed in guilt again with the thoughts of what occurred.

Trapped in his thoughts DJ begins to think about Chasity and her accusations about Trail. He Feels awkward discussing his feelings about a woman. In his mind, he rehearses how to start the conversation. He wonders if he should even question what happened between the two of them.

Finding the words to respond DJ quips "Bro on the real the party was nice, but that liquor had me acting out of character." Laughing at his comment Trail responds "I already know how that goes my G. But what happened though?" With a serene look he replies "I messed up big homey.

I know you said not to fall for Chasity, but I ended up falling for her. The bad part is I went up in that party drunk. I was calling her hoes and everything else in front of everybody for no reason. I just messed it up bad."

Grinning as he takes another gulp of his drink Trail snaps "So why are you down on yourself? I'm still waiting to hear what you said wrong."

Changing to a serious mood he gives a stern look and slightly pauses before responding "She a good woman though G, I mean a real good woman. I don't know what I was thinking." With the grin no longer on his face Trail retorts "You really like this shawty huh lil bro?" Looking into his eyes he understands how serious DJ's feeling are toward Chasity.

Trail reaches over to shake DJ's hand. DJ returns the gesture. Taking another drink, Trail looks at his cup and says "Nothing but respect fam and I'll lay off the negative comments about ya girl. I didn't know you was feeling her like that."

Looking back over at him Trail slaps DJ on the leg and continues "Bro I did tell you not to fall in love though and you went and did it anyway." Breaking into laughter he goes on "I will say you got you a bad chick and I'll tell you like my guy told me." Looking over at his kitchen "Slip her some of that G-Juice and you can do whatever you want to her, whenever you get ready."

Looking confused DJ turns in his direction and asks, "What's that?" With a devilish grin Trail quips "You behind the power curb my man. You need to catch up. It is that GHB. Gotta make sure it's crushed so when you slip it in, they drink they can't tell the difference."

Not knowing how to respond DJ just looks at him in astonishment. Amused from DJ's reaction he continues "Trust me fam it works. Ole girl in the room came over last night and I used it with her, and we had a good time."

Hearing his story prompts him to recall Chasity's accusation she made of Trail raping her. Finally gathering the nerve, he hesitantly asks "So what did go down between you and Chasity? Did she get on that G-Juice with you?"

Smiling he says "You got a lot to learn fam. That is the best part. A lot of these chicks not on the drugs like that so at the end of the day they don't gotta know. If they on that drank, they don't care. All they want to do is have a good time anyway."

Not getting an answer to his question about Chasity, DJ sits quietly sipping on his drink. Thinking to himself as his brother always tells him, *when you don't get an answer you've gotten your answer."* As they continue to talk DJ begins to zone out and images of Chasity pouring her heart out and crying without any support cloud his mind.

Thinking of her laying on a bed helpless and being raped by Trail begins to rip at his heart. Starting to feel guilty about not being understanding and supportive of her DJ looks over at Trail who continues to grin and sip his drink.

Chapter 27

Mind swirling with the information he just heard DJ nervously laughs. Looking at him in curiosity Trail asks, "What's so funny lil homey?" DJ Sarcastically responds "So with that G-Juice you don't have to do no work to get the cooch huh."

His jubilation toning down Trail props his feet on the coffee table and after a slight pause answers "Let me tell ya. In case you haven't heard it before, I'll put you on some game. In this life the key is to work smarter and not harder."

Suddenly a grimacing noise comes from the bedroom. Trail tells DJ to hold on for a second and walks toward his room. He turns on the light as he enters and notices Fannah moving around.

Walking over to her he lightly shakes her. With her eyes slightly opened he lets her know that her clothes are on the dresser next to the bed.

Fannah rolls over after hearing Trail's voice. She gives a half-hearted attempt to raise herself but still woozy she quickly plops back down on the bed.

Laughing at her clumsiness Trail kisses her forehead while saying "There is no rush, take your time, relax and get some rest. I'll make you some food." Exiting the room, he turns the lights back off before closing the door.

Walking over to the kitchen he asks DJ "You want something to eat? I'm about to cook a little something." Kindly rejecting his offer, DJ answers "I'm good. I'mma just get my drink on to get my head clear."

With the moaning continuing DJ looks over at the bedroom door. Watching his reaction to the noise, Trail calms his concern and quips "She good fam. She just a little hung over. I'm bout to whip up something to put on her stomach so she can shake back."

Seeming to be appeased with the explanation DJ takes another sip of his drink before again turning his attention to the shoes lying on the floor.

Glancing back Trail observes that DJ is focused on something. Inching toward the living room he peers toward the direction that DJ is transfixed on and sees Fans shoes.

Walking back into the kitchen to continue cooking breakfast he remarks "You know that's Fan in there." Hearing the name, DJ lays back in his seat and continues to sip on his drink. Looking toward the kitchen he starts to ask what Trail is cooking but before he can get the question out an open bottle laying on the counter catches his attention.

Fixated on the bottle he's able to make the words out. Labeled with a makeshift marking he reads "G-Juice". His mind swirls into a 3D state of unbalance. He switches from thoughts of how much Kevon likes Fannah, to him accusing her of being with Trail, to her now being in Trail's room.

Delirious DJ envisions Fan helpless in the room drugged and raped. Continuing to drink he gives a concerted effort of trying to not become frantic and alert Trail of his actual thoughts.

Grabbing another drink from the refrigerator Trail looks into the living room and says "looks like you almost on E over there. You want another drink?" Accepting his request, he nods. Going back into the refrigerator he grabs a drink and tosses it over toward him from the kitchen "Heads up. Catch."

Opening his drink while still cooking Trail says "You remember Fan, right? The girl from the barber shop?" Nodding to his comment DJ starts to become antsy and quickly opens his drink. Snickering he jests "I don't know why I asked. She best friends with your girl. So of course, you know her."

In the room, Fannah is trying to collect her thoughts but draws a blank as she wonders "What happened. How did I get here? What am I doing here?" She places her hands on her head and massages it to calm her throbbing headache. Pushing up off the bed the covers slip down revealing her bare chest.

Looking at her uncovered breasts puts her in a sudden panic prompting her to reluctantly raise the covers. Looking further underneath she discovers that she is completely naked. Slowly regaining consciousness, she feels her crotch area throbbing.

Reaching down to ease the pain she massages the area with her hand. She feels her hand drenched, which causes her to instantly bring her hand up to view. Semen and blood cover her hand causing her to burst into tears.

Gathering the energy to roll over and finally making it to her feet Fannah becomes nauseous. Looking back at the area she laid in, semen and blood cover the sheets. Tears flow down her face as she wipes away the secretion and blood that oozes down her legs.

Now desperately assessing her surroundings, Fannah recognizes photos of Trail. The photos begin to bring back memories of the previous night.

Starting to become afraid she bursts into tears before frantically searching for her clothes. Looking around the room she sees her clothes folded on a dresser. She immediately stumbles over, picks them up, and begins to get dressed.

Looking around for her shoes her mind focuses back on the blood and semen that's covering her hands. Becoming afraid she tries to retrace the events of the night. Vaguely recollecting parts of the night, she remembers Trail forcing himself on to her.

With her headache subsiding her memory slightly becomes clearer. She remembers looking at his face while he undressed her tears continue to flow from her eyes. She recalls telling him to stop and pushing him away before things went black.

With fear, anger, and embarrassment engulfing her, Fannah gives up the search for her shoes and stumbles toward the door. Fumbling with the knob she finally gets the door open. Upon entering the room makes eye contact with DJ. Neither expecting to see the other they are caught in a momentary trance.

Breaking the awkward silence Trail retorts "You finally got up. I'm almost done making your food." Gaping in his direction with disgust Fannah quickly turns her attention toward the front door.

Not responding to his comment, she begins to walk when she notices her shoes lying on the floor. Stopping to pick them up she continues toward the door and is suddenly stopped by Trail.

Jogging to catch up with her he lightly grabs her arm and asks "Why are you in a hurry? I just cooked breakfast for you." Not turning around and obviously frightened she counters "I don't want anything to eat."

Jerking away from his grasp, she pleads "Can you please take your hand off of me so that I can leave!" Not obliging her request, Trail continues to hold her arm and responds "You shouldn't be driving. C'mon and get some food first."

Attempting to pull away she reiterates "No! I'm not hungry so can you please just let me go!" Noticing that the situation is escalating DJ interjects "Rail. The food won't go to waste. I'll eat it. Just let her make it bro."

Turning toward DJ after his comment he focuses back on her and mocks "We all good bro. I think she just a little tired from last night...Ain't that right Fan?" Spanking her on the butt he continues "I will see you later and hit me up when you get home." Unable to control her tears they stream down her face as she runs out of the apartment.

Walking back toward the kitchen he glances over at DJ and chuckles "You Captain Saving these hoes all of a sudden now huh lil homey." Uneasy he takes another drink before answering "Naw, just looked like lil mama was trying to make it somewhere."

Finishing up with the food Trail makes DJ a plate and brings it over to him along with another drink. Starting to eat he looks up and snickers "I just bust ole girl cherry fam. That was her first time. So, you know I had to represent."

Taking a bite of his food he continues "I know I said I wasn't going to talk on it anymore but between me and you I was your girls first too."

Generating a sinking feeling in his stomach DJ starts to realize that everything that Chasity was telling him was true.

Glancing over at Trail he feels the admiration he once had for him disappear.

Reminiscing on the fear Fannah exhibited and the tears flowing from her face DJ looks over at Trail. Eating his food, he tries to conceal the feeling of disgust that has overcome him.

Chapter 28

Entering the apartment Fannah slowly walks over to the couch and curls up in a ball. Hearing the noise Chasity walks out of her room to find out what is wrong.

Chasity notices the door is wide open, so she walks over to close it. Then she sits down next to Fannah who is curled up on the couch.

She scoots closer as she begins to rub Fan's back. Then she asks, "Is everything ok?" Understanding that something is bothering Fan. Chasity wonders if it has anything to do with Kevon. Curious she asks, "Did Kevon ever get in touch with you?"

Startled by the question Fan doesn't respond but looks up contemplating in her mind why Chasity asked. Having her attention, Chasity goes on "He called last night looking for you."

Worried she continues "It was strange because he called my phone and I don't even know how he got my number. Plus, I was concerned because I know you usually always answer your phone."

Pausing for a minute and noticing the dried tears on Fan's face she warily continues "He was saying something about he thought he saw your car somewhere." Now with a mortified gaze on her face Fan curls back into a ball.

Thinking that Kevon did something to hurt Fan, Chasity remarks "Ohhh No! Uhh! Is that why he was looking for you? To hurt you? I'm not having that...I'm calling the police!" Getting up to go grab her phone Fan grabs her hand and cautions "No! Kevon didn't do anything to me."

Sitting back down Chasity asks "So what's wrong then Fan? I've never seen you like this." Not responding she reaches for her hand. Worried that this may be something serious she extends her hand. Grabbing her extended hand, Fannah grips it tightly and begins to cry.

Pulling her out of her curled ball position, Chasity holds and embraces Fan with both arms. Consoling her she says, "It's ok Fan." As the tears pour down Fan's face, she buries her head in Chasity's shoulder.

Sniffling she manages to murmur "It was Trail. He raped me." Pausing for a minute and unsure of what she heard Chasity raises her up and asks "Fan. What did you just say?" Chocking up Fan wipes away tears from her face and whimpers "Trail. He raped me."

Feeling as if she were reliving her own nightmare, Chasity stares at Fan placing her hands on her face wiping away her tears. Starting to cry herself she embraces her again saying "I'm so sorry. I'm here with you no matter what."

After a few moments she releases her grasp on Fan and shrieks "We have to call the police." With a terrified look Fan responds "Police?" Chasity grabs her hands and replies

"Yes. The police. He needs to be in jail. This guy can't continue to keep getting away with this type stuff."

Her feelings of hurt and anger now turning to fear she pulls her hand from Chasity's grasp shaking her head warning "Chasity, I've known this guy for a long time and he is not the person you want to make an enemy out of." Empathizing with her she pleads "Fan! He is already your enemy. Look what he did to you. He did the same thing to me and no telling who else."

Understanding the feeling that Fan is going through she decides to finally share her story. Calming down she grabs Fan's hands again and says, "You remember that party you took me to a while back?"

Not receiving a response, she continues "I think Trail was having a birthday party or something like that?" Sensing where the conversation is going, Fan begins to feel remorseful and shakes her head in agreeance.

As Fannah confirms her memory of the situation she continues "I really didn't want to go to that party because I didn't know anyone, but I went to be there for you. That was my first-time meeting Trail. I thought he was so unattractive and never gave him any inclination that I was interested, but for some reason he continued to flirt with me."

Pausing for a moment to hold back tears she continues "I knew he was the one whom invited you. I wasn't sure what your relationship was with him and I figured the flirting was harmless, so I didn't say anything." As she is talking Fan's mind drifts to the conversation she had with Trail. Recalling that he said Chasity was flirting with him.

Listening to Chasity's story and comparing it with what she knows of Trail she begins to understand why Chasity referred to Trail as being evil. Noticing that she doesn't have her attention Chasity snaps her fingers shouting "Fan, Fan, are you there?" Coming out of her fog Fan responds, "I'm listening to you."

Shaking her hands, she goes on "But anyway during the party I was fine but then he started bringing me drinks and I started feeling woozy. I remember telling him that I wasn't feeling well and needed to find you so that we could leave."

Interrupting her she says "Wait. What? You were looking for me to leave?" shocked she continues "When you disappeared Trail told me you had hooked up with one of the homeys and to tell me not to wait up for you." Releasing her hands, she starts to tear up.

Seeing that Chasity is distraught about the story Fan says "I know it's tough. You don't have to talk about it." Beaming at her in the eye she says "It's not that. All the way until this day I blamed you for what happened because I thought you left me there alone. I knew that I shouldn't have been drinking so I took my share of the blame, but I had no idea he lied to you."

Confused she replies "Lied?" Taking a breath, she responds "Fan! Trail took me to a room in that house and told me to get some rest and that he would come and get me once you were ready to leave."

Taken aback Fan listens on "Next thing I knew I blacked out and I was in and out of consciousness seeing him naked and taking my clothes off. I tried to yell but I didn't have the strength. When I woke up, I was alone and naked laying in a strange bed."

Astonished after hearing Chasity's story Fan looks at her speechless. After a moment, Fan wraps her arms around her professing "I'm sorry Chasity. I'm so sorry." Having held her emotions in to be strong for Fan she breaks down. During their embrace she cries "I was a virgin before that happened."

Her eyes widening as she hears that comment. Hurt, tears continue to down her face. Chasity now feels guilty for her false perception of her friend. As she thinks of how she took her loyalty and trust for granted she holds her tighter saying "I'm really sorry."

Freeing their hold from one another Fan remarks "He did almost the exact same thing to me. He gave me some water to drink but after drinking it I became woozy and..." Unable to relive the details Chasity takes her hand saying "Trust me. It gets easier but right now it's going to be extremely difficult for you to talk about. What we do need to do though is go to the police."

Attempting to calm Fan, Chasity reassures "Don't worry we can support each other. I'll have the courage to tell my story too." Nodding Fan replies "Ok. You are right." Getting up to go get her phone from her room Fan drifts into thought.

Once she returns Fan blurts "DJ saved me." Stunned by her comment Chasity stops dialing and looks at Fan asking "I don't understand. What does he have to do with this?"

Shaking her head, and nudging Chasity, Fan replies "Your DJ. He was over Trail's apartment when I was trying to leave. Trail grabbed me and I felt like he was going to try to do something else to me, but DJ jumped in and told him to let me go."

Shocked by Fan's statement Chasity fumbles with the phone and continues to dial the police. Waiting for someone to pick up Fan continues "For some reason I think he was acting out of love. I don't think what we saw the other night was really him."

Meditating on her words Chasity thinks back to DJ's voice mail and what he shared with her. Grinning she recalls what she shared with him. Interrupting Chasity's thoughts someone answers "What's your emergency." After a slight pause she answers, "I want to report two rapes."

Chapter 29

Getting to the barbershop DJ walks in uncharacteristically early. With the big game tomorrow everyone mocks "you gone get em tomorrow for us right supa star" as he passes them. Making it to his booth he sees that he has a line of customers waiting.

Before beginning to cut, DJ pulls out his appointment book and fills in the available slots. The patrons look at DJ in awe. As usual, they suspect he'll hook up his friends and the people he knows first before getting to them.

DJ is normally dressed in baggy pants and a sweatshirt but today he's wearing a pair of jeans along with a fitted button up short sleeve shirt.

He calls up the first customer on his list. He has an obvious change in his attitude and attire. The customers as well as the other barbers notice the sudden improvement and look at each other in confusion.

He takes his time with his first customer's haircut as he is attentively catering to his request. Finishing up, he gives the customer a mirror and asks if he is satisfied with the haircut.

Receiving a thumbs up from the customer DJ takes the cape off, cleans him up, and lets him know the total. Getting up from the chair the customer looks at DJ with admiration for the great customer service and professionalism he just received.

Digging into his pocket he retrieves the money to pay for his haircut. As DJ attempts to give him the change the customer waves him off giving him an additional tip before walking out.

Waiting on his next appointment the barber in the booth next to him asks "So what's up DJ? What's with the grown man outfit and professional way you conducting yourself all of a sudden? You giving up on the streets or something? Or are you just getting your mind right for the big game tomorrow?"

Smirking DJ responds, "Why can't a brutha just be about his biz?" Raising his eyebrows, the barber quips "Bruh are you messing with me right now." Still smirking he responds "Man I'm just on some other stuff right now. Ain't nothing out there in them streets for me." Giving him a fist pound, he remarks "Preach! Enough said my brutha." As they continue to cut hair.

Suddenly the barber shop begins to rattle. Some of the new customers look around with concern as the regulars laugh and some bounce along with the pulsations. Hearing the sound instantly causes DJ to tense up.

As the noise gets louder one of the newer customers ask, "Am I the only one who's worried about all this shaking?" Hearing the concern of the customer, one of the barbers calms him by answering "It's only music. That's Trail. The owner of the barber shop. He just likes to show out and play his music loud. Nothing to worry about."

With the pulsating sound now gone the barber shop stops rattling. Moments later Trail walks into the shop. Dapping everyone up as he walks by one of the barbers asks, "Rail what happened to those bad ass broads you were with the last time you came up in here?" Snickering at the question he answers "Man you know how I do. I had to cancel them hoes."

Bursting into laughter the barbers dap him up and responds, "You a wild boy." Feeling offended by the comment DJ does not join the laughter and continues to cut his customer's hair.

Making it to his booth Trail extends his hand as DJ unenthusiastically returns the gesture and daps him up. Noticing that his mood is different Trail remarks "I see you focused on getting your money lil homey. When you get a break, I need to holla at you for a minute about some other business."

Nodding without giving eye contact DJ continues cutting hair. Walking away Trail shouts, "I'll be in the lounge waiting when you get ready."

Becoming antsy DJ looks over at his appointment book and asks his next few customers if he can push them back thirty minutes. With all of them agreeing to change their appointments he finishes up his current customer, brushes himself off, and walks toward the lounge.

Nervously walking into the lounge, he spots Trail sitting at the bar sipping on a drink watching the game. Walking over he sits in a seat next to Trail and orders a water from the bar.

Concentrating on the game Trail glances at DJ before turning his attention back to game and cracks "I see you playboi, dressing up grown man style. You switching up the game on me huh?"

DJ takes a gulp of water and says "Naw man. I've been making a lot of mistakes so I'm just trying to clean everything up a lil bit."

Turning away from the game Trail looks at his glass of water and chuckles "Look at you with that H2O, you ain't even on that real drank no mo. I ain't mad at ya bro. Do ya thang."

Trail turns his barstool in the direction to face DJ. With a serious look Trail says "Alright down to business lil homey. You know the game tomorrow is a big deal, right?" Thinking over what Kevon has been cautioning him about DJ becomes anxious but manages to nod in agreeance to Trail's question.

Receiving confirmation by his head nod that he is engaged in the conversation Trail motions for the bar tender to join them at the bar. Not ordering drinks DJ becomes confused.

Wondering why the bar tender is involved with their conversation he becomes attentive. The bar tender places a box on the counter and stands by as Trail pulls the box toward him and opens it up.

Satisfied with its contents he pushes over toward DJ and says, "Open it". After DJ takes note of what's in the box, he quickly closes it. Now staring at Trail in disarray DJ asks, "What am I supposed to do with that?" Leaning on the counter Trail laughs "That's yours."

Opening the box again DJ counts the money inside then sits the money back in it and closes it before asking "For what? What is this money for?"

Trail motions for the bar tender to go away so he can continue his talk in private. Rocking back and forth he remains silent until he exits the lounge.

To be assured that it is just the two of them Trail scoots closer and says, "This is what I have been talking to you about the entire time playboi."

Now staring at him he continues "Getting paid. This is just half of what you're going to get off the game tomorrow. Once you do your thing and make sure you all get that W then you'll get the other half."

Mulling it over DJ responds, "So what if I don't want anything to do with this money?" A little agitated at his comment Trail replies "Look. I went through a lot to get you hooked up with this deal."

Pausing for a moment he goes on "So at the end of the day you don't have to take this money BUT if you don't make sure you all win that game tomorrow it will be a lot of people with power upset and that won't be good for anyone."

Feeling the tension, they stare at one another for a moment before Trail continues "This what Bump got caught up in. He didn't do what he was supposed to do and them boyz came for him."

Starting to feel uneasy at the mention of Bump, confusion starts to set in DJ's mind. His initial thought was that Trail had his back when he had an altercation with Bump. Now listening to Trail's comments his mind wanders. Recalling each incident with Bump, DJ begins to form a different version of what actually happened to Bump.

DJ places his hand on the box. He knows if he doesn't take the money it will make him a target. Pulling the box closer he asks, "So that's all I have to do is make sure we win?" With a grimacing laugh Trail shakes his head.

Taking the money out of the box and stuffing it into his pocket DJ responds "Ok. Easy enough." Getting off the bar stool he walks back toward the barber shop. Holding his hand out Trail calls "Hey! Can we shake on it?" Seeing his extended hand DJ walks back toward him and returns the gesture as they awkwardly shake hands.

Chapter 30

Arriving back from the police station after filing the police report Fannah and Chasity walk inside their apartment. Displaying a look of embarrassment Fannah says "That was very uncomfortable...Tell me why I feel like the guilty one?"

Agitated she continues "I mean they questioned me, took tests, took samples, touched all on me. Dang it's like I was the one who committed a crime." Throwing her arms up in frustration she snarls "I'm about to go shower. I'm sick to death with all this filth covering me."

Going into her room she rips off the clothes she was wearing and vehemently throws them in the trash. Grabbing her hygiene supplies she turns on the shower.

Feeling underneath the spigot until the water is the right temperature, she enters letting her hair get wet. Pulling her hair back and looking down at her body she drops down onto the floor of the shower and bursts into tears.

Sitting on the couch Chasity notices the shower has been running in Fannah's room for a while. Getting up and walking into her room she sees the fumes coming from Fan's bathroom. Walking inside she notices the clothes that she was wearing balled up and discharged into her garbage can.

Glancing around Chasity sees Fan sitting on the floor of the shower in tears as the water flows down on her head. Running to the shower Chasity turns off the spigot. Grabbing a towel from the counter she goes back over to the shower and picks Fan up from the shower floor.

She wraps the towel around Fan as she escorts her over to her bed. Sitting on the bed she helps her dry off. Draping the towel back around her she walks over to her dresser and rummages through searching for pajamas. She locates the pajamas and assists Fan with getting dressed.

Sitting next to Fan on the bed Chasity lays her head onto a pillow and says, "everything will be ok." Unable to rest Fan raises her head, sits up on the bed and grabs the pillow. Sitting upright she places the pillow on her lap.

Noticing that she is shaking Chasity slowly takes the pillow from her lap, places it back on the bed and lies her head back down on the pillow and remarks "I'll sit here with you until you feel better."

Sitting on the bed Chasity continues to console Fan. Wallowing in her own sorrow she manages to hold back tears as she massages Fannah. Fannah hears Chasity sniffling. She begins to feel guilty knowing that Chasity was at the police station right by her side filing a report.

With no more tears to shed, Fannah buries her head in the pillow. Her thoughts turn to the night Chasity was raped. She thinks about how Chasity must have felt having no one there to comfort her. As the guilt mounts, she remembers watching Chasity pouring her heart as she described that horrific night and she regrets not being there for her.

She listens to Chasity as she continues to sniffle. Chasity rocks back and forth continuing to comfort Fannah. Fannah turns over on the pillow. Looking up, she notices that Chasity has tears flowing down her face.

Sitting up, she wipes her tears away and says "I'm so thankful to have you as a friend. I am so sorry for everything." Pausing, she gives her a sympathetic look before asking, "How have you dealt with it all and been so strong?"

Wiping her tears away Chasity grins and responds "You don't have to apologize girl. And to tell you the truth I haven't dealt with it...I guess that's why I've never been able to trust a guy and have never had sex with anyone after that incident. Maybe in some way I feel responsible for it all."

Wiping tears away she continues "I don't know. I know it sounds stupid, but I can't explain it. I just feel like I was drinking at the party with other guys and we all know what happens at parties right? So, I figure had I not been drinking then the rape would never have happened."

Holding Chasity's hand while watching the tears come down her face Fannah somberly replies "Oh my goodness Chasity. That is so terrible." Wiping tears from her face Chasity softly says "See. I was trying to tell you that I haven't dealt with it yet."

Ashamed of how she has treated Chasity, Fan scoots closer and wraps her arms around her. As they console one another Fan asks, "So have you ever told anyone else about what happened?"

Starting to feel disappointed Chasity pulls away from their embrace and places her head in her hands. After a moment she bellows "The first time I felt the courage to tell anyone was the other day. I felt you and DJ had been so manipulated by Trail and I wanted to help. I wanted to try to convince you all that he wasn't the great guy you all were making him out to be."

Smirking Fan retorts "So that must mean you really like him then huh?" With a slight grin she hesitates before replying "I thought I loved him but maybe I don't know what love is."

Sarcastically giggling she continues "Or maybe I don't know how to be in a relationship...I mean I thought he was different but when I heard him call me those names...I just thought. Maybe it is me. Maybe I am the problem. You know."

Shaking her head in disagreement Fan responds "I told you. He was drunk. You saw him drinking straight out the bottle and you could smell it on him. Plus, you've said before that he can be aggressive."

Tapping Chasity's arm, she questions "Right? Then you mix that with love, heartbreak and Trail's lies." Calming down she proceeds "But I do think you really got to know the real guy. He actually opened up and showed you the real him. That wasn't him and nobody is perfect."

After making her statement she instantly thinks back to Kevon and how trusting he was of her. How in return she disrespected him and should have been more honest with her dealings with Trail.

Noticing that she is caught in a daze Chasity asks, "Are you ok?" Looking back at her she replies "I should have listened to you about everything. I really messed up with Kevon. He is such a great guy for me, and I screwed it up."

Grinning she grabs Fan's hand saying, "Looks like we both found the guy of our dreams huh." Not returning the grin she looks down replying "The difference is you are still good.

Chasity's eyes dart over to Fannah's phone as she continues to listen to her "DJ knows he messed up and is trying to make it up to you but I was the one who messed things up with Kevon and it seems like there is no way that I can even dream about making it right again."

Now staring at her phone lying on the dresser, Chasity reaches over grabbing it and begins dialing. Shocked by her impulsive action she says, "Who are you calling on my phone?"

Putting her finger over Fan's lips she whispers, "Be quiet." Hearing a ring on the other end she waits for an answer. After a few rings, the voicemail prompt comes on.

Pulling the phone away from her ear she looks at it and without leaving a message she hangs up and dials again. This time it goes directly to voicemail. With a feeling of dejection Fannah sighs "I'm guessing you are trying to call Kevon."

Without verifying her comment Chasity replies, "hold on." Jumping off the bed she places Fannah's phone back on her dresser. She runs to her room and quickly returns with her phone.

Starting to feel let down as she watches Chasity begin to dial on her phone she whines "Chasity. I'm telling you it's a lost cause. I knew he wouldn't answer my calls and even if he did, he's not going to talk to me after the way I treated him."

Again, putting her fingers over Fan's lips, Chasity grins as he picks up the phone answering "Hello." Giddy she pulls on her arm and says "Here. Take the phone. It's Kevon. He answered!"

Reluctantly Fan grabs the phone with no expectation nonchalantly saying "Hello, Kevon...It's me Fan." Waiting for a response there is now a silence. Unsure if he hung up, she continues "Are you still there?" Breaking his silence, he jests "I'm kinda busy right now. Can I call you later?"

Looking at her disheartened expression Chasity waves her arms and whispers "tell him how you feel." Giving her the thumbs up, she shakes her head confirming that she is heeding her advice.

Taking a deep breath, Fan sighs before putting her ear back to the phone and says "Hold on Kevon. You have every right to be upset with me, not trust me and maybe not ever talk to me again." Voice starting to crack she continues "but for what it's worth I really want you to know that I do love you."

Pausing to stop herself from crying she goes on "I was stupid for the way I've been acting but from our times together and our conversation I've opened up to you and let you in more than I've ever let anyone in ever."

Clearing her throat, she goes on "Please know that I am sorry. I don't want things to end between us this way. I'm willing to start over with you. I am new to relationships. I know I messed up and I am woman enough to admit it to you but that doesn't mean I don't love you."

Holding the phone, she waits for him to respond. Tears in her eyes she looks over as Chasity is silently asking "What is going on?" Shaking her head, she shrugs her shoulders suggesting that she doesn't know.

Clearing his throat, he finally replies "I don't know what's what at this point. I just need some time to figure everything out...I hear what you're saying but there is a lot going on right now and this situation with us is confusing...I still love you, however I think I just need some space right."

Sensing a glimmer of hope, she exults "That's fair Kevon. I just thank you for listening to me and I do genuinely love you more than anything." Not sharing her joy, he mutters "Ok. I'll talk to you later."

Hanging up and giving the phone back to her, Fannah jumps onto Chasity, hugging her and sobbing "I don't know what I'd do without you." Hugging her back Chasity quips "I take it the conversation went well?"

Releasing the hug, Fan looks at her and says "This is the hardest thing I've ever had to deal with in my life and I thank God that you are here with me. Despite how I have treated you."

In a reassuring tone Chasity responds "Come on now. You didn't know. I never said anything. You had the courage to talk about it and do something about it as soon as it happened. So, I can't fault you for not acting on something you knew nothing about. We good girl. I love you."

Chapter 31

The crowd is roaring as the home team, Pine Grove Bulldogs, run onto the field. Circling up at midfield the coach gives a pregame speech. During the speech he tells the players how important this game is.

Pine Grove is ranked #3 in the state. They are playing against the #1 ranked team. The coach attempts to motivate the team by letting them know that they have home field advantage.

He encourages them to use the energy from the fans to push them to victory. With the players fired up they huddle for a loud chant before separating into pre-game warm up lines.

Earning a role as the team Captain and playing in his first game back from his suspension, DJ leads the warmup exercises. While counting off during the exercises DJ's eyes drift off into the crowd. Knowing that Kevon has never missed any of his games he scans the crowd hoping to see him in the stands.

Disappointed that he does not spot Kevon, he scans the crowd again hoping that Chasity is there. With no luck in his search for Kevon and Chasity, DJ scans the stands one last time and discovers Trail sitting in the crowd.

As DJ and Trail notice one another, Trail points in his direction and throws him the deuce. Relieved that he has someone there for him, DJ gives him a return head nod.

Suddenly, the referee blows the whistle signaling for the start of the game. Winning the coin toss Pine Grove elects to receive the ball.

Feeling as if he has butterflies in his stomach, DJ backs into the end zone awaiting the kickoff. Waving his arms in an up and down motion DJ gets the crowd into the game.

Seeing the ball in the air DJ runs to catch it. Scanning the field, he spots an opening. Without a pause he quickly squeezes through the hole and is surprised by the open field ahead of him.

Pushing off a tackler he sprints up the field and is pushed toward the sidelines. Tip tapping on the sideline without going out of bounds he catches his balance. Now sprinting down the sideline he only has the kicker in front of him.

Attempting to avoid the kicker DJ accelerates. As DJ approaches, the kicker dives to make the tackle but misses. Seeing the end zone, DJ looks back with no defenders chasing and jogs toward the goal line. Flipping into the end zone he scores the first points of the game.

Celebrating after scoring the touchdown, DJ jogs down the sideline to his team's bench. Ecstatic, once he reaches the bench, his teammates pull him to the ground. Piling on him they congratulate him for his amazing touchdown.

With the crowd in a frenzy, Pine Grove kicks the ball to the opposing team. Amped from the crowd noise, the home team flies down field and tackles the visiting team's kick-off return man on their own 10-yard line.

Now on defense, DJ is matched against the visiting team's best player. With a 4-inch height advantage, the team's best player lines up opposite DJ. Wanting to take advantage of the height difference the opposing team calls an audible. Sending the other receivers to the opposite side of the field, DJ and the taller receiver are now locked one on one.

Recognizing the audible DJ laughs to himself, thinking they are not aware that he is one of the best high jumpers in the country. Understanding how to offset the height difference DJ prepares for the play. Seeing the ball being snapped, DJ backs off a few yards and waits for the quarterback to release the ball.

Once DJ sees the release, he accelerates to the ball, elevates over the taller receiver, and intercepts the pass. With no defenders between him and the goal line, DJ high steps into the end zone for the score. With a comfortable lead the coach sits DJ.

With DJ on the bench the visiting team gets the ball down the field and into field goal range. Brining the kicker onto the field the visiting team kicks and makes a field goal. The made attempt makes the score 14-3 as the first quarter comes to an end.

With the home team holding a 14-3 lead, the second quarter begins. Pine Grove receives the ball and the offense sputters. Unable to make a first down they punt the ball back to the opposing team.

Pine Grove brings DJ back in the game to play defense. Noticing DJ enter the game, the opposing team decides to move their best receiver to the opposite side of the field, away from DJ. Understanding the shift, DJ calls a defensive back audible. With no one on his side of the field DJ decides to blitz the quarterback.

Once the ball is snapped, DJ pretends to drop into coverage but quickly rushes the quarterback. Not expecting the blitz, the quarterback does not see DJ coming. After delivering a crushing blow that jars the ball loose DJ sees the ball laying on the turf.

Realizing that the ball is still live, DJ jumps to his feet. Running to the ball he picks it up and sprints to the end zone untouched for another score.

Leading 21-3 the Pine Grove coach decides to sit DJ again. With DJ out of the game, the opposing team's best receiver takes advantage and begins to make jaw dropping catches.

Anxious to get back in the game, DJ walks over and asks the coach to put him back in the game. Attempting to calm DJ, the coach lets him know it is almost half time and the team will be ok.

On a third and seven play from their own 45-yard line, the opposing team continues to target DJ's substitute. Again, taking advantage of his absence the visiting team's best receiver makes a fingertip grab for a 25-yard gain.

In scoring range the visiting team is now on Pine Grove's 30-yard line. With 35 seconds remaining in the first half, Pine Groves coach reluctantly puts DJ back in the game.

Seeing DJ come back in the game the opposing team, resorts to a trick play. As DJ and their best receiver are again locked up one on one, the visiting team lines up in a shot gun formation. They spread the receivers to seemingly attempt a long pass.

When the ball is snapped their best receiver motions, as if he is running a deep route, but suddenly turns toward the quarterback. Seeing the play develop, DJ yells "Reverse, reverse." With the defense being sucked to the opposite side no one is in position to react.

Sidestepping a potential block DJ chases the team's best receiver. Not noticing DJ chasing from behind, the team's best receiver crosses the line of scrimmage and sees no defenders between him and the goal line.

Crossing the 20-yard line he is expecting to easily make it into the end zone. Five yards later he is tackled from behind. Stunned that he was chased down he looks back and sees an exhausted DJ laying on the ground panting heavily.

With 15 seconds remaining in the first half the visiting team opts not to use their last time out. Lining up for the next play they notice that DJ is exhausted. The Pine Grove coach motions to call a time out to get DJ out of the game. Waving him off DJ says "Let me play. I'm good."

Ceding to DJ's demand, the coach decides not to take a time out or sub him out of the game. Instead he looks on as the time ticks down.

Snapping the ball, the visiting team targets DJ, as their best receiver is matched against him one on one and streaking toward the end zone. Watching the quarterback release the ball the fans stand to their feet.

Their best receiver and DJ both elevate toward the ball at the same time. Falling to the ground they both roll over and DJ has the ball.

Screaming hysterically the crowd is going crazy. Making it over to the sideline DJ begins to limp. The offense trots onto the field to kneel the ball and bring the first half to a close.

Satisfied with his performance, DJ now becomes concerned with his health and if he will be able to play in the second half of the game.

Assisted by the training staff, DJ limps off the field but takes a moment to glance toward the crowd again in search of Kevon or Chasity. Not seeing either he holds his head down and continues to limp toward the locker room.

Catching his attention, he looks back at the crowd again and notices a guy sitting next to Trail who looks familiar. Taking note that Trail is giving him a thumbs up and clapping along with the crowd, while the guy sitting next to Trail is frowning and does not seem happy.

Strolling his memory, he struggles to recall where he knows the guy sitting next to Trail from. Drawing a blank he becomes frustrated that he cannot remember who the guy is. Suddenly a sharp pain engulfs his leg causing him to focus on his injury.

Sitting at his locker in pain, the coach walks over and tells him that he has a strained hamstring. Holding his leg, he asks "So what does that mean? I can still play right?" Shrugging, the coach pats, him on the shoulders.

Taking a deep breathe the coach responds "DJ you have done a complete 360. You have gone from being one of the hardest players to coach to one of the best. Plus, your teammates love the new you. You have given it all you have, plus some."

Tapping DJ on his shoulders, the coach continues "It is because of you that we are winning this game. It is possible that you can play on a strained hamstring, but you could cause more damage. I recommend just take care of yourself." Leaning back into his locker area DJ slams down his helmet on the floor.

His thoughts quickly transition to the last game he played in when he got into an altercation with Bump. Replaying that incident in his mind, he recalls the guys who pulled onto the school campus to come to Bumps defense. Jolting his memory, he matches the face of one of the guys that were in the cars with the guy sitting next to Trail.

Thinking to himself "That's where I know him from." DJ's mind begins to race, wondering to himself why is Trail sitting next to one of the guys who Bump was affiliated with. Unable to make sense of it he thinks back on Kevon's advice to him, *"these dudes out here gone tell you what you want to hear to get you to do what they want you to do. Pay attention."*

DJ rehashes all the words that Trail has spoken to him over the time that they have known each another. He then begins to piece together what Kevon meant with his advice.

Embarrassed by his loyalty to Trail, DJ says to himself "Everything was about Trail. It was always about him. I was a pawn on his chess board. He was only telling me what he thought I wanted to hear. What was I thinking?"

Reclined as the trainers ice his hamstring, DJ thinks back on Chasity being raped, Bump being killed, Fan being raped, and the money Trail gave him.

Aware that Trail may be plotting another scheme, DJ begins to fear for his safety. Understanding that he made a deal and accepted the money, his focus transitions back to the game.

Walking back onto the field the fans are loudly cheering and celebrating their teams 21-3 lead. Understanding this is one of the biggest games in the school's history, the players begin to pump up the fans.

Disappointed that the coach decided not to let him play, DJ paces the sideline. Wearing an ice pack, he joins in with the crowd and cheers on his teammates.

The visiting team starts on offense and quickly exploit DJ's absence. They score on the first possession of the half, driving the length of the field. After kicking an extra point, the score is now 21-10.

Receiving the kickoff, Pine Grove's offense sputters again. Unable to gain a first down they punt the ball back to the visiting team. Understanding their disadvantage due to DJ's absence, Pine Grove attempts to make it a defensive game by double covering the visiting team's best receiver.

The visiting team decides to take advantage of their best receiver being double covered. Spreading their offense, they begin to pick apart the Pine Groves defenders.

Being picked apart in the passing game, Pine Grove brings in an additional defensive back. Now with one less linebacker to protect against the run, the visiting team begins to gash Pine Grove with running plays.

Ending the third quarter the running back runs up the middle for a 25-yard touchdown, making the score 21-17 after the successful extra point is made.

Discombobulated the Pine Grove players are in disarray. Walking to the sideline, they blame one another for missed assignments. Looking to the coaches for guidance, the players receive no assistance. Irritated with the teams play and lack of coaching, the players begin bickering amongst themselves.

Before the fourth quarter begins, DJ calls the defense over into a huddle and yells "This is all about you eleven guys out there on the field. We are up by 4 points. That means they need a touchdown to beat us. They don't win if they don't score!"

Inspired by his message the blaming and bickering comes to an end and the players start pumping each other up.

Starting the fourth quarter, Pine Grove's defense steps up. With the offense still unable to score the game becomes a defensive game, with neither team being able to score.

Halfway through the fourth quarter the visiting team starts to become frustrated with their stagnant offense. Instead of punting on a fourth and nine, the visiting team goes for it at midfield.

Setting up for a passing situation the quarterback receives the snap and drops back. With everyone covered he slings it toward his best receiver who is double covered.

Elevating over both defenders he catches the ball and lands on his feet. As one defender falls after the catch, he pushes the other down and sprints to the end zone.

In a frenzy the opposing team's bench goes wild. Kicking the extra point, they now lead 24-21. Down on themselves the Pine Grove players return to the bench with their heads down. Seeing the lost confidence, DJ walks down the sidelines.

Slapping each defensive player on the helmet he yells "That's the best receiver in the nation! Keep your head up, we are good. You played that the best you could. Nothing you can do about the past. We only down by a field goal. We got this!"

Understanding that a loss would not be in his best interest, DJ looks back at the crowd to gage Trails temperament now that they are losing. Observing that Trail is no longer standing and cheering he becomes anxious.

Confused he sees that the guy sitting next to Trail is now in a better mood now that they are losing. Shaking it off he becomes intent on getting the coach to put him back in the game.

Turing his attention back to the game, DJ sees that their offense has again sputtered, and they must punt. Watching them walk back onto the field DJ detects that the Pine Grove players are losing motivation. The visiting team begins to easily moving the ball down field, and close to field goal range.

Seeing the disposition of the defense, DJ runs over to the coach begging to get back in the game saying, "Coach if they get into field goal range and make a field goal the game may be over."

Waving DJ off, the coach looks on as the visiting team continues to drive down the field against his sluggish defense. Seeing the game slip away the Pine Grove coach turns to the bench and asks "DJ, do really think you are able to play?"

Without answering, DJ rips off the ice pack on his leg and puts his helmet on. Holding him back from running onto the field the coach calls a time out with 3:30 remaining in the game.

Before the coach can talk DJ interrupts, "Y'all better suck it up and get your head in the game. We got three and a half minutes to show these guys that we are the #1 team in the state." Reenergized from DJ's speech, the team all put their hands in the huddle and chant "1, 2, 3, WIN!"

Noticing DJ run onto the field, the visiting teams coach motion for the quarterback to call an audible. Getting a feel for what is about to take place, DJ drops back off the line as they snap the ball.

With DJ back in the game the safeties are shading to the other side of the field and allowing DJ to play his man one on one with no help.

Watching the running back block and release on a fly up the middle of the field DJ leaves his man. Getting behind

DJ the team's best receiver vigorously waves his arms noticing that he is wide open.

Looking back, the visiting team's best receiver sees that the quarterback has already released the ball. Watching the pass go in the direction of the running back. He watches as DJ beats the running back to the pass. After intercepting the pass DJ is immediately tackled.

Needing a field goal to tie the game, the Pine Grove offense stalls again. Without gaining a first down they punt the ball with 2:55 seconds left. Starting to become frustrated, DJ looks over at the offense in disappointment. Wondering why the offense has not made a first down the entire second half.

Receiving the punt, the visiting team fair catches the ball with 2:50 remaining in the game. Jogging back onto the field to play defense, DJ contemplates in his head the possibilities of what can happen if Pine Grove loses this game.

Anxiety building, DJ is determined to pounce on any opportunity he sees to win the game. Snapping the ball, the visiting team begins to kneel and run the time down.

Understanding the visiting team is attempting to run the time out and end the game, DJ feels himself becoming desperate. The visiting team has a fourth down with 48 seconds remaining and choose to bring on the punt team.

Pine Grove in response brings their punt return team onto the field. DJ, who is usually the punt returner, sneaks closer to the line of scrimmage as the visiting team continues to let the clock run down before punting the ball. Running the clock down to 10 seconds they snap the ball to punt.

Once he sees the ball snap, DJ sprints toward the line of scrimmage and elevates over the top of the blockers. As the visiting team kicks the ball, DJ is there to immediately block the punt.

Scrambling to the blocked punt, DJ beats the kicker to the ball, picks it up, and easily runs into the end zone as time expires on the clock. The touchdown gives Pine Grove a 27-24 victory after the made extra point.

Flooding the field, the team pommels on DJ as the crowd erupts with joy. Holding his sore hamstring DJ makes it to his feet celebrating with his teammates. Suddenly his facial expression turns from excited to serene.

Looking toward the stands for Trail's approval, DJ instead notices Trail shrugging his shoulders. Concerned as to what is occurring his views Trail being surrounded. He sees the guy he was sitting next to in addition to other guys who have now showed up, which he also recognizes from the incident with Bump.

Chapter 32

Conversing in the stands Prince turns to Trail asking, "What happened." Shrugging his shoulders, Trail returns a blank stare. Becoming agitated Prince turns and walks away as his entourage follows. Before exiting, Prince turns and shouts "You need to meet me in the parking lot."

Nodding in response to his request, Trail glances toward the parking lot noticing cars driving up. Keeping an eye on the vehicles, Trail recognizes members of the Chop Down Boyz. Paying attention as they jump out of the cars and dap up Prince.

Reaching toward his back Trail feels for the .45 that is holstered in the rear of his pants. Somewhat reassured after confirming he has his gun on him, Trail walks toward the parking lot to meet up with Prince.

Dapping up members of the Chop Down Boyz, as he walks through the parking lot, Trail is met by Prince who opens a rear car door inviting him inside. Looking around at the Chop Down Boyz, Trail cautiously enters the vehicle. Closing the door, Prince walks to the other side to join Trail in the car.

Sitting in the back of a luxury SUV, Prince orders the driver to drive. Driving away Prince pours a drink and offers one to Trail. Nervously accepting the offer, Trail watches Prince as he pours the drink. Grinning as he finishes pouring the drink Prince hands it to Trail.

Taking a sip of his drink, Prince slowly leans back in his seat and takes a deep breath. Turning back toward Trail, Prince asks, "Can you explain how I personally paid off the Pine Grove quarterback and offensive coordinator to lose the game…"

Calming himself he continues "They do their part…but the guy who you said you have under control AND I give you money to make sure there are no issues from is the only one who doesn't do his part?"

Giving a seething stare Prince continues "In fact this guy does the exact opposite. Despite ALL of the efforts of the quarterback and offensive coordinator to do what I paid them to do, this dude takes it upon himself…in pain might I add…to go above and beyond to win the damn game!"

Remembering their last few conversations, Trail is now visibly nervous. Searching for a plausible comeback Trail counters "Like I've told you before its Kevon…DJs brother is in his head. Ever since Kevon got out of the game, he is trying to convince DJ not to get money with us either."

Not giving eye contact Prince replies, "So is that also the reason you were cheering when they were winning and giving him the thumbs up sign every time, he made a big play?" Not having an answer, Trail takes another gulp of his drink to buy time while he thinks of a credible excuse.

Hearing the silence, Prince turns to Trail and observes that he is deep in thought. Attempting to calm himself, Prince reaches toward his inside jacket pocket.

Noticing his movement, Trail begins to panic and slowly slides his hand underneath his shirt. Being careful he subtly slips his hand toward his back placing it on his gun.

Pulling out a cigar, Prince pushes in the car lighter on the console in between himself and Trail while cutting the end tip of the cigar. Blowing a silent breath of relief, Trail takes his hand off his gun and sinks into his seat.

Suddenly bothered by a headache, Trail also feels a delayed reaction in his body movements. Feeling nervous, Trail takes another sip of his drink, to calm himself.

Grabbing the car lighter after it pops out, Prince lights his cigar. Blowing a puff of smoke, Prince asks "Remember I told you that I know about everything that happens in this city?" Starting to feel his face turn numb, Trail manages to nod in agreeance.

Taking another pull on his cigar Prince continues "First of all I don't believe you paid DJ to lose the game. Just like you didn't pay Pickles to win that last basketball game."

Blowing out cigar smoke he laughs "As a matter of fact I think you did just the opposite. I think you took my money, paid Pickles to lose the basketball game and gave DJ my money to win the football game. Then you probably went and bet against me which let you double up right? Wait, don't answer, I know, it was Kevon's fault, right?"

Becoming anxious, Trail manages to take another sip of his drink. Attempting to sit up in his seat, Trail feels his arms and legs beginning to turn numb. Dumping the ashes of his cigar in the ashtray Prince gives him a devilish grin.

Picking up his drink, Prince remarks "Funny thing is I just don't think Trail screwed me over. I know he did...See I did some investigating of my own. Initially when you said we had an issue with Kevon I checked it out myself. As a matter fact Kevon came to me."

Puffing smoke from his cigar Prince continues "He wasn't going to get in the way. He only wanted to make sure his lil bro was taken care of. But what I had a question about was Pickles. Kasyn was plotting with someone on another plan. Do you know the answer to that question?"

Raising his glass, Prince takes a sip of his drink and goes on "You don't have to answer. I think we both know the answer to that question. And you know what else? It wasn't Kevon or DJ who killed my guy Bump either was it?"

His drink dropping out of his now numbed hand, Trail becomes desperate and attempts to reach for his gun. Continuing to try to reach, Trail discovers he has no feeling or reflex in his hand or arm. Powerless his body flops back into his seat unresponsive.

Pulling out a knife from underneath his seat, Prince looks over at Trail, as he is unable to move and cracks "Another funny thing is I gave you the game and took you under my wing. Then I hear that you were trying to take me out!" Looking down at his knife he continues "Oh and here is the best part. I just heard today that my daughter was raped."

Peering at him to see his facial expression Prince, notices that Trails eyes are widened. Wiping his knife on his pants Prince quips "G-Juice huh. I taught you that back in the day. Never did I think my daughter would be a victim of the game I gave to you."

Shaking his head, Prince continues "I guess what goes around comes around huh? GHB. That is what the police test results found in my daughters' system the day after her rape. GHB!"

Motioning for his driver to pull the car over, Prince leans toward Trail putting the knife to his neck and says "You know how you feel now, you piece of shyt. That's how you left my daughter."

Backing away grinning with the knife still pointed at Trails neck Prince chuckles "A teacher never teaches his students everything he knows for a reason...the bottom of the glass. Always check the bottom of the glass. Opening the door on Trails side of the vehicle, Prince mutters "That's your final lesson." Stabbing him in the chest, Prince pushes him out of the car into the ditch.

Closing the door, Prince motions for his driver to pull off. Wiping Trails blood off his knife, Prince places the knife in a bag and picks up his phone. After dialing the number, Prince waits as the phone rings.

Getting an answer "Hello!" Prince responds "Time to keep your life. Five blocks down from the school, on the back road, down from the old paper company. He in a ditch. Finish him or you will be finished."

Chapter 33

Enjoying a laugh together, Fannah pauses, giving Chasity a stern look. Frowning her face, Chasity asks "What is that look for?" Pounding her arms on the bed Fannah exclaims "What about you? While you are busy fixing my life what about everything that is going on with you? And what about you and DJ?"

Rolling her eyes, Chasity quips "What about him?" Throwing her arms in the air Fan replies "You know what I mean. You love that boy and he loves you. You know it. So why are you trying to be so hard?"

Squinching her face, Chasity begins to speak when her phone suddenly rings. Picking up her phone Chasity looks at the number and smiles without answering. Snatching Chasity's phone away, Fannah looks at the missed call and asks, "This is DJ's number isn't it?"

Not receiving a response to her inquiry, Fan continues "Why aren't you answering his calls Chass? I just saw the twinkle in your eye when you looked at your phone and saw that it was him calling."

Still not responding, Chasity takes her phone back. Minutes later her phone rings again. Knowing that she is not going to answer, Fannah tries to grab her phone from her to answer.

Putting the phone behind her back, Fannah jumps on top of Chasity to try and answer her phone, at which time she screams "No. I don't want to talk to him right now." As they jostle for the phone they are interrupted by a knock at the door.

Looking toward the door Fannah shrieks, "It's him." Jumping off the bed, Fan runs to answer the door. Looking out of the window blinds, Fannah sees that it is DJ. Seeing that DJ is patiently waiting for someone to answer, Fannah quickly opens the door. She immediate asks "Are you still drunk?"

In a docile disposition DJ shakes his head "No". Hesitating he remarks "Fan I don't know what got into me that night. I was wrong. Not blaming it on the alcohol, but it did not help the situation. Bad part is that I let what someone else told me about you and Chass get the best of me."

Looking toward the ground in disappointment, DJ pleads "I disrespected you and Chass, I am here to apologize to both of you. Will you accept my apology?" Grinning Fannah grabs his arm and retorts "Boy get in here."

Pointing toward the couch Fannah says "Make yourself at home, give me a sec." Running into her room she says excitingly "Guess who's in the living room."

Plopping back onto the Chasity answers "Fan. Not even two days ago this guy was calling us names and being disrespectful to us in front of our guests."

With her excitement fleeting, Fannah jumps on the bed muttering "So you know who it is?" Shaking her head "Yes" Chasity responds, "I heard his voice."

With a frustrated look Fannah remarks "Chasity, are you serious, right now? You just not too long ago agreed that he was the love of your life. You said he was the best thing that ever happened to you and now your holding grudges?"

Getting off the bed, grabbing Chasity by her arms, Fannah pulls her off the bed as she asserts "Look what I did and how I took your friendship for granted but you forgave me right? Plus, how am I supposed to have hope that Kevon will forgive me for everything I did, and you aren't willing to forgive Demyre?"

Reluctantly allowing Fannah to pull her off the bed, Chasity begins to crack a smile. Seeing her smile, Fan laughs "See, your happiness is coming back, and you haven't even talked to him yet. Plus, he just gave you that huge apology, so you know he did not drive all the way over here just because he felt guilty. He's sincerely sorry."

Walking behind Chasity, Fannah pushes her into the living room and closes her door. Hearing the door close, Chasity looks back and giggles to herself. Seeing DJ, she walks over to him. Feeling uneasy, DJ respectfully stands to his feet.

Taking a seat on the edge of the couch Chasity coyly asks, "So what's up?"

Rubbing his hands on his pants to remove the sweat from being nervous, DJ skittishly says "I don't know where to start...but let me start by apologizing. I apologize for everything I did and everything I said to hurt or disrespect you." Holding her head down she murmurs "Mmmm hummm."

Watching Chasity drop her head, DJ starts to feel as though she does not feel that his is sincere in his apology. Edging closer to her he continues "I love you. I truly do. I know because when I am playing football, Watching TV, driving around or evening eating I find a reason to think of you."

Calming down and becoming more confident, DJ goes on "I told you that I would never let anything happen to you the night at the Park. I didn't honor that commitment because I was the one who did something to you."

Clasping his hands together he continues "I said some terribly things that I can't take back. I only ask that you let my actions prove that I am more than a night full of reckless decisions and verbal assaults. That wasn't me."

Letting him see her crack a smile she remarks "So what was all that about anyway? I know you told me you have another side, but I never thought I would be on the receiving end of the Demyre, dark side."

Becoming relaxed after seeing her smile, DJ leans in and lightly grabs her hand. Sitting down on the couch he gently pulls her as she follows his lead. Pulling her from the edge of the couch to the area closer to him.

Looking her in the eyes he says in a soft voice "I'm really not good with all this mushy stuff. I know I have never been in love before either. Oh, and a relationship. This is a first too." Smiling while looking into her eyes, he continues "I'm giving it all to you. All of me."

Holding her hand tighter "I want to always love you and I want you to love me. Even though I am finding out the hard way that love can make you do some crazy things. What you saw the other night that won't happen again."

Releasing her hand and rubbing his face in disappointment he continues "Trail kept trying to put it in my head that you were a ho. So, when you said he raped you the picture I saw was you all having sex."

Turning toward her, he goes on "At that point I guess I became selfish and didn't think of what had happened to you. I was being insensitive and to be honest like you said, Trail had me fooled and I believed what he was telling me."

Slowly grabbing her hand, he goes on "I was in love...I am in love with you. I didn't know how to react to hearing that the woman I am in love with..." breaking down and unable to continue she scoots closer to him rubbing his hands.

Holding her hands tighter, he gathers himself. Looking back toward her, he continues "Again I'm not familiar with how this relationship stuff works. I did not know how to be there, how to support you during a difficult moment, and how to believe you when you open up and tell me you were raped."

A tear rolls down his face. Wiping it away he says "That is what I am apologizing for. Not being there for you when you needed me. I am sorry babe. I was wrong, but I can swear to you on my life that it will never happen again. I placed my loyalty into someone I thought was my friend over someone I knew I loved."

Listening attentively, she grips his hand and replies "Ok. Ok. It is fine, honestly the things you said really hurt me but now I understand and accept your apology." Turning toward him, she becomes silent.

Raising their held hands to her lips, Chasity kisses his hand then places them in her lap and says "You know you aren't the only one who has hang-ups. Loving someone is not easy for me either. It's hard for me to put my trust in a guy, but I opened up for you and decided to be in this completely."

Sighing "It is scary because I honestly believe you when you told me you would protect me and never hurt me you know..." Pausing again to look into his eyes, she continues "If it had been anyone else it would not have hurt as much but because it was you..."

Rubbing her hands and consoling her, he asks "Can we just please start over? I am hurt just thinking about the hurt I caused you. I do not want to live in the past. I want to make your present, future and forever happy."

Reaching over to hug him she whispers "Yes." Wrapping his arms around her in return he answers "Thank you. I promise to give you the best of me." Smiling he jokes "The good thing is, you have seen the worst and it can only get better."

Losing herself in his arms she breathes a sigh of relief. Kissing him on the cheek she pulls away from their embrace and remarks "Ever since I was raped I do have commitment and trust issues so if we are going to do this I need you to know that and work with me ok?"

Shaking his head in agreeance she continues "Also I thought about coming to your game but with everything that was going on with us I just didn't think it would be a good idea. So, I apologize for that, but did you win?"

Chuckling he responds "From the conversations we've had I could tell that experience scarred you. It only makes sense that you would have trust issues with guys."

Kissing her on the cheek he goes on "That was never an issue with me. I am and will always be willing to show you the respect and patience that you deserve from a guy and we can get through whatever issue we encounter, together."

Now giggling he nudges her replying "And yes I was looking for you at my game but don't worry I understood why you weren't there. And yes, we won but it's a long story." Pausing he looks toward Fannah's door and then back at her and asks, "Is she ok?"

Turning toward Fan's door and back toward DJ, Chasity replies "She will be. She has been through a lot and thank you for helping her out. She told me what happened." Shaking his head in disgust he responds, "I don't know exactly what happened but from what I put together it wasn't good at all."

Looking back at her door again, Chasity gets up and pulls DJ up saying "Let's go check on her to make sure she's doing ok." Knocking on Fan's room door, Chasity does not get a response. Knocking again she yells "Fan. Are you ok?" Still not getting an answer Chasity opens her door and sees Fan on her bed crying.

Bursting the door open, Chasity goes in and sits on the bed next to Fan and asks "What's wrong?" Standing in the doorway DJ asks, "Is there anything I can do or anything I can get you?" Not answering either of them Fan puts her face in the pillow and continues to cry.

Scooting next to Fan, Chasity picks her head from the pillow and places it in her lap and consoles her saying "It'll be ok." Wiping her face, Fan balls up next to Chasity with her head on her lap.

Grabbing a pillow and placing it in between her legs, she murmurs "It hurts. I was a virgin. I didn't think my first time would be like this." Not knowing what to say Chasity continues to comfort her. Balling tighter in a ball tears start stream down Fan's face."

Stunned by her revelation Chasity is caught off guard and is unsure how to provide empathy in this moment. At a loss for words Chasity continues to comfort her by holding her head in her lap and rubbing through her hair.

Looking down at Fannah, Chasity is relieved that she is now calm. Glancing toward DJ, Chasity notices that he is in shock. Standing awkwardly in the doorway to Fan's room, DJ is in awe of what Fannah has just revealed.

Not accustomed to being in a situation where he is not in control, DJ feels out of place. Feeling empathy for Fannah, DJ walks over to the two and says "I know this is difficult for you Fan. Is there anything I can do? Do you want me to stay? Or if you need time to yourself, I can leave. Just let me know. Whatever you want."

Forcing a smile, Fan responds "Thank you. I will be ok." Unsure of what to do he walks over and kisses Chasity on the cheek and whispers "I love you" before patting Fannah on the shoulder and reaffirming "Call or text me if you need anything."

He then waves and walks toward the door. Watching him walk out Chasity yells "Hold on Demyre." Raising Fannah's head up she Squeals "Girl I will be right back" as she runs behind DJ.

Meeting him at the door she blurts "Kevon can help her." Giving her a confused look, DJ quips "Huh?" Sighing she goes on "Fan talked to Kevon earlier and I saw the look in her eye. He makes her happy and she needs him during a time like this."

Nodding he replies "Ohhh, Ok. I get it but me and him are not talking either. Shhhh I messed up with him too and he's not answering my calls."

Sighing again she retorts "Demyre, we got through a pretty difficult time and you know it was Fan who is to thank for it? She made it her business to call you and keep telling me to give you a second chance."

Looking down after hearing her comment he starts to feel guilty. Seeing that he is feeling guilty she goes on "I didn't say that to make you feel bad, I'm just asking if you can try to talk to him for her please?"

Shaking his head, he replies "Ok! I will." Giving her a hug, he continues "I will let you know how it goes...and I love you." Watching him as he walks out the door, she responds "Thank you and I love you more."

Chapter 34

Driving home, DJ feels like he is on cloud nine. Excited for the new opportunity with Chasity. Thinking of ways to make her happy, his happy thoughts are interrupted by grief. Suddenly saddened by the way he has treated his brother.

He relives the lectures, support, and protection his brother has given him over the years. He sees images of the sadness he saw in his brother's face after their argument when Bump was shot. The look of disappointment he witnessed on Kevon's face at the party, now float through him mind.

Now trapped in an unknown situation with Trail and his affiliates, DJ thinks about the outcome of his football game. Thinking of the warnings he received from Kevon, DJ's gleeful feeling completely dissipates. Trying to think of one friend he has that he can call for help, he draws a blank.

With his mind in a haze, DJ recalls the phrase "All I ask is that you make sure to watch a person's actions instead of listening to their words" play in his head.

Sarcastically giggling to himself, DJ thinks back to the things that Fannah told him about Kevon. Still in thought he replays all the things his brother has done in efforts to keep him out of trouble.

Realizing what his brother was trying to tell him, DJ again looks back on his last game. He is gaining a clearer picture of why Trail left the game without speaking to him. He was starting to understand why he was hanging around guys that were affiliated with Bump.

Gaining clarity to the recent events in his life, DJ thinks to himself "Trail was just telling everyone what they wanted to hear to get them to do what he wanted them to do."

Feeling stupid for how he jilted his brother for Trail, DJ picks up his phone to call. Embarrassed he hesitates. Remembering his promise to Chasity, he decides to go through with the call.

Dialing the number, he listens to the phone ring before hearing the answering machine pick up. Not leaving a message, he hangs up and tries again. Listening to the phone ring, DJ again gets the answering machine.

Now deciding to leave a message "KV, this DJ. Give me a call when you get a chance. It's important." Hanging up after leaving the voice mail, DJ continues driving. He makes a detour and decides to drive over to Kevon's apartment to try talking to him face to face.

Pulling up to Kevon's apartment, he sees that Kevon's car is in the parking lot. Knowing that he is probably inside he begins to get out while thinking back to the last two encounters they have had. Recalling the negative and hurtful words he spewed at his brother during those two occasions he pauses.

Gathering himself he becomes intent on making amends for his hurtful words and unappreciative behavior. Making it to the door he bangs with his usual knock to identify himself. Waiting a moment and realizing he is not coming to the door he calls his phone again.

Hearing the phone ring inside the apartment, DJ knows that Kevon would not leave without having his phone. Now knowing that he is in the apartment he knocks harder yelling "KV, open up the door man! I need to talk to you!"

Waiting a few more minutes, he gives up and begins to walk toward his car when suddenly he hears the door open. Turning back toward his apartment he sees Kevon standing in the doorway. Intimidated by the placid look on his face DJ walks toward Kevon asking "Bro can I come in? I need to talk to you for a minute?"

Without responding to his question Kevon flings the door open. Walking back inside of his apartment, Kevon takes a seat on his sofa. Taking his action as a sign to come in DJ jogs back toward Kevon's apartment. Upon entering he closes the door behind him.

Coming in and taking a seat, DJ uncomfortably attempts to find the correct comment for an apology. Interrupting the awkward silence Kevon remarks "So what's been up? I listened to your voice mail when you said something was important."

Startled from the comment, DJ mutters "I just been thinking about everything that has happened over the last few weeks and I'm just trying to turn everything around."

Giving a confused look, Kevon attentively listens as DJ proceeds "I'm just seeing life for what it really is and people for who they really are." Gleaming at him with a grin, Kevon responds, "About damn time." With a look of curiosity, Kevon asks "So what was it that sparked your change?"

Relieved by his welcoming tone DJ replies "It was a lot of things. Probably a lot to do with being selfish and closed minded. I was just looking at things from my point of view and what I seen every day."

With a sigh, DJ relaxes as he continues "You have to get it how you live in the streets you know. So, me not ever seeing you out there putting in work I guess I just had this picture of you being square."

Attempting to speak DJ interrupts "That whole situation had me in my feelings. I felt you did not have my back when things popped off with Bump. So, when I hooked up with Trail and he start telling me what I wanted to hear I was sold."

Becoming tense, DJ continues "Then you came in and seemed to be jealous of the relationship I had with Trail. In hindsight I will say I do understand now that it was not jealousy at all. I'm just saying at the time I took it as you were hating. I was doing me and had a homey that was looking out for me when you couldn't, is how I felt."

Taking a breath, DJ pauses to now give Kevon a chance to respond. Noticing that Kevon is now quiet, attentively listening, and has no facial expression DJ continues "I just had it all wrong. I see that you were just trying to look out for me in your own way. I also learned what you meant by, listening to people's actions over their words."

Sitting up in the sofa Kevon now has a more jovial demeanor and laughs "If that's your way of apologizing bro then apology accepted."

Still laughing, Kevon continues "What about Chasity? You put her out there bad. I think you should make your way over and apologize to her because she was hurt, and you know she definitely cares about you."

Waving his hands and giving a thumbs up sign DJ responds "Done deal. Yes, I almost messed up bad, but I got an understanding woman. I am blessed for her to have come into my life. So yes, I apologized to her, and even though it took a little while, Chasity ended up forgiving me. I will say Fannah helped."

Hearing the name Fannah visibly seemed to frustrate Kevon. Quickly attempting to change the subject Kevon responds, "I am glad Chass forgave you bro, because you did mess things up pretty bad."

Paying attention that Kevon is attempting to elude any conversation of Fannah, DJ jokes "You don't have to remind me how bad I messed up, but I just thank God that she FORGAVE ME."

Circling back to the conversation of Fannah, Kevon goes on "You know I also apologized to Fan and she forgave me for how I acted."

Seeing that he is unresponsive to the conversation about Fan, DJ continues "Fan helped me get Chass to understand that PEOPLE make mistakes and you can't hold that against them."

Not getting a reaction, DJ pleads "Nobody is perfect KV. Don't make Fan pay for being human and making a mistake." Understanding that he is adamant on discussing Fan, Kevon retreats into silence.

Noticing that he is beginning to clam up on the subject, DJ goes on "Come on Bro. You were just talking about how it is good to forgive and how great of a woman that Chass is for me right?" Receiving no response, DJ continues "Anyway, Fan is that same type of woman for you and maybe even better."

Still not getting a response and now starting to feel guilty about his part in the collapse of their relationship, DJ retorts "Look! You just forgave me, and I was dead wrong in damn near everything I said to you. I was especially wrong for what I said about Fan."

Kevon turns in DJ's direction and becomes attentive to what he is now saying. Feeling a little jittery after gaining his attention DJ continues "Fan was never messing with Trail like that. I said that out of anger."

Having his attention, he goes on "Trail talked trash about her, so I ran with it. Like I told you earlier, the dude played me. Had me believing everything he said...So to be honest if you want to be mad at someone it should be me and not her."

Sitting up in his seat Kevon clears his throat and decides not to continue eluding the conversation as he answers "I understand what you are saying but we family and it's always love. Plus, the situation with you and Chasity is different than me and Fan..."

Interrupting him by profusely shaking his head, Kevon stops as DJ blurts "Trail raped Fan!" Stunned Kevon looks at him in astonishment. Anticipating him to continue and dismiss the comment as a joke, DJ stares back at him with a stern expression.

Coming to grips that DJ is not joking, Kevon asks "What are you talking about? When did this happen because she never told me anything about him raping her?"

Not flinching and holding eye contact DJ answers "This just happened. After their party, the other night he drugged her up and raped her. You haven't been answering her calls so she couldn't tell you."

In shock Kevon leans back on his sofa and retreats to an unnerving silence. Never seeing him in this type of mood DJ suggests "If nothing else just give her a call and check on her. You know it would make her feel better if you checked in on her."

Noticing that Kevon's demeanor is unchanged, DJ changes the subject to lighten the mood and says "I'mma roll over to the barber shop later and grab my stuff. Based on everything that's happened, there's no need for me to keep working there."

Still not receiving a response, DJ decides to leave hoping Kevon will think over what they talked about and call give Fan a call."

Getting up, DJ walks over to Kevon and grabs his hand. Shaking his hand, DJ says "Thanks for chopping it up with me and I will hit you up later. I didn't mean to lay all that on you." Pausing he sighs "Just think though, if you are taking what I told you like that, imagine how Fan is taking it, you know."

Kevon looks up at DJ with a nod of agreeance. Feeling he has gotten through to Kevon, DJ walks toward the door. He reaches the doorway but before exiting DJ turns and says, "Bro thanks for looking out for me."

Grinning DJ proceeds "I know I probably didn't deserve it and gave you so many reasons not to... but believe me when

I tell you that the BS is behind me." Pausing again before exiting DJ bellows "Don't forget to call Fan."

Chapter 35

Lying across her bed, Fan dozes in and out of sleep. Waking up from a bad dream and afraid to allow herself to doze back off she forcibly attempts to stay awake. Exhausted she unconsciously begins to moan. With her moans becoming louder and louder she catches Chasity's attention who then comes into the room and asks, "What's wrong?"

Waking from her stupor, Fan stops moaning as she looks around her room. Spotting Chasity she looks up at her without responding. Staring at Fan's blood shot red eyes, Chasity feels helpless. She is unable to think of what she can do to assist her in feeling better.

Thinking that she may be having flashbacks of her horrific incident with Trail Chasity says "I know its hard Fan but try not to think about it. Try to think of the positive things in your life."

Laying back down on the bed, Fan murmurs "What positive things? My dad disowned me, never met my mom who they say was a prostitute, and the best thing to come into my life I ruined." Shocked by her comment Chasity takes a deep breath.

Embarrassed from her surprised reaction to her comment, Fannah continues "I took Kevon for granted and disrespected him. Nobody deserves that, especially him. I do not know what hurts worse, me being so naïve as to trust Trail and allow him to do those things to me, or the fact that I let Kevon down, hurt him, and ruined his trust in me."

Still shocked from her comment, Chasity remains quiet and attentively listens. With a tear now forming. Fan continues "Had I just been honest with Kevon and allowed him to be the man in my life that he wanted to be, none of this would've happened."

Pausing for a minute Fan proceeds "Maybe Trail was right. Maybe I wanted him to do that stuff to me. Maybe because I came over to his apartment that late at night half drunk, I deserved it."

Becoming frustrated that she's blaming herself, Chasity interrupts "I know this is hard on you, but you are taking this way too far. Trail is SICK. He is sick Fan. He stalked you out and took advantage of you."

Her voice getting louder "I mean this sicko did the same thing to me. And guess what? I blamed myself too, but it is not our fault! It is not our fault!" As Chasity begins to choke up, there is a brief silence as they both are now stuck in their thoughts. Suddenly, Fannah's phone rings.

Looking at her phone wondering who could be calling, Fan picks it up and looks at the number. Her saddened mood quickly turning to a happy one, Fannah looks up at Chasity as the phone continues to ring. Noticing the quick change in her mood, Chasity glances over at her phone to see whose calling. Looking at the number she says "That's Kevon! Why aren't you answering?"

Smiling, Fannah continues to just look at the phone without answering. Noticing that she is too shocked to answer, Chasity snatches the phone out of her hand and answers "Hello Kevon. Fan is right here."

Pushing the phone back into her hand Chasity mutters under her breath "Say Hello Fan...You've been talking about him all this time so don't get quiet now girl."

Grinning, Fannah puts the phone to her ear and answers "Hello" In a distant voice, Kevon responds "How are you? Are you doing ok?" Giddy from the sound of his voice she gives a short reply "Yes."

Sensing that she may be down or just doesn't want to talk, Kevon retorts "Well ok. I was just calling to check on you. I know this may not be the best time to talk with you, so I guess I'll talk to you later?"

Realizing that she is giving short answers and giving him the impression that she does not want to talk, Fan becomes frantic in her attempt to keep him on the phone.

Responding "No, no, Kevon. Please can you stay on and talk with me for a little while? I really want to talk with you." Reassured that he didn't catch her at a bad time Kevon goes on "Oh ok. It just seemed like you didn't want to be bothered and I can definitely understand based on what you've been through."

Feeling better Fannah begins to open up "I was just surprised to hear from you that's all. I didn't mean to come off as if I didn't want to talk with you."

Hearing him sigh into the phone she continues "So Kevon I just want to let you know again that I am sorry. I truly do apologize for everything. I know I betrayed your trust. And I know I have to live with that."

Hearing him about to speak she thinks that he is skeptical about her apology as she interrupts "Wait! Wait! There is more. I should have never made time or had another man in my life when we vowed to be committed to each other."

In desperation she rambles "Look. I am not trying to give you any excuse for anything I did. I just ask that you understand that I know I made a mistake...actually, I made a few mistakes, but nothing was intentional. I just did not value what I had. I didn't value you the way I should have and the way I want to if you will allow me."

Getting an opportunity to speak, he replies "Fan this isn't about me. What you have been through is horrible and no one should have to go through that. You know we were friends before any of this. So as a friend I wanted to make sure to reach out and make sure you were ok." Sniffling in the phone she responds, "So just friends now?"

Feeling she took his comments the wrong way, Kevon answers "I don't mean it like that but it's like I said the other day, I still love you but right now this is about you and getting you ok." Pausing for a second he continues "By the way. We are friends. You know you could have told me this happened to you the last time we talked right?"

Feeling cornered she quickly responds "I didn't want you to feel sorry for me. Or feel that I was trying to get you back out of sympathy for me or something."

Sighing in the phone, he remarks "Fan, WE ARE FRIENDS! Before we were in a relationship, we had that bond. So, you feeling like you can't talk to me about any and everything is also a problem that we should talk about. Of course, not right now. Right now, the focus is on you. We need to get you everything you need to get over this. That is my priority."

Grinning Fan replies "Kevon you are everything to me. That is one thing, probably the only good thing that has come out of everything that has happened. That you are everything to me and just like you said when we were in the park. From now until forever right?"

Relieved by her good attitude Kevon responds "I really admire the way you are handling this. You seem to be handling it well." Evading the compliment, she retorts "You are here talking to me on the phone after everything that happened. There are not too many men who would be interested in their girlfriends' well-being after all that"

Clearing her throat, she corrects herself, "I mean X-girlfriend or friend, or you know what I mean. Seriously though no other man would care after everything that has happened between us. So, I take it all as a blessing. A blessing to let me know who genuinely cares about me and unfortunately the hard lesson of who does not.

Feeling comforted that the incident hasn't pushed her into depression Kevon gives her some inspiration "Well Fan, life is a lesson and you only loose when you don't learn from the lessons. Obviously, you have learned." Comforted by his positivity Fan decides to ask, "So I know it's soon but how you feel about us?"

Chuckling to himself he responds, "I already told you I love you Fan and..." Interrupting his phone beeps as he says "Hold on for a second. Someone keeps calling me." He clicks over to answer his call. Fan remains on hold while looking over at Chasity smiling.

Clicking back over he says "Fan can I call you back? I have to take this call." Slightly deflated Fan remains poised and replies "Sure. I'll wait for your call and I do appreciate you calling to check on me." Quickly hanging up to take his call she manages to say I love you as the phone clicks.

Chapter 36

With his packing complete before leaving, DJ walks toward the lounge of the barbershop to have a drink. Having a strange feeling, DJ aimlessly darts his eyes from the bar to the dance floor and back before finally walking over to take a seat.

Suddenly a voice asks, "what are you drinking?" Without looking toward the voice, DJ responds "Let me get a cranberry juice with a lemon please".

Bringing the drink and setting it in front of DJ the server asks "You sure you don't want a real drink? If you worried about the cost you do not have to worry about that, everything on the house for you." Taking money out of his pocket and placing it on the counter DJ responds, "I'm good, but I don't drink anymore."

Pulling the glass closer to him he looks at it for a few seconds before picking it up and begins to swirl the glass around as to mix the drink. Chugging the drink, he slams the glass to the counter and continues "Thanks for the offer though."

Smirking after hearing his comments the server takes his glass and propositions "The offer still stands, anything you want is on the house?" Pushing the money for his drink toward him he responds "Nah, I'm sure. That drank don't do me any favors."

Turning toward the server, DJ freezes. Now staring at the server, he mutters "weren't you at our homecoming game with Trail?"

Smiling he counters "Ahhh, you remember. Yes, that was me. They call me Prince." Walking closer he stops in front of him and extends his hand. DJ reaches out and shakes his hand in return. Releasing the handshake Prince reaches into his inside jacket pocket and pulls out a paper bag and places it in DJ's hand.

Looking down at the bag, DJ cautiously opens it and stares inside before attempting to reach inside and grab the contents. Grabbing his hand before he pulls out the contents, Prince warns "not here...wait til you get to yourself".

Slowly dropping the contents back into the bag, DJ pulls his hand out of the bag. Folding the bag, he inserts it into his back pocket. Now focusing his attention back on Prince, he asks "Is this the other half of the money that Trail said he was going to give me if I made sure we won the homecoming game?"

His eyes widening, Prince responds "Excuse me. What was that again? Did you say Trail gave you money to win that game?" Shaking his head in agreeance DJ takes the bag from his back pocket and pushes it back toward Prince.

Looking at the bag as it lay on the counter, Prince responds "Don't be silly lil man. This is part of the transaction. You do your part and I keep my end of the bargain."

Pushing the bag back over to DJ, Prince continues "I tell you what. You keep that and this barber shop. It is mine but I cannot maintain it with everything else I have going. So, along with this package you get the barbershop too."

Giving a confused look DJ replies "For what? Why are you giving me all of this?" Pausing for a moment DJ goes on "I appreciate the offer but no thanks. No thanks to this money for the homecoming game win, No thanks to the barber shop, and no thanks to the free drinks."

After another short pause DJ continues "Prince I have been thinking about this and when Trail gave me that money, I did not feel right about it. I felt trapped. I see how the game go now. You trying to use and take advantage of us young dudes because we don't know the game."

Shifting toward Prince, DJ continues "I see now what you all be doing. I see how easy it is to get caught up in the money, but I don't want any part of it." Rubbing his hands together DJ asserts "My bad for any inconvenience but I'm good. I will get the money that Trail gave me back to you ASAP."

Now laughing, Prince slowly walks closer to DJ before stopping inches away. He calmly rests both hands on the bar space in front of him and in a seething tone says "Look, this is all about business. Life is a business, marriage, divorce, kids, vacation, cars, money, LIFE, DEATH! These are all business decisions DJ."

Walking around the bar and taking a seat next to him, Prince continues "Let me tell you a story. When I was seven years old, I had a hook up on this special kind of candy bar. It was delicious."

Looking at DJ with a menacing laugh Prince continues "It was better than the others out there. Little kids wanted to buy them from me. So, I started selling them. A little while later even the other kids who were selling other candy bars were not making money off their candy. So, they came to me and started buying my candy bars and selling them."

With DJ's full attention Prince goes on "Everyone was happy, and BUSINESS was good. Eventually it was getting so good that they wanted more up front but did not have all the money to buy as much as they wanted or needed. So, I loaned it to them, and they paid me back."

Pausing he sits up in his seat and stares at DJ until they make eye contact. Grinning Prince goes on "Here's the good part. There's a ten-year-old boy who decides to borrow a large amount of candy bars from me and not pay me back."

Making a muscle gesture Prince proceeds "He was bigger and stronger than me so physically I was not able to take care of the situation on my own."

Tapping on the counter Prince continues "So I faced a dilemma because other people who had loans from me saw what was happening. Had I let him take my candy bars and not give me my money others would've started to think they could do the same."

Sucking his teeth, Prince goes on "Now at the time I had older brothers and cousins who were high school dropouts and had nothing better to do with their time than to cause trouble and chaos. So, at this point I'm sure you can guess what happens next."

Now with his arms folded "long story short the ten-year-old not only gave me the money he owed me but he had to pay me ten percent from all the money he made from then on out."

With a sinister grin, Prince gazes over to again catch eye contact before continuing "If I remember correctly while my brothers and cousins were MAKING SURE I got my money from the ten year old he offered to give my candy bars back"

Prince shrugs his shoulders. "Is this starting to sound familiar? Back then he told me that he hadn't sold all of the candy bars and didn't have all the money to pay me what he owed."

Unfolding his arms he laments "Now had I settled for him giving my candy bars back without completing his part of the initial transaction that would've had others thinking they could get something from me and have the option to give me the candy bars back."

Shaking his head, Prince continues "I can't give anyone that option. I give them good candy bars and they return them later and now they are less valuable than when I originally gave it to them."

He moves his head from side to side "No, No, no, if that happens, I make less money because I have less valuable candy bars. I'm sure you would understand why I wasn't able to let that 10-year-old off the hook."

Taking a deep breathe Prince gets up and walks back behind the bar grabbing the money for the drinks and shoving it into his pocket. Picking up the bag he states, "See I hear everything you said but I was making business decisions at seven years old."

He points at DJ and shakes his head "So when someone makes a business decision at sixteen, seventeen, and eighteen years old you have to excuse me for not shedding tears when you say they didn't know the consequences at that age.

Slapping the bag in the palm of his hand, Prince says "At the end of the day it is not a good business decision for me to let you give the money back and walk away. I mean if I let you do that everyone would think they could do that to me right?"

Placing the bag into his pocket he continues "At that point I would stop making money because no one would take me serious as a businessman. If I hold up my end of the bargain it is just out of respect that you do too."

Patting on the bag that is now in his pocket Prince jests "You don't have to physically have this money or the money I already gave you but what did happen is that I gave it to you and you participated. Now if you give it back, I'll take it back as a gift...so thank you."

Seeing the dejected look on DJ's face, Prince attempts to give him some encouragement interjecting "I can see the dilemma you may think you are in but you have to always look at the bright side of things youngsta."

Mustering a slight grin, Prince suggests" Just as the ancient theologian Thomas Fuller once said, *"the darkest hour comes right before the dawn."* In other words, this is your chance to make the right decision unlike others before you. You can turn your dark moment into the light and get your happiness and success."

His grin now disappears from his face "On the flip side and in case you haven't realized I know a lot of people. And I am sure you would not want the media, colleges, pro scouts, or your family and friends to find out you have been taking money to rig games, would you?"

Winking his eye, Prince shouts "So at this point you have two decisions you can make. One is to man up and make good on your part of the deal and be set for life. Or two, not make good on your deal and have your entire life ruined."

Giving DJ a piercing stare, Prince retorts "Your dad made his decision, Trail made his decision and your brother made his. They also had choices just as you do now. Unfortunately, they didn't make the right one."

Dazed from Princes threats DJ sits speechless. Slapping the counter Prince yells, "You need to pay attention! Now you can learn from those before you who made bad decisions, or you can follow the decisions they made and end up like they did. Again, this is not personal. It's only business and in life you have to make some tough business decisions."

After a slight pause Prince continues to stare into DJ's eyes before scathingly muttering, "Stick around, relax in here for a minute to think about what we talked about. We will be in touch I got some business to take care of."

Chapter 37

After hanging up with Fannah, Kevon clicks the phone back over answering "Now what were you saying about my brother?"

In a panicked voice, Kasyn responds "Dude I heard them Chop Down Boyz coming for him because of what happened at his last game." Startled by his comment Kevon replies "Hold on for a sec, I'mma need you to back up and let me know what you are talking about.

Still in a frenzy, Kasyn goes on "This is what I was telling you about the other day when you were taking me home, but you didn't want to listen..."

Pausing, Kasyn continues "Look! Word was already out on DJ because he was the reason Pine Grove beat Hidden Valley when they were supposed to lose. Now that he went all out to win the Homecoming game the other day, when they were supposed to lose...shhhh I'll just say that wasn't a good move for him."

Taking a moment to take in the information he just received, Kevon slowly responds "My brother isn't involved in the game and never was so why are they coming for him?"

Sighing into the phone, Kasyn exults "Involved with the game! Dude! Money done exchanged hands. DJ into them boyz for some G's."

After a brief silence, Kevon calmly remarks "This just don't sound right...Man. I know Trail, and them Chop Down Boyz working together. We were just talking about the BS that Trail got us jammed up in that we didn't know about."

With agitation becoming apparent in his voice, Kevon continues "DJ is a loyal dude and I know back then he was especially loyal to Trail. So, if that is the case there's no way he would've took money to LOSE and then turn around and go all out to WIN. Nah, I know my brother better than that."

Clearing his throat, Kasyn replies "I hear you man. I am just telling you what is going on. At the end of the day he took the money and the game did not go the way it was supposed to go. And unfortunately, he don't have anyone on his team to take the heat for him like I did for you."

Irritated by Kasyn's comment Kevon remarks "What are you talking about! We back to that? Didn't we put that behind us? I thought we were over it...So why are you bringing it up again?"

Without hesitation Kasyn quips "We are over it. I'm just giving you something to compare his situation to, so you'll know how serious this is."

Concerned for his brother Kevon begins to sense that something bad may happen. Unsure of what may happen to him he asks, "So what else have you heard?"

Jumping at the opportunity to provide information, Kasyn answers "from what I hear they will be waiting for him to come back to the barber shop and they are going to set him up."

Startled by his comment, Kevon begins to wonder to himself how does Pickles know all this information? Who is giving him this information? And is he involved with any of this?

Intent on not drawing attention to his suspicion of Pickle's motive, Kevon cautiously asks "Who did you hear this from and what kind of set up do they have out on my brother?"

Bothered by his question, Kasyn responds "Bruh the streets talk. That is what I am telling you. Everybody talking about it. You have not been out the game that long. You know how it go."

Apprehensive after the questions, Kasyn evasively continues "And as far as the set up...Ain't no telling with Chopdown. If you ask me, I really think they just gone scare him up and try to get him in the same situation they got you in."

Not satisfied with the answer, Kevon gingerly replies "I understand but I can't let him get trapped up in the same situation I got myself into. I mean that's the purpose of me being the older brother."

Agitated, Kevon asks "What's the point of me going through and overcoming a bad situation if I can't pass it down to my little brother and he learn from it?"

Sympathizing, Kasyn replies "Kevon, I hear ya bro. On the real I felt it was only right for me to come to you and let you know what is going on. I'm not the enemy here."

Taking a deep breath, Kevon exclaims "Calm down Pickles, I never said you were the enemy. I am just venting. Nothing against you, it has just been a rough couple weeks for me you know. Seems like the more I stick my neck out to help people the more people line up to chop mine off."

After a short pause Kasyn counters "I feel your pain. But on the real, right now this is more about DJ than you...At this point who knows when these dudes gone decide to pull up on DJ."

In a serious tone Kasyn warns, "Because at the end of the day DJ works over there where Chop Down hang out. For all we know he might be there now and in trouble."

Hearing Kasyn talk about the barber shop, Kevon's mind replays his last conversation with DJ. Remembering that he told him that he will be going over to the barber shop to pick up the rest of his things.

With a change in tone Kevon abruptly blurts "Barber Shop huh? Ok, I'm making my way over there so that I can make sure nothing happens to DJ." Relieved, Kasyn counters "That's a good idea and if you need me to do anything just let me know. You know I got your back."

Listening to his verbal support, Kevon darts toward his dresser drawers grabbing a pair of jogger pants and a sweater. While getting dressed Kevon begins to have an uneasy feeling. He wonders why Pickles is taking such a vested interest in supplying him with this information concerning DJ.

Finally dressed, Kevon leaves out of his apartment and asks "If you want to help you can let me know who got the hit out on my brother. That way I know who to look out for and who to tell him to look out for."

Slow to respond to his inquiry, Kasyn finally says "Man I don't know who the person making the call is. All I know is that it's those Chop Down Boyz and you know how deep they roll."

Expecting the vague answer, he receives Kevon replies "That's cool man. For some reason I think Trail is somehow involved in this." Staggered by his comment Kasyn responds "Bro, you are out of the loop for real, Trail got stabbed and left for dead by Prince. I'm thinking the last thing on his mind right now is your brother."

Shocked by Kasyn's statement, Kevon says in bewilderment "What! When? Why did Prince try to kill Trail?" Evasively Kasyn counters "I'm telling you all I know but the issue now is DJ. He could be next..."

Snapping back to the present situation, Kevon replies "Ok, You right. Thanks, and I appreciate you for passing this info on to me and I'm sure DJ will appreciate it too."

Pausing before hanging up Kevon goes on "By the way, the other day, you said Fan wasn't worth it, and that I should leave her alone right?"

Wondering where he is going with the conversation Kasyn answers "Yes. She was always around Trail. Girl was just playing you bro."

Sarcastically laughing, Kevon responds "Turns out she was worth it way too much because Trail found her worth it so much that he raped her."

Waiting for a response Kevon hears the phone drop and soon after he hears a dial tone. Assuming that the news shocked him, Pickles hangs up and calls DJ's phone. The phone immediately goes to voice mail. Now thinking the worst, Kevon runs to his car and drives to the barber shop.

While driving, Kevon finds himself in a fog and confused. He begins to question Pickles' friendship and loyalty. Wondering to himself "Is Pickles trying to help or does he have some other motive? Is he someway still involved with Trail and the Game?"

Skeptical of the information he received from Pickles, Kevon goes against his instincts that are telling him not to drive over to the barber shop.

Flashing in his mind, Kevon remembers one of the last things DJ said was he was done working at the barber shop and he was going to go there to pick up his stuff.

Replaying his conversation with Pickles, Kevon recalls Pickles saying that the Chop Down Boyz had plans to set DJ up at the barber shop. With that conversation replaying in his mind, Kevon quickly phases out any inhibitions on if he should drive to the barber shop. Becoming anxious to get there he accelerates and begins to drive faster.

Chapter 38

"I see you over there cheesing girl. What were you all talking about?" a curious Chasity asks. Still giddy Fannah evasively responds "I know you had something to do with him calling...and I'm not mad. I really appreciate it."

Happy for her friend, Chasity jokes "I don't know what you're talking about? I didn't have anything to do with that...but anyway don't try to avoid my question."

Rolling her eyes, Fannah remarks "Sure you didn't Chass. So, I wonder how else Kevon would know what happened to me then huh?" With a coy smirk Chasity replies "You do know that Demyre was in here when we were talking about all of that? Plus, you also know that they are brothers, don't you?"

Playfully pushing Chasity, Fannah responds "Whatever. We both know DJ and Kevon were not on speaking terms. So, if DJ did contact Kevon, once again YOU had something to do with it." Shrugging her shoulders, Chasity retorts "Ok, Ok, so I did. Happy now. So, are you all good? What did you all talk about?"

Calming from her giddy mood, Fannah takes a moment before replying "It was ok. I knew I messed up and it is going to take time. I am not sure if it'll be like it was, but I think he understands. Or at least I hope he knows that I sincerely care about him and I do regret what I did. At least I can say that our friendship has not been ruined."

Smiling after listening to her comment, Chasity reaches over and gives Fan a hug. Half-heartedly returning the hug Fan pushes away and continues "I wished none of this would've ever happened but if nothing else I am reassured in how much Kevon cares about me."

Becoming silent after her comment, Fannah holds her head down and covers her face with her hands. Moving closer to her, Chasity asks "What's wrong now? I am not understanding you girl. You just got some great news and now you are sad again?"

Removing her face from her hands she looks up and mutters "That's just it. He has always felt this way and I took it for granted. I messed it up because I was both too naïve to listen and to be the girlfriend I should have been. I was just too dumb and naïve."

Taking a deep breath, Fannah goes on "Kevon is being so supportive and at this moment I guess that is what I really need from him more than anything else right?" Before Chasity can respond, Fannah's cell phone rings. Thinking that it is Kevon calling, Fannah cheerfully bounces on the bed and picks up the phone answering "Hello."

Happy for her Chasity looks on as she answers but notices the smile on Fan's face quickly fades. Her smile is now replaced by a pale and blank trance. Worried about her sudden change in demeanor, Chasity asks "Fan! What's wrong?"

Not answering, Fannah continues to hold the phone to her ear. Concerned because Fan is not answering or responding, Chasity places her hand on Fan's shoulder.

Chasity commences, to shake Fan while continuing to ask what's wrong. Still not receiving any response, Chasity grabs the phone from Fan and clamors "Hello! Is this Kevon?"

With an ominous laugh the caller replies "Naw sweetness this ain't no Kevon." Recognizing the voice Chasity becomes speechless. Hearing no response, the caller continues "Are you still there sweety? Cat got your tongue." Gathering her thoughts, she shrieks "Why are you calling her? She doesn't have anything to say to you Trail!"

Chuckling at her comment Trail laughs "Come on now. I thought we were better than that. You remember the party back in the day when we had a good time together? I can understand you trying to cover it up by saying it didn't happen so that your girl won't get mad at you."

Grunting, Trail continues "You knew me and Fan were dealing with each other. So, you were trying to be a loyal friend. Ain't nothing wrong that. Now it is a different story taking your lies to the police. C'mon now, don't you think you're taking this cover up a little too far?"

Starting to become afraid, Chasity nervously replies "How could you. You do that to my friend and have the nerve to call here... AND yes. YOU RAPED ME! You sick sack of crap. Just like you raped Fan and no telling who else. You deserve to rot in jail!"

In a menacing voice, Trail responds "Rot in jail huh? --- Now in order for me to go to jail for a crime, that would mean there would have to be living witnesses. Someone would have to be alive enough to repeat these lies that you and your ho friend are running around telling the police?"

Frightened after listening to his threat, Chasity becomes speechless. Still in a stupor Fannah looks on as Chasity becomes silent and begins to tremble.

Inspired by her courage, Fannah comes around and manages to gather enough courage to grab the phone back from Chasity and shout "Look Trail please just leave us alone."

With the continued grimacing voice, Trail says "Leave you alone? You two hoes trying to put me in jail for giving you a good time. Lying and telling the cops I raped y'all? Now after all that you want to tell me to leave you alone?"

Sighing in the phone, Trail hesitates before continuing "We had something good. We both wanted it. So why are you trying to let your slut friend, and your soft ass boyfriend convince you to lie on me? I mean at the end of the day dude just jealous of us like YOU told me remember?"

Groaning again, Trail pauses. After a few moments he catches his breathe and mocks "You told me he had the issues. So, because your lil boyfriend couldn't be close to you like I was he couldn't take it right…"

Interrupting Trail, Fannah blurts "Kevon doesn't have anything to do with this. You drugged me and raped me. I was a virgin. I would have never had sex with you. You drugged me and raped me. My mistake was thinking I could trust you. I was wrong to think you were my friend. You are an evil human being!"

Breathing heavily into the phone, Trail responds now in a seething tone "This is what is going to happen. You and your little lying ass friend are going to go back to the police and tell them everything you said about me is a lie…do I make myself clear?"

Waiting a few minutes for a response, Trail only hears Fannah breath into the phone. Understanding she is not going to respond, Trail continues "I know you hear me!"

Anguishing after yelling, Trail's voice softens as he mutters "Just so you have some incentive, here is something you can look forward to…if you get the police off my ass maybe nothing tragic will happen to your little boyfriend when he comes to the barber shop to try to help his little brother!"

Listening to Trail's threat, Fan's concern for Kevon instantly overrides her own safety as she yells "LEAVE KEVON OUT OF THIS! He has done nothing to you! He doesn't have anything to do with this!"

Hearing Fan's emphatic response, Trail is satisfied he has her attention. In agony Trail replies "You brought him into this. It could have been you and me, but this is how you want it to go. Now I am giving you a way out. This way we all get what we want."

Taking Fan's silence as consent, Trail goes on "At this point I can care less about either one of you. I got my own stuff to worry about. So, what happens next is up to you and your lil friend."

Hearing a dial tone after his threat, Fannah becomes visibly distraught. The phone falls from her hands as she and Chasity stare at on another speechless.

Chapter 39

Driving toward the barber shop to check on DJ, Kevon starts to think about Fannah. Reminiscing on the first time they met, the first time he talked with her, and how complete he felt when she agreed to be in a relationship with him.

Replaying her apology in his head, a smile covers his face. Realizing the importance, Fan plays in his life, he starts to feel guilty that he has not been more empathetic in understanding her desire to make it work between the two of them.

As he continues to reflect, his guilt begins to turn into animosity toward Trail. Wondering to himself, why would he lie and take advantage of him in that high school game that got Pickles suspended?

He wonders why he would he try to take advantage of DJ, who wanted to do nothing but have his back? And why would he rape Fan, who was loyal to him as a friend and is one of the nicest people in the world?

Hitting his steering wheel, Kevon becomes angry "What kind of evil person is he really" Unable to come up with a logical answer, Kevon's hatred toward Trail becomes stronger and stronger prompting his eagerness to arrive at the barbershop to ensure his brother is safe.

Driving toward the barber shop, Kevon again tries to call DJ to warn him not to go and that he is in danger. Dialing the number waiting for an answer he receives the voice mail.

Not leaving a message, Kevon dials the number but again and again he gets an immediate voice mail. He is becoming increasingly concerned so he hits the gas, speeding up the car.

Anxious with his mind racing, Kevon decides to return Fannah's call. Confident that talking with her will calm him, he dials her number. His mind instantly switches to what she has been through. Remembering his guilt about her situation, Kevon suppresses the urge to talk about what he is going through and instead intends to comfort her.

Listening to the phone ring, Kevon becomes engulfed with happiness. Thinking that everything in his life is coming together. He's happy he is finally getting through to Demyre. He's happy about his newfound bond with his brother. He's also thankful for the great relationship he has with Fan and feelings of fulfillment knowing that he has found the love of his life.

In the midst of his happy thoughts, Fan answers "Kevon!" Caught off guard but happy to hear her voice, he responds "Hey Fan. I apologize for getting off the phone so soon earlier. It was an emergency that I had to deal with."

Hearing Fan begin to comment, Kevon interrupts "Hold on for a second. Before we get into my emergency, I have something else that I want to talk with you about." Impatiently heeding her urge to warn Kevon about Trail's threats, Fannah concedes to his request and answers "Ok."

Pausing for a moment, Kevon goes on "I think you already know that I love you and I know that you love me. What I also know is that what we have is special. I don't know how to personally support what you've gone through because I've never been close to anyone who's suffered through anything like that."

Clearing his throat, Kevon continues "What I can say though is that I want to go through it with you, and I can promise you'll have my unconditional love and support through it all. We are friends, but I want us to go through this situation and this life together as one."

Finishing his statement, Kevon waits for her response. After a few moments with no response, Kevon asks "Are you still there? Is everything ok?" Sniffling, Fan responds "Kevon! Yes! Of course! I am sure you already knew the answer to that before you asked. I love you so much and I'm simply happy you are accepting of me despite what I've been through..."

As he is about to comment, Fan interrupts "Before you say anything, I have something I have to tell you." Curious as to why she isn't in a more jovial mood, Kevon responds "Ok. I'm listening."

Without hesitation, Fan blurts "Trail just called me...He threatened me and Chass. He said that if we don't recant our report to the police that he was going to...ummmm..." Hearing the panic in her voice Kevon interjects "He is going to do what?"

Pausing, Fannah quickly quips "Kevon he said that something is going to happen to you if we don't go to the police and say that he didn't rape us...And he even mentioned you being at the barber shop. How did he know you were going to the barber shop?!?"

Deliberating on her comments, Kevon thinks back to his conversation with Pickles. Thinking to himself "How did, Trail know he was going to be at the barber shop"

Attempting to seem unbothered by her comments, Kevon responds "Fan don't worry about me. I will be fine. Just make sure you and Chass are good----but Pickles just told me that this guy named Prince stabbed and tried to kill Trail."

Surprised by Kevon's comment, Fannah repeats "Prince?" Speaking louder with the thought that she may not have heard him, Kevon repeats "Yes Prince! I am not sure exactly what happened, but I am sure Trail will be looking for Prince and not trying to come for me. Either way do not worry yourself about me ok. I'm good."

Pulling up to the barber shop, Kevon parks and tells Fan "So I just made it here. It's pretty quiet but I see DJ's car parked. I'm going to go in and make sure he is good." Still concerned, Fan asks, "That's fine but can you talk to me until you make it to DJ please?"

Giggling, Kevon retorts "You are funny. Guess you are trying to be my protector huh?" Not amused by his comment, Fan replies, "I guess, but seriously I just don't understand why you are so calm with everything that is going on."

Still humored by her concern, Kevon exits the car while saying "You are right. Let me put on my scared face." Walking toward the barber shop, Kevon looks around and gets an uneasy feeling as it is an unusually quiet day for the area of town that the barber shop is located.

Pausing for a moment, Kevon tells Fan to hold on as he continues to walk before stopping in his tracks after a glare temporarily obstructs his view. Blinking his eyes to regain focus he turns toward the glare long enough to see the muzzle flash. Pow! Pow! Pow! Pow! Pow! Five shots later he lay on the ground in a pool of blood.

Hearing the gun shots, DJ runs from the barber shop and sees Kevon lying on the ground in blood. Running to his aid, DJ grabs Kevon off the ground and holds him in his arms while yelling for someone to help.

Out the corner of his eye he observes a familiar face running from the scene. Turning his attention back to his brother, he tries to calm him. Begging for him to breathe and stay with him.

With blood spewing from his mouth, Kevon starts to shake uncontrollably. Yelling for help, DJ continues to hold his brother in his arms until he stops moving. DJ shakes Kevon and yells "stay with me!"

Once he realizes that Kevon is no longer breathing, DJ looks around and begins to yell at the top of his lungs, "SOMEONE HELP! SOMEONE HELP! CALL 911! HELP ME, MY BROTHER HAS BEEN SHOT!

While screaming for someone to call 911, DJ hears screaming seemingly coming from Kevon. Hopeful he looks down but notices that the sound is coming from his phone.

Pulling the phone from his hand he puts it to his ear and asks, "Who is this?" Hysterical she screams "This is Fan! WHAT IS GOING ON?" Saddened, DJ cries "Kevon has been shot; someone shot my brother."

Chapter 40

Locating his pre-paid phone, he begins dialing. Getting an answer on the first ring and without hesitation he immediately begins to yell "What in the hell are you doing Pickles?" Out of breath he replies "What are you talking about? You really gone just call my phone talking crazy?"

Frustrated, Trail responds "You know exactly what I'm talking about. KEVON! Y'all just shot him. The plan was to just scare him, not kill him. Shyt already hot for me in these streets. We agreed to go after Prince and just scare Kevon.

I'm on the run for rape dude. RAPE! And did you forget one of the girls is Kevon's girlfriend. The same damn Kevon that just got shot to death. So, who do you think they gone be looking for?"

A slamming door sound echoes in the background. Still panting and out of breath Kasyn responds "You calling me talking crazy. You just need to calm down. Did you forget I just saved your life? And not to mention you are the one on the run, not me."

Calming down he replies "What's up with you? First you murk Bump without anyone calling for the hit and now Kevon...you are outta control." Chuckling he responds, "You were the one trying to impress DJ."

Catching his breath, he goes on "If you gone act tough don't be surprised when shyt get real. Did you also forget you were the one who wanted Fan so bad and wanted Kevon out of the way, remember all that?"

Shocked at his comments Trail remarks "What the hell! I know you aren't serious...I wasn't trying to kill nobody for no reason. I was on the up and up. The barber shop the hottest ticket in town. I'm putting dudes on and they turning over the money."

Stunned by his reaction he continues "We decided on this. Not just me and with this gambling thang, everybody was eating. Prince was the only problem, you know that. There was absolutely no reason to murk anyone else...you tripping."

Chuckling even more he responds "Prince was a problem for you. Who said he was a problem for me? What beef do I have with him? I didn't have a problem with Bump. And as far as Kevon. Everyone knows we were best friends."

Startled by Pickles' sudden change in personality he asks "Why Kevon? You two have been friends from jump." Catching his breath, he replies "That actually wasn't me. Nah, I didn't cosign that move at all. Prince was the triggaman"

In a disappointed tone he proceeds "Unfortunately plans change. Just like ours had to. Plus, you know I was the man back then, I put him on. I mean we did do him dirty putting him in the middle of that scheme but when we got caught, he could've took the rap. He was new and hadn't even had a charge yet. He would've just gotten a warning.

Becoming angry his voice starts to get louder "But for what we had going, I called you before each of our games remember. I told you the play. I talked to him about it too, but he wasn't down. He was serious about getting out the game."

Sucking his teeth, he snaps "I thought we were cool, and he would help me, but he was done. I couldn't keep pulling them licks off by myself. Especially with him on his own agenda trying to impress that chick. So, he sealed his own fate with them dudes. I tried to put him on game."

Pausing, his voice lowers before continuing "Plus he was starting to ask too many questions. Asking about me still being in the game. Asking about me being affiliated with Prince. Asking about me being affiliated with you."

Feeling he hit a nerve he reiterates "Yeah, he was on to us. He figured out that you told him one thing and I told him something different in the game that got us caught up in high school. I'm sure you didn't want him to keep asking questions and get you and Prince mixed up in it too."

Upset after hearing Prince's name he chides "You think I give a damn about Prince and what happens to him! Did you forget he left me for dead? And since you wanna bring him up. While you thinking you on his good side you was gone be next. After he got DJ in his pocket, he didn't need you anymore. You think I was getting close to the dude because I needed a new friend?"

After a slight pause, Kasyn growls "So you don't think I'm up on that? DJ is one of the best prospects in the nation right now. He loved his brother." With a taunting laugh he mocks "It is amazing how fast fear can change a person's decision. Especially when something tragic happens to a loved one."

In a confident tone he goes on "But like I say Kevon didn't deserve that. He'll get his justice. When plans change though, you have to change with them. Can't fold under pressure."

Changing his tone, Kaysn continues "Speaking of didn't deserve. Those girls. Those two girls you raped. Now that was just wrong. They were innocent dude. Why would you take advantage of not one but two innocent girls like that? Now they really didn't deserve that.

Momentarily speechless from shock Trail manages to clear his throat and replies "WHAT! Dude you are the one who told me that Chasity wanted me to come in that room and hit." Shocked he continues "You didn't even tell me til the next day that you spiked her drink. Do you remember that?"

Upset he snarls "And at The Grounds when you told me that Fan was down with it? You told me she plays hard to get. Wow! You even told me she be on that drink and like to get loose on the juice too" Suddenly realizing that he has been double-crossed he is instantly overcome with a feeling of embarrassment and fear.

Hearing the fear in his voice Kasyn laughs "No use in being remorseful now...I mean c'mon dude. You know what rape is. You let Greed control you. The money, the cars, the women...you just want it all. You actually thinking you could have it all is the worst part."

Hearing the silence from the once boisterous Trail empowers Kasyn as he goes on "Instead of having a strategy and making a plan you were easy to manipulate by your greed. You have to learn the game before playing it."

Feeling the defeat in Trail's tone, Kasyn boasts "It won't do you any good now, but to win you gotta have something on someone… Have to have that leverage. You didn't and your greed caused you to misjudge me."

Becoming embolden he gloats "You pegged me for a quiet pawn. Someone you were gonna walk over and have do your dirty work. And you know what, you were partially right. Yes. I did your dirty work BUT my hands are clean so you may as well have done it yourself."

With his mood changing from embarrassed to vulnerable, Trail asks "So since you are such a brilliant thug what are you getting out of any of this? You could've killed me already right! So why not? Why go through all this? Did you ever think I can now blow up your spot and put you and Prince on blast?"

Giving a sinister chuckle he remarks "Well as the great Tupac once said and I quote, *revenge is the sweetest thing next to getting coochie,* --- so that is what fifty percent of this is about --- revenge. Revenge on you for underestimating me but also, revenge on Prince."

Becoming more brazen, Kaysn's voice gets louder "The other half is just about power. I wasn't down with moving on Prince. That was all you, but since you wanted it so bad, I saw my chance to let him know the Play. Let him know so I can get that spot once you out the way."

Laughing out loud he continues "Prince ole skool. He makes sure to have his plan in place and know what's going on. He saw you coming before you started the plan. You got so impatient you couldn't tell the difference."

After a slight hesitation he scoffs "Like I told you earlier you have to have something on someone if you want to win. You didn't have anything. Plus, if you were dead who could we pin Kevon's death on? So, since that's done you are no longer needed."

Continuing to laugh, Kasyn says "You are going to like this one but I'm sure by now you already know. Fannah is Prince's daughter. You raped the big homey's daughter dude. Don't you find that funny as hell!!!" speechless Trail holds the phone and does not respond.

Finding humor in his silence Kasyn continues "Oh and as for your comment about blowing up my spot...I don't think you'll get that chance."

Hanging up the phone after his statement Kasyn arrives at Trail's apartment. Seeing the television and lights on he quickly picks the lock. He pulls out his gun as he enters Trail's apartment expecting to surprise him.

After entering the apartment his phone rings. Grabbing it out of his pocket and seeing that Trail is calling he begins to answer before being interrupted... "Thought you were the one who always plans things? Did you really think I'd be posted up at my crib with twelve waiting on me? But here are a few things that you might find funny."

With his voice a little more confident Trail says "I put cameras on the outside of my barbershop so the dude who shot Kevon was on candid camera. Everything that went down recorded and downloaded to my security system."

Satisfied with his silence Trail continues "Also, everything we've been talking about was recorded. Oh, and you are going to like this one. My apartment has a silent alarm with cameras so any second now twelve should be rolling up. But I'm sure you already planned ahead."

Chapter 41

Sirens sound from every direction. The police are the first on the scene. Two officers rush over toward DJ who is still holding Kevon in his arms. Still shaking him while yelling for him to say something, the police officers' step in attempting to calm him and escort him from the scene.

He begins to act in an erratic manner hindering the police officers from amicably removing him from the area. The medical personnel have just arrived. With no other alternative, the police resort to forcefully separating DJ from Kevon to allow the medical personnel to perform life-saving measures.

With reality beginning to set in, DJ looks on as the medical personnel attempt to resuscitate his brother. DJ is mentally paralyzed and oblivious to the questions the police are asking. His eyes are transfixed on his brother as they place him onto a gurney and put him inside an ambulance.

Sympathizing with his situation the police officers understand that he is not in the mind set to answers questions and they begin to interview other bystanders. Watching the ambulance pull away DJ continues to stand in a trance. Recognizing him from the football team one of the police officers' quips "DJ! Do you need a ride to the hospital?"

Still not answering, the police officer continues "Come on. My car is right there we'll follow the ambulance to the hospital." With the ambulance out of sight DJ slowly snaps out of his trance. Getting into his car the police officer insists "Come on DJ. I'll take you to the hospital." Hearing his name and realizing he does not know which hospital his brother is going to he takes the police officer up on his offer and gets into to the police car.

Riding to the hospital he embarks on a feeling of regret. He realizes Kevon was the only guy who genuinely cared about him and his well-being. He feels remorse for the harsh words he said to Kevon and the days he spent hating him.

He realizes there may never be another day to spend with his brother, never be another day to tell him how much he appreciated everything he's ever done for him, never be another day to tell him how much he means to him all starts to sink in at once. As he leans back in his seat, tears form in his eyes.

Dozens of thoughts rush through his head about his brother and all of the talks they had. All the times Kevon tried to reach out to him. All the times he tried to give him advice and how each time he shunned his attempts.

His thoughts drift toward Trail and the loyalty and trust that he gave him that should've been given to his brother. Sitting in silence the regret and remorse continues to tear away at DJ as tears now visibly stream down his face.

Noticing the tears and empathizing with how DJ watched his brother being gunned down in front of him the officer nudges him saying "DJ, think positive. We have great doctors here. I have known your brother for a while, I am a fan of his too."

Trying to cheer him he jests" I've been to all his games. Just like he pulls through on that court, he is going to pull through this…"

Without a response from DJ he continues "My heart is with you. Kevon is a great person. He has looked out for me in the past and you aren't the only one praying for him to pull through. Don't worry though, no matter what I got you, whatever you..."

He is suddenly interrupted by a call that comes across the police radio. *Break in at DogWood Complex Building 8 Apartment #26.* Catching his attention, he recognizes the address and apartment. Moments later the police officer gets a call on his personal cell phone.

Listening in, DJ can hear him repeat to the caller "So am I sending the false alarm order out on that call or do you have someone else working it?"

DJ watches the police officer nod in agreeance and hang up the phone. His mind focuses back on his brother as they finally arrive at the hospital.

Parking the car, the officer looks over at DJ and exclaims "My bad for that interruption, but like I was saying Kevon like family to me. You being his little brother makes you family too. Just know you can hit me up for whatever you need."

Shaking his hand and thanking him DJ gets out of the vehicle and nervously walks into the emergency room. Upon entering the hospital, he notices Chasity and Fannah are already there and they immediately bombard him with sorrowful hugs and apologies.

In tears they both tightly embrace him. Caught off guard he returns their gestures. After a few moments he pulls away and calmly Chasity says, "They aren't letting anyone back there." Comforted by her presence he looks into her eyes and whispers "Thanks for being here Chass."

Taking his hand, Chasity walks him over to the waiting room area and takes a seat next to him. She pauses for a moment before she drapes her arms around him. Walking with them Fannah takes a seat facing them as they all sit in silence. After a few moments Fannah breaks the silence and blurts "Trail did this!"

Looking up DJ stares at her emotionless. Slapping her hands together in tears she weeps "I told him not to go. Trail called me and threatened that if we didn't drop the charges, we pressed on him that something would happen to Kevon at the barber shop!"

As tears stream down Fannah's face, Chasity gets up and sits next to her in an attempt to calm her. With a blank look DJ says "It is not your fault Fan. Trail just a shady dude. Had I not gotten involved with him Kevon would have not been at the barber shop in the first place. So, don't blame yourself."

Seeing that she is still distraught he continues. "You do know he stalked you right? He used me and everyone he could to make sure you and Kevon would not be together. He was jealous. As a matter of fact, he actually lied and was telling everyone you was his girl."

Becoming angry he shouts "I mean he made sure you all were together all the time. So, I even believed him. That's why I made those horrible comments at the apartment. It was because of everything he was saying. He got over on all of us. We have to see it for what it is. He gone get his though. Believe that."

Starting to feel guilty again after hearing his comments Fannah thinks back to Chasity's warnings of her spending too much time hanging out with Trail and how it was giving off the wrong impression.

Sinking into Chasity's arms she weeps "You were right about me hanging around him too much and giving off the wrong impression...It is my fault...This is not right. Kevon did not deserve any of this?"

Emotionally drained, DJ can't manage the energy to continue to comfort her and resorts to watching her weep in Chasity's arms. He drifts into his own remorseful thoughts of what ifs and what could have been with his brother.

Entering the waiting room, a strange voice asks, "Are you all doing ok?" Recognizing the voice Fannah raises from Chasity's arms. She looks in the direction of the voice and is instantly caught in an incapacitated gaze. Noticing her trance DJ turns to view what has caught her attention.

Turning in their direction DJ catches eye contact and immediately turns away. Laughing to himself he walks over to DJ and reaches for a handshake.

Introducing himself he chides. "What's going on DJ or is it Demyre? I'm Prince, remember me? It hasn't been that long has it? Returning his handshake DJ doesn't respond.

Understanding the tragic situation DJ is dealing with Prince pats him on the shoulder and offers his prayers before walking over toward Fannah.

Still staring at him in awe Fannah watches him walk toward her. Holding his arms out he remarks "Are you just going to stare and not give your dad a hug?"

After hearing that comment Chasity and DJ's heads perk up and swiftly look toward Fan. Stunned Chasity asks "He's your dad? I thought you said you didn't know who your dad was?" Speechless Fan continues to stare at Prince without speaking.

Confused as to what is going on DJ asks "He is your..." Before he is able to finish his question the doctor walks into the waiting room and asks, "Are you all are here for Kevon?"

Rising to his feet DJ walks over toward the doctor followed by Chasity, Fan and Prince and responds "Yeah. He is my brother...what's going on with him?"

Looking him in the eyes the doctor asks "Do you want to talk here in front of everyone or would you prefer to speak in private?" Fearing for the worst he reaches for Chasity's hand while shaking his head and responds, "I'm good, go ahead and just say what you have to say."

Staring at the doctor and waiting for her next words DJ's mind wonders into thoughts of regret. He thinks back to his game when he fought Bump and got upset with his Kevon when he was only looking out for him. He also thinks about how he gave so much of his trust and loyalty to Trail and so little to his brother."

Chasity rubs his back noticing his despondent mood. Still in a daze his flashbacks continue. He remembers how he didn't show up at the basketball game that Kevon wanted him to come to, how he turned his back on him after the fight and shooting at the park, and how he embarrassed his brother was of him for how he acted at the party.

Feeling remorseful as he grips Chasity's hand tighter his mind focuses back to the doctor as she looks down at her medical board. Looking back up she says "I'm sorry. Your brother didn't make it. Kevon is dead."

Chapter 42

After hearing the doctor say that Kevon is dead DJ's legs buckle in shock. As he wobbles back and forth Chasity comes to his aid by grabbing his arm. Holding him around the waist she escorts him to a chair.

Sitting next to him she controls her emotions understanding that she has to be strong for him. Not knowing what to say she sits quietly next to DJ with her arm around his waist, rubbing his folded arms.

Standing in shock Fannah attempts to walk over to take a seat before stopping at a wall. Unwilling to continue walking to take a seat she slides down a wall. Landing on the floor, she sits motionless.

Sympathetic to the news they just received Prince walks over to DJ placing his hand on his back and says "Everything will be ok. Your brother is in a better place."

Not looking up or responding to Prince's gesture DJ continues to hold his head down and grieves in silence. Understanding DJ's loss and the severity of the moment Prince walks away after offering his condolences.

Assured that Chasity will be there to comfort him he turns his attention to Fannah who is sitting on the floor distraught. Walking over to comfort her he grabs a chair and pulls it close to where she is sitting. Taking a seat in the chair he says "Life goes on. Everything will be ok Fannah."

Reaching out for her hand she pulls away and blurts "Why are you here? What is in this for you?" Caught off guard he responds "Fannah. I'm just here to make sure you and DJ are good."

Folding her arms in anger she replies "Why would you even open your mouth to say something like that? You left me when I was a baby and now out of the blue when I'm an adult you come to make sure I'm good?"

Listening to her tirade he allows her to vent. Waiting a few moments for an answer that she doesn't receive she proceeds "And you don't even know DJ. So why would you say you are here for him or me? You can just leave! We don't need you here."

Sitting back in his seat he giggles for a few moments before saying "You are mad at me? Do you know why Kevon is laying in that hospital bed dead? Huh...do you?" Startled by his loud tone she listens without having an answer to his question.

Amused by her sudden silence he goes on "Trail was jealous of him. And guess why he was jealous...it was because of you, not me! You played that guy and had him acting stupid. Stupid enough to kill a guy just because he didn't want to see that guy with you."

Pausing for a moment to witness the guilt in Fannah's face he proceeds "Now you have the nerve to sit up in my face and blame me like you are innocent..."

Listening to his comments Fannah begins to feel guilty. Sitting up against the wall she brings her legs against her chest wrapping her arms around her knees. Looking toward Kevon's hospital room she slowly covers her face with her hands and begins to sob.

Hearing her cry Chasity and DJ look in her direction. Noticing the agony that Prince is putting her through DJ walks toward Prince blurting "What the hell are you doing to her? Don't you see she hurt dude? You need to let up!"

Now turning his attention toward DJ, Prince stands to his feet. Foreseeing the altercation that is about to occur Fan jumps in between the two. While wiping tears she attempts to calm the situation by asserting "It is ok DJ, I'll handle this."

Chasity grabs DJ and begins to walk him back to a seat. Relieved that the situation between the two has been deescalated Fannah turns toward Prince. Continuing to wipe her tears away she rants "So what now? I'm grown...are you supposed to be dad now? You missed everything and now I'm supposed to be happy you are here?

Sitting back in his seat staring into her tear filled eyes he responds "look you have every right to be angry with me but until you allow me to explain you'll never know what you are angry about."

As a tear runs down her chin she retorts "EXPLAIN! You have your nerve. You were not there. I don't need an explanation to figure that out. A dad is supposed to be there to protect his family, provide for his kids, and to keep them safe from everyone and everything. You did none of those things."

With her sorrow turning into anger she goes on "You were not there for anything. And what's worse is you show up on one of my worst days in life and have the nerve to blame me for my boyfriend being killed? The one man who actually gave a shyt about me because lord knows you didn't. You show up here to blame me? That's what you do after all this time? That is low, even for you."

Grinning Prince looks up at her quipping "I originally came here to show a little support but since my gratitude is unappreciated how about I take you up on your offer and just leave."

As he rises to his feet she interjects "Again! How surprising. This is what you are good for. Causing a situation and leaving it for someone else to clean up. You just up and leave. So easy for you. So easy to run. You are a great example of a real man and a real father."

Without pause Prince raises his hand and strikes Fannah across the face knocking her to the ground while yelling "I am still your father. Do you understand me! You will respect me."

Seeing her lay on the floor, DJ runs over and pushes Prince to the ground. Running behind him Chasity comes to Fannah's aid. Filled with anger DJ lashes out "What the fuck is wrong with you! You picked the wrong day to test my gangsta! My brother not gone be the only one flat lined up in this hospital today."

Attempting to get up from the ground, DJ approaches Prince yelling "How about you hit me and see how this play out for your lame ass!" With his fist balled he cocks back to throw a punch. Before swinging Chasity and Fan quickly run toward DJ, they grab and pull away with the help of a security guard."

Hearing the commotion other security guards rush into the waiting room area. Observing that Chasity and Fannah are struggling to restrain DJ they give them assistance. Finally getting DJ into a different room they proceed to calm him.

After ensuring that DJ is calm Fannah walks back into the waiting room with her hand over her bruised face to confront Prince. As security guards are guiding Prince out of the hospital, she rushes toward him.

Livid she vents "How dare you hit me! I am not the problem, you are. You failed me; I did not fail you. I looked for someone to protect me my entire life because my dad failed me. Looking for someone who wasn't and didn't care to be there for me made me a failure. You made me a failure."

Hindering security from escorting him out of the hospital Fannah stands in front of them exclaiming "No. No. You need to hear this" Pointing at Prince she goes on "You walk around wanting the world to think you are this great person. You come here to portray yourself as a great father. You are not!"

Interrupting her rant Prince prompts security to continue escorting him out of the hospital while waving toward Fannah. Jumping in between him and the security she screams "I am not done! You failed; you failed your daughter. Where were you when I actually needed you? Do you know what I've been through? Do you know I was raped?"

Pushing him she shouts "You quick to blame me for killing my boyfriend but I bet you did not know your daughter was raped, did you? If you really cared you would make sure I was ok, but instead you make me feel worse."

Security now holding her back she continues to yell "I would think you'd care and try to be my dad, but I shouldn't expect you to be something you've never been to me. You've always been nowhere to be found. So, continue to be that to me, be nowhere to be found. I don't care, because as of this day you are dead to me!"

Continuing to be led out by security Prince seems unfazed by Fan's comments. Instead his concentration turns toward DJ. Catching eye contact with him he gives a grimacing grin before bellowing "I gave you a choice. It must be in the blood because you, your dad and your brother keep making the same bad choices."

Chapter 43

Waiting at the hospital to see Kevon one last time before leaving, DJ silently lays in Chasity's lap. Startled he hears her phone ring from her pocket. Snapping both of them out of a daze he taps her on the leg and lets her know someone is trying to call.

Pulling the phone from her pocket she notices that it is Trail's phone number. Shocked she nervously sends the call to voicemail. Seconds later it rings again. Staring at the phone in a tranced state she doesn't answer. Seeing the angst in her eyes DJ raises from her lap and asks "What's wrong? Who is it?"

Speechless she doesn't answer and continues to look at her phone in shock as it continues to ring. Noticing that she has drifted into a stupor DJ takes the phone from her. Tapping the answer button, he begins to yell into the phone "Hello! Who is this?" hearing the dial tone he realizes he answered too late.

Handing the phone back to Chasity, DJ looks at her in concern and says "They hung up! Who was that?" Before she is able to respond Fannah's phone rings. Seemingly startled and frightened Chasity looks over and shrieks "Don't! It's Trail!"

Instantly petrified Fannah looks down at the phone, letting it ring without answering. She slowly looks up at Chasity and asks, "This is who has been calling your phone?" As Fan and Chasity stare at each other in fear DJ reaches over Chasity grabbing Fannah's phone answering "Hello!"

After a slight pause he responds, "Is this DJ?" Recognizing the voice, DJ replies "You got a lot of nerve calling here right now! You kill my brother, raped Fan, and then I find out you raped Chasity!"

His voice getting louder he shouts "Why the hell you calling their phones? Where you at?" Interrupting he interjects "Calm down man. I didn't call for no drama. I don't have long so just hear me out."

After a slight pause he goes on "I just want to apologize. I know why you pissed off. Just so you know I'm taking responsibility for my part in everything. I am here at the police station about to turn myself in but before I do, I want you all to know the truth about everything."

With his rage tempered DJ becomes attentive to what Trail has to say. Hearing in his tone that DJ is no longer yelling and shouting he asks "Is Fannah and Chasity there with you?" Hesitating he nonchalantly answers "They here."

Taking a deep breath, he asks "Can you put me on speaker phone? I want to talk to you all at the same time...And truss I'm not on no bull. I know what you all are going through, and I just want to get this off my chest. I ain't trying to hurt no one. Just hear me out."

Taking the phone from his ear DJ looks at Fannah and Chasity. Watching attentively, they both curiously stare back at him. Pointing toward the phone he quips "This dude has something he wants to tell all of us. Are you all ok with it?"

Shaking their heads in agreement DJ pushes the speaker phone button and retorts "You are on speaker phone. So, let's hear it."

Clearing his throat, Trail says "First off, I know I don't deserve forgiveness from any of you for the stuff I've done but I am going to apologize and ask for your forgiveness anyway. I'm going to start by letting you know that I was set up. Chasity remember when we were at that party back in the day?"

Not receiving a response, he goes on "Well Pickles told me you were in the room waiting for me and that you had gotten your drink on because that puts you in the mood. I believed him."

He raises his voice to speak over the noise as sirens go off in the background "Just like I believed him when he told me that YOU...Fan, wanted me and that's why you kept going out with me." Sinking in their chairs Fan and Chasity stare at one another in shock.

Hearing them gasp he pauses before continuing "Yeah, he also told me that you liked it rough and play hard to get. He told me you like when a man is aggressive. So, when you all pressed rape charges on me I didn't understand because that's what I was doing. I was being aggressive thinking that's what you wanted from your man."

Taking another pause, he goes on "I thought we were all cool. I mean you all kept hanging out with me and no one said anything to me about the situation after it happened, so I thought we were good. I thought we were just trying to keep it on the low."

Voices in the background interrupt Trail as he continues "Alright I don't have much time but, Pickles even told me that you liked to get juiced up so that you'd enjoy sex better. You know I was really into you. So, I was willing to try any and everything I needed to do to get you."

Stunned, Chasity, Fan and DJ all look at each other in amazement. Breaking the silence DJ quips "Dude! You know what rape is. Don't try to play that victim shyt here." Immediately responding "Ok, it's cool, blame me. I'm not saying I was right. I just want you to hear my side of the story."

Taking a deep breath, Trail proceeds "The dude I looked up to and taught me everything I know tried to kill me in the end. Prince put me and Pickles onto the G-Juice. I didn't even know he had a daughter. The dude taught us the game. Sometimes he even participated and watched us run game on other girls."

Sighing he goes on "I guess deep down he even knew himself what we was doing was foul. When he found out what happened to you Fannah, he tried to kill me. On top of that Prince and Pickles set me up. Pickles killed Bump, and Prince was the one who pulled the trigger and killed Kevon."

Interrupting DJ shouts "WAIT! Dude I saw you running from the scene when my brother got shot..." Before he can finish Trail interjects "I know, YES I was there when it happened, but I was coming to stop it."

His tone now softening he continues "I'm a hood dude and down for whatever but I don't just kill people just because. Prince has gotten out of control. He uses everyone and now I see how they used me to be the fall guy for everything."

Speechless they all continue to stare at one another in awe. Taking a pause, Trail continues "Pickles didn't want Kevon dead. He wasn't going to kill his best friend. We all just wanted to scare Kevon because he had gotten out of the game and we needed him."

After a pause he continues "Kevon didn't talk about it, but we all came up in the game together. Kevon was bout that action back in the day, but he started to fall back when you started getting older DJ"

Background noises get louder as Trail takes the phone from his mouth murmuring "I'm almost done." Placing the phone back to his mount he continues "It is almost time for me to go but Fannah he had really fallen for you. So that's why he cut the game off completely. He got out for you all."

His tone changes as he proceeds "Yeah I was jealous but none of us wanted him dead. That was all Prince. He felt like he knew too much, that he wasn't loyal to him anymore, and he wanted to prove a point."

Speaking up DJ jests "Wait, why you? If he was your big homey and you had his back why would Prince want you dead? Trail quickly responds "I HAD his back. I felt Prince had gotten too big, too powerful, and too reckless so I started plotting to take him down. I'll tell you, bad things happen when you go up against bad people with power and Prince is a bad man with lots of power."

Hearing a vague noise in the background seeming to say, "time up" Trail clamors "I'm going to have to go but before I do DJ Imma tell you, I saw what happened with Kevon. It happened by the Barber Shop, so you know how to find out if what I'm saying is true or not."

With haste in his voice Trail continues "Prince left me for dead and Pickles was supposed to finish me off. After finding out how they set me up and almost killed me, I just wanted to save Kevon. He was done with this life. He just wanted to help you."

Sighing into the phone he mutters "Obviously I got there too late to stop what they did. The things I did didn't work for me. I'll be doing time once I turn myself in but hopefully this helps you and gives you some closure. Before I go. Chasity, Fannah and DJ forgive me again and I wish you all the best."

Listening to the dial tone after Trail's call ends Chasity and Fan sit emotionless. Sitting up DJ places Fannah's phone on her lap and hastily makes his way toward the exit. Caught off guard by his sudden action Chasity runs behind him.

Catching up to him she pulls at his shirt asking "Where are you going? We have to see Kevon before they move him." Anxious he replies "Babe, I love you. I just need you to be there for Fan when she sees Kevon. Then you all go over to your apartment, lock the doors, and keep your phones with you. I have to call in a favor. I'll call you later ok?"

Confused Chasity remarks "Babe, I'm afraid. What is going on? We just lost Kevon and with everything that is going on I don't want to lose you too. Can you just please stay with me?"

Masking his fear with confidence DJ says "Chass, I told you I got you right? We've made it through our storm and nothing else will separate us. You have to trust me. Plus, you know how to keep track of me. Be strong for Fan and you all go to the apartment. I'll talk to you later."

Gently grabbing her face, he gives her a kiss on the lips and briskly jogs out of the hospital.

Chapter 44

Wiping tears from her eyes Chasity looks back at Fannah. Feeling bad she walks over to Fan and nudges her. Looking up with a blank stare Fannah murmurs "I am ok. I just want to go in and see him one last time." Wondering to herself if she will be strong enough to handle it, Chasity asks "Are you sure Fan? Do you think you will be ok?"

Staring at Chasity with a puzzled look Fan yells "So you and your boyfriend are all happy and alive, but it is a problem for me to go and see my dead boyfriend?" Confused by her outburst Chasity stands in shock as the emergency room door flings open.

The doctor walks out and approaches asking, "do you all want to come see Kevon before he is taken in for an autopsy?" Shaking their heads in agreement the doctor directs them to follow her.

Walking toward the emergency room Fannah stops Chasity. Tears forming in her eyes she cries "You don't want to come see him, and I don't want you to come! I will be fine." Turning back toward the doctor she requests they continue walking without Chasity.

Confused, shocked, and hurt Chasity walks toward the waiting room and takes a seat. She is torn between disobeying her friends request and going to be by her side despite her anger. She decides to walk toward the emergency room door when she is interrupted by a text from DJ.

After reading the text Chasity hastily begins to type into her phone when the emergency room doors burst open. Fannah runs out of the doors toward her with tears in her eyes. Once she reaches her, she tightly embraces her and begins to sob uncontrollably "I'm sorry! I'm sorry! You were right. I'm not ready."

Reciprocating the embrace, Chasity comforts her "It is ok, no matter what I am here Fan, I will be here for you. I know you are hurting. Let's go home."

Driving home they embark on silence. Antsy, Chasity picks up her phone and finishes answering the message she was typing earlier. Now looking over at Fannah, seeing her in disarray, she speeds up to get her home.

Arriving at their apartment Fannah looks over at Chasity and says "Thank You! You have been by my side through a lot and you didn't deserve that treatment in the hospital. I am just hurt, and I don't know what to do."

Turning the car off Chasity gets out and walks over to the passenger side and opens her door answering "C'mon Fan. You know you don't have to apologize. I love you girl. Let's go in so you can relax."

Once inside Fannah walks to her room and plops on her bed. Following her inside Chasity goes to the kitchen and makes two drinks. With the drinks in hand she walks over to Fannah's room and peeks inside.

Seeing Fan's face down on the pillow she tips toes inside and sits next to her on the bed. Attempting to get her attention she quips "Fannah! Get up girl, I got something to cheer you up."

Rolling over she looks up and sees Chasity swirling two shot glasses filled with alcohol. Raising up to grab one of the glasses she giggles "Sis you always think taking shots cures all the problems huh?"

As they share a laugh, Chasity responds "Maybe it isn't but it is always a start." Raising the glasses in the air they clank them together simultaneously yelling "salud" as they each drink the entire shot.

After a slight pause Chasity looks over to Fannah and bellows "I think some of this is my fault. Fan, I'm sorry I didn't tell you about Trail before now...I honestly didn't know who to tell or what to say or even how to react."

Huffing she goes on "I was afraid! I mean I never was raped before and didn't know anyone who had been. I was even wondering to myself if it was rape or was it my fault that it happened!?!"

With a puzzled look on her face Fannah begins to speak before being interrupted "I know, it sounds like this is coming from nowhere, but this has been on my mind for some time now. I just want to get it out."

After a slight sigh she goes on "I actually looked up to Trial and thought he was a good friend. I trusted him. I hung around him. I drank around him, and he made sure I was ok plenty of times...the same way he was treating you. That's why I kept trying to warn you because at that time I never thought he would do anything like that to me."

Dropping her head in sorrow she continues "I feel like I didn't do enough to stop him from hurting you. It happened to me and I feel had I did something about it none of this would have happened to you or even Kevon for that matter."

Voice starting to crack she whimpers "I was never the girl to flirt with guys or need attention before then. It ruined how I felt about myself. There was always this feeling that I'm not good enough. That I have to do more or be more to stand out. That day ruined my life and that awful feeling never goes away."

Turning back toward Fan she goes on "Maybe I was too afraid or ashamed to tell you what happened to me. Do remember all those times you got upset with me? You always thought I was always in your business. Or maybe you just thought that I was trying to get in your business to holla at a guy you were interested in?"

With a blank stare Fan doesn't respond as Chasity continues "I wish you had known then that I would have never done you like that. That was just my way of trying to protect you. Maybe it wasn't the right way, but it was all I knew how to do."

Beginning to sniffle she murmurs "I remember each time you looked at me like I was a thot or insinuated that I wanted your man because I flirt. I laughed on the outside and played along with it only because I wanted to be there for you."

Saddened Chasity sighs and continues "So I took it but each time it hurt me, and I cried on the inside. I was a virgin when I was raped by Trail. I never cared what others thought of me, but you knew me, so it hurt when you would make those comments."

Reaching over and grabbing Fan's hand she proceeds "We have been through so much together and I know you always have my back. Just knowing that you are like a sister to me I grinned and took the negative comments. I know you didn't mean any harm?"

Pulling away from Chasity, Fan takes a deep breath. Looking at her for moments with a sorrowfully expression she says "Prince wasn't there for me. He wasn't a father to me. He wasn't a dad. He was nothing. That's why I never said anything about him. That's why I said I didn't know who my dad was because I don't. He wasn't there for me and til this day, I truly feel he did something to my mom."

Choking up she goes on "There was no mom or dad for me when I was growing up. No dad to tell me I was his princess and that I was special. Nobody to tell me I was beautiful and didn't need a man to validate me."

Rocking on her bed she goes on "I just had my grandma. I didn't have a man around who would warn me not to accept disrespect from a man. I didn't have a dad there to protect me. It is no excuse, but I guess I did invite attention from guys. Even horrible guys like Trail."

In frustration Fan holds her head in her hands as she continues "I quickly learned most guys aren't men and only are out for one thing. But that didn't stop me from trying to fill the void. Maybe I was naïve and looking for love in all the wrong places."

Lifting her head from her hands in disappointment she goes on" Or maybe I didn't know what love was. Then Kevon came into my life. Things changed. He filled that void in my life. He showed me what love was."

A slight smile engulfing her face she continues "Me and Kevon had such a connection. It was something about him. I just knew he was the one. He gave me friendship, companionship, and everything in a man that I needed.

A slight grin comes across her face as she proceeds "He filled my wants, needs, desires and all I did in return was betray his trust. I continued to befriend Trail who was only using me. Maybe Prince is right to blame me..."

Wiping her face, she looks up and goes on "None of this is your fault, Chass. Please know that, but what about you? I thought we were close enough to where you knew you could talk to me about anything. You could have told me what happened to you. You have always been there for me. You should have let me be there for you."

Sighing heavily, she grabs Chasity's hand asserting "I apologize again for how I reacted at the hospital. I know you were just trying to be there for me." Sniffling she goes on "I guess I just felt guilty. Guilty because of what I did and the situation I caused."

Reaching out to comfort her Fan interrupts "Chass, it is ok. I do think me, and Kevon had some closure, but I just have to live with my actions. I believe in karma and this is mine. But you, you have been great to me and you have been there for DJ."

Grabbing her hand, she exults "This is how karma works. You do the right thing and good things happen to you. You should be happy because I am happy for you. You deserve it." Smiling she leans and they hug each other tightly.

Separating from their embrace their moods shift. Expressing concern, Fannah looks at Chasity and asks "What about DJ? We are here reminiscing and being here for each other, but he just lost his brother. How is he? Who is there for him?"

Concerned Chasity responds "I think he is ok. I talked to him earlier. I didn't want him to leave alone but he insisted. He said that it was something that he had to take care of. I love that man to death, and I do trust him. People are being killed and I am just afraid. I just want him to be safe and come back to me alive."

Chapter 45

Bouncing from side to side, passerbys watch the Cadillac Deville as it drops to three-wheel motion. Because it's dropped so low the rear of the car now scrapes the ground as it slowly pulls up to the corner and comes to a stop.

Laughing as he watches everyone stare at the spectacle, he just made Prince tells Kasyn whose standing at the corner, "Get in! Let's get in some traffic."

Reluctantly, Kasyn opens the door and enters his vehicle. In a seemingly great mood Prince continues to laugh while turning two switches on the dashboard of the car to the up position. The car is now in a 3-wheel motion. It begins to rock from side to side before finally coming to a high resting position on all four wheels.

After the switching motions are complete, there is a slight pause and the car is motionless. Suddenly, Prince slams down on the gas pedal making the wheels screech and instantly they take off.

As Prince weaves the car through traffic Kasyn warily asks "What's with all of the stunting lately? You are the one who always tell us to stay low key."

Continuing to laugh Prince responds "I'll tell you like this lil homey. Sometimes you have to live your best life! When you work hard there is a point when you need to look back on your accomplishments and allow yourself to reap the benefits of that hard work."

Noticing that Kasyn isn't sharing his enthusiasm he continues "Look at it like this, everything we have been planning all this time has all come together. I just left the hospital and Kevon is out of the way for good."

Making a slashing motion toward his neck he says "He is outta there. He paid for what you say he did to you and now you don't have anything or anyone standing in your way. You can now be this cities basketball superstar. That NBA next right? That is what you wanted right?"

Giving Kasyn a nudge, he goes on, "Plus Trail is gone to the upper room so you that guy in the streets right now. Now, I did have a talk with DJ. I gave him the layout but lil dude don't want to play by the rules. So, he is our only loose end." Giggling to himself "But the way you been handling up I know you gone get that situation taken care of."

Starting to become concerned with Kasyn's somber and dismissive mood, Prince's mood shifts. Slowing the vehicle down he leans back in his seat and asks, "So what's up Pickles?"

Looking in his direction he goes on "Something is on your mind. I mean I got the call on the police scanner about the break in at Trail's apartment. I called off the patrol to give you all the time you needed to take care of that." Curiously glancing over at him he goes on "you did take care of that right?"

Staring straightforward not making eye contact Kasyn nervously replies, "Trail is still alive." With his mood quickly spiraling downward he composes himself to ask "What do you mean still alive? I'm not understanding!"

Upset Prince shouts "He have all of the information that can ruin us. YOU AND ME...and you didn't make sure to get him taken care of? That was the second time you let him make it!"

Still staring forward, Kasyn responds "He wasn't at the apartment Prince" pausing he continues "Trail not stupid. Why would he be at his apartment? Dude running from two rape charges and you left him for dead. He knows people know where he lives so why would you send me to his spot thinking he would even be there anyway?"

Unable to control his rage Prince pulls the car over to the side of the road and yells "You disrespectful piece of shyt! So now you questioning my moves? Is that what you're doing?"

Veins popping from his forehead he yells "Matter fact why are you just now telling me this?" Not allowing him to answer he blurts "Why in the hell are you in this car and not looking for him? Huh! Talk!"

Before Kasyn is able to respond Prince continues "I'll tell you why! Because you are a dumb, envious, untrustworthy sack of shyt. You don't think I know what you have been doing?" Shaken by Prince's verbal attack Kasyn looks up with a puzzled look as fear begins to set in.

Grabbing his pistol from under his seat Prince lays it in his lap bellowing "The game in high school? The one you always laid the guilt on Kevon for? The one that almost destroyed everything! That was all you. You and Trail tried to screw me. You deserved what you got. And all this time you had the nerve to lay that guilt on Kevon."

Opening his console, he retrieves a gun magazine and inserts it into the pistol that is laying on his lap continuing "The Bump thing. You knew that was my guy. He was bringing in money. The word was sent to scare lil homey straight, but you take it upon yourself to kill him!"

Looking in Kasyn's direction with his hand now on his pistol Prince proceeds "To top it off you and Trail scheme to flip the games I set up. Then you try to put all the blame on Trail."

Prince points the pistol in Kasyn's direction saying "The funny part is you thought I didn't know about any of that did you? You thought after Trail got killed all your secrets were going to die with him?"

Calmed by his silence he goes on "You have got to be the dumbest person to ever walk this earth or the bravest son of a bitch I've ever met." Waving the gun, he goes on "Either way I'm sure you know you done messed up, don't you?"

While switching the safety to the off position on the gun Prince says "You thought killing Trail was your boss move? Now laughing he continues "You playing games and don't even know what game you playing."

His face turns red as he scoffs "This chess not checkers. I gave you a chance to be special but you not special. You just a pawn. You dudes out here jumping and crossing each other, you playing the wrong game."

Sucking his teeth while pointing the gun at Kasyn's head, he snaps "The hate, the envy, the jealousy, the backstabbing! You do it to yourself. I was going to let you think you had something going."

Shaking his head, Prince continues "You really thought you were getting over on me. See this wasn't supposed to end this soon, for you anyway." After a slight pause Prince smirks while looking into Kasyn's eyes and quips "Unfortunately you sped up your expiration date. Checkmate."

Chapter 46

With the gun pointed at his head Kasyn slowly turns toward Prince. Mustering a slight grin, he retorts "You think you know me. What is more important is that I know you. To be more specific I know the things you've done."

Turning to look down the barrel of the gun he continues "What that means to you is that you are in no position to issue any demands or threats."

Expecting fear, Prince is surprised by Kasyn's confidence. Pushing the gun into his forehead Prince counters "You obviously don't seem to understand who is in what position at this point."

With the gun still pointed at his head Kasyn calmly responds "Old man you are living in the technology age. Everything can be traced, recorded, and shared. You made all your bets and hits on your personal phone. Bump was afraid you were going to try to kill him for losing that game. So, he got smart and started recording and downloading your conversations."

Remaining calm with the barrel pointed at his head he goes on "Trail did the same thing. He got all of the information about the bets stored. That is why he started double crossing you because he knew he had something on you. He started making plans to take you down and be the boss himself."

Thinking to himself that he may need Kasyn to gather all information on him, Prince switches the lever of the gun back to the safety position. Hearing the gun lever switch Kasyn begins to relax.

Less nervous, Kasyn continues "Not to mention Kevon had been on game as you know but what you didn't know is that he put his little brother on game too. After that homecoming game when he saw you and Trail together, he started putting the pieces together."

Rehashing all his encounters with DJ, Prince begins to understand his position. Noticing the deep thought that Prince is in Kasyn goes on "Yeah! DJ also started recording phone conversations."

Still calm he jests "If you were paying attention you would have noticed each time he talked to you he never implicated himself. He stayed quiet and fed into your ego. After that you go gassed to admit everything you have done, are doing and plan on doing. He allowed you to indict yourself and he has it all stored."

Humored by his silence he confidently continues "Why would I finish Trail off when you would have been able to put that body on me? May as well leave him alive. Let him be a witness to your attempted murder when you left him for dead."

Looking him in the eyes he proceeds "Bump was a different story. He knew who I was, and he knew I was connected to you when you had me ride with you to that football game. Crazy part about that game is that set everything in motion."

With his tone rising he adds "Bump lost that game, plus he got into a fight with DJ. Anyway, other than that no one else who knew me, knew that I was connected with you. And this was the way YOU set it up."

A slight grin covers Kasyn's face as he proceeds "Everyone knew you had issues with Bump because he lost that game. I knew he was afraid for his life and was about to start talking. Which means him living would be a problem for me. He could connect me to everything we were doing."

Seeing the knot in Prince's throat Kasyn goes on "He was the only one who knew that I was connected to you. No witness, no case, with him dead. At least for me, but for you his death would point back to you and Trail, leaving my hands clean."

His grin now turns into a smile as Kasyn gloats "You talk about me not being about that murder game. Back then, you were the one without the heart. You had people do your dirty work. Bump was your cash cow and you just wanted him scared up a little bit."

With the gun still pointed at his head Kasyn's tone lowers as he asserts "The problem with it is you got greedy. Your greed blinded you. You didn't see all of the roads led back to you. You thought you were untouchable and made too many enemies in the process."

Taking a heavy breath his smile dimmers as he blurts "Kevon didn't have to die. You are right. I didn't have the heart to kill my best friend. All he wanted to do was look out for his brother. I did think the clout he was getting should have been mine. He owed me more credit than he gave me. He was a good person, a good friend, and a good brother."

Shrugging his shoulder, he mocks "Plus you right. We did set him up. So, I felt that we were even. He wasn't going to be a problem though. You just felt he had to go. It was also important that you came in to see it done yourself."

Breaking down, he pauses before shouting "YOU KILLED MY BEST FRIEND! He was just supposed to be scared up a little and that's it! But even in death he made a way to get back at you by putting his brother on game."

Lowering the gun Prince's mind begins to race. With the gun no longer at his head Kasyn looks up and brags "DJ has all the information that puts his brother's death solely on your shoulders. Not mine, not Trail's but yours."

Trying to catch eye contact Kasyn goes on "Trail is a street dude but he pretty smart too. After you gave him that barber shop, he made a rule. That barber shop was a safe zone. Nobody talked about or did any street business there."

Watching how that comment visibly made Prince nervous he jests "Trail made a point to not have any guns, drugs, betting, or anything like that go on at or around the barber shop. It was just supposed to be a place to get a cut, holla at some chicks, and kick it."

Not expecting a response, he continues "When was the last time you were at the shop? Maybe you don't remember the last time, but Trail installed top notch security. So, I'm sure someone can let you know when you were there last."

A smile spreads across Kasyn's face as he jokes "As a matter of fact, someone can tell you when the last time you were there, AND what you were doing when you were there."

Fed up with the conversation Prince taps the gun on the steering while yelling "You little shyt! You are not a boss. You think you got this figured out but whose got the gun? Did you forget who got the money? Who do you think runs this damn town?

Tapping his gun on the steering wheel again he goes on "I guess you just forgot all that huh? That's what I got and what do you have huh? Your little wonderland plots and schemes that won't mean a damn thing once you're 6 feet in the dirt!"

Remaining calm Kasyn interjects "So that's your plan? You think you are going to just kill me and this all goes away?" Pausing for a second he quips "What then? You screwed over everyone who had your back. Now you think all that money and power you have will make everyone take the fall for you?"

Watching him in thought Kasyn continues "And did you forget you picked me up in the middle of town. Everyone seen me get in your car. You are the last person I was seen with. If you kill me, how are you going to explain that?"

Continuing to tap the gun on the steering wheel Prince looks over to Kasyn and asks "So what do you want? Since you have all of this figured out what is your plan?"

While folding his arms a slight grin comes across Kasyn's face before quipping "About time you come to your senses." Giving him a menacing gaze, he continues "After putting a gun at my head, I hope you don't think my plan is to help you!"

After a pause he goes on "Give me the gun and we can talk." Looking at the gun and glancing back up at Kasyn, Prince unloads the magazine and hands the gun to him yelling "Here is the gun but you a damn fool if you think I'm about to give you this magazine."

With a look of desperation, he continues "I am not going to sit here and let you kill me in my own car. So here is the gun, now what is the plan?" Snatching the gun Kasyn responds "There are cameras at that barber shop that run 24/7. Trail has a security room that has the security monitoring device."

Noticing that Prince is confused Kasyn proceeds "The recording of you killing Kevon is downloaded on that device and the only way to get rid of it is to get that device and destroy it."

Slightly relieved Prince retorts "You talked like you was down with DJ. So, what are you getting out of helping me?" Shaking his head in amazement he counters "Do you not remember I was there with you that night? I didn't kill Kevon. However, you did give me the gun to get rid of after you killed him."

Without responding, Prince turns the keys on the ignition, cranks the car, and puts it in drive. As they drive toward the barbershop, Prince asks "Please tell me you got rid of the gun?"

Emotionless he snaps "You think I am just helping you just to help you? I wasn't about to run around with a burner with a body on it...I had to stash it and get the hell out of there. I wasn't expecting you to kill him right there, in the middle of the day."

Becoming anxious, Kasyn growls "We need to just hurry up and make it there so we can cop the evidence and destroy it. After that, DJ will be our only loose end."

Chapter 47

Pulling up to the barber shop, Kasyn blurts "that looks like DJ's car." Now transfixed on the car, Prince parks next to the car and glares through the windows checking to see if DJ is sitting inside. Canvasing the area as they sit in the car, they both exit the vehicle, circling DJ's car confirming he is not inside.

After confirming, DJ is not in the car, they look toward the barber shop. Smirking Kasyn scoffs "You know what this means." Shaking his head in disbelief, Prince replies "I guess DJ will have to get taken care of sooner than later now."

Turning toward Prince, Kasyn counters "You the one with magazine. You can pass it to me, or you can take the strap. Don't matter to me."

Shrugging his shoulders, Prince reaches his hand out for the gun. Looking down at the gun, Kasyn gives the gun to Prince. Satisfied, Prince inserts the magazine into the gun.

Looking down at the gun and then back toward the barber shop, Prince takes a big sigh. Stuffing the gun into the back of his pants he proceeds to walk toward the barber shop. Watching him walk toward the barber shop, Kasyn pauses for a moment before slowly trotting behind him.

Arriving at the door, Prince mutters "I think he's in here. The door is open." Twisting the doorknob, Prince pushes the door open and enters. Tipping through the main area they hear rumbling in the lounge.

Pointing, they both walk toward the lounge. As they turn the corner to enter the lounge, they see DJ. With DJ unaware of their presence, they advance toward him.

Seemingly in a hurry, DJ exits the lounge and bumps into Prince. Caught off guard, DJ steps back and begins to stare at them both. Shocked, DJ asks "What's up? What y'all trying to do?"

Giggling, Prince retorts "I told you last time I saw you what it was gone be when I see you again." Turning his attention to DJ's hands, Prince questions "What is that you have in your hands?" Grasping on it tighter, DJ doesn't respond.

Sliding his hands towards his back, Prince retrieves his gun. Pointing it toward DJ, Prince demands "I think we both know what that is."

Silence embarks the room as Prince continues "I'mma need you to hand that over NOW!" Receiving no reaction from DJ to his threat, Prince cocks the gun and yells "Now I'm not asking, I'm telling you to give me the damn system.

Without flinching, DJ continues to stare at Prince before slowly bending down and placing the system on the ground.

With it now out of his possession, Prince begins to walk toward him shouting "Move!"

Gesturing with the gun for him to back away from the system, Prince continues "How did you think this was going to play out, huh? You thought you was going to take this to the police and then what?" Pausing as he looks down at the system, Prince yells "Do you not know who I am yet?

Giving a devilish grin, Prince picks up the system, raising it in the air and smashing it to the ground. Unsatisfied, Prince picks it up for a second time and slams it harder which smashes it into pieces. Now satisfied with the destruction, Prince begins to stomp on the remaining pieces of the system as he clamors "What's your move now?"

While viewing the scene, Kasyn pulls gloves from his pockets and places them on his hands. Smirking toward DJ, Kasyn bellows "Prince I got something to clean up outside." Looking back toward Kasyn, Prince hesitates for a moment.

He suddenly realizes the throw away gun he used to kill Kevon is stashed outside. Gathering his thoughts, Prince responds "Yeah! Go ahead and handle that. I'll tie up the loose end here."

Watching Kasyn exit, DJ turns his attention to the shattered pieces laying on the ground. Rubbing his chin, DJ murmurs "So what is your plan? How are you going to explain my dead body laid next to some broken pieces of a security system?"

Unfazed by the gun and shattered security system, DJ states "Does that make sense to you? Why would anyone believe some killers broke into a barber shop, broke the security monitoring equipment, and then killed me? Ain't no money in here. You should know that. Where is the motive?"

Scratching his head with the gun, Prince replies "You know what. You are right! It makes no sense for your dead body to be found in the barbershop."

Pointing the gun toward DJ, Prince continues "But what would make sense is if you came back to the same place your brother was killed, with a gun, and felt so much guilt about him being killed that you took your own life in the very spot he died."

Motioning with the gun for DJ to walk outside, Prince goes on "Now who wouldn't believe that." With a deceitful smile, Prince mocks "As a matter of fact, I'm sure some would even feel sorry for you and understand why you committed suicide."

Exiting the barber shop they see Kasyn sweating and breathing heavily. Looking toward Prince, Kasyn pants "Let me finish this." Keeping his focus on DJ, Prince continues to point the gun in his direction. Waving the gun, Prince demands DJ to walk toward the area Kevon was killed.

Now looking over at Kasyn, Prince chides "What the hell wrong with you?" Walking toward him he responds "I had to take care of that situation. Now give me the strap so I can finish this one."

Turning toward Kasyn, Prince replies "Nah, you sloppy. Ain't nothing else to talk about, this is getting done." Pointing the gun toward DJ, Prince laughs "I guess this runs in the family. You, your brother and even your daddy. It ends the same."

As he begins to squeeze the trigger, Prince pauses. Taking his finger off the trigger he lowers the gun and looks back at Kasyn. Thinking there may be other cameras in the area, Prince decides to be cautious.

Figuring he will let Kasyn take the risk, Prince jests "Aight Pickles, you want it, you got it. This is your last chance to get it right." Handing the gun to him, Prince continues "Get it over with. You got just as much to lose as I do."

Taking the gun from Prince, Kasyn begins to walk toward DJ. Folding his arms Prince taunts "You trying to do it at close range and get blow back?" Agitated, Prince goes on "You don't know what you doing, just stop."

Walking after Kasyn, Prince gets louder yelling "Pickles! Enough of the games. Toss it back to me so I can finish this myself." As Kasyn gets closer to DJ, Prince becomes anxious.

Catching eye contact with DJ, Prince notices a smile engulf his face. Now nervous, Prince stops walking and becomes motionless. Making it to DJ, Prince witnesses Kasyn hand him the gun.

With a feeling of defeat, Prince snaps "What is this? Pickles you damn sell out. No way either of you make it out of this alive." Prince takes a step backward continuing "What do you all got? Nothing. No proof, no weapon, just the words of some loser wanna be street thugs."

Shaking hands, DJ pats Kasyn on the back as Pickles jogs away giggling to himself. After watching Kasyn jog off, DJ turns his attention back to Prince chuckling "I see no one has taken the time to update you on how technology works."

Seeing the confused look on Prince's face, DJ continues "All you did was break the monitoring system. Everything that was on it got uploaded to the cloud. My cloud." Now pointing the gun toward Prince, DJ continues "Remember the gun you killed my brother with? What makes you think it is gone?"

Continuing to walk backwards, Prince retorts "None of what you say matters. No one will believe a word you have to say. You are a game rigging, bribe taking, street thug." Waving good bye as he turns around, Prince mocks "You don't have the heart to pull the trigger, but I will see you again and next time I won't hesitate to send you to your brother and daddy."

Running to his car, Prince jumps in. Cranking it up, he begins to pull away. Without notice blue lights flash. Looking behind him, Prince notices a police car blocking him in.

Putting the car in park, Prince continues to look behind him and notices the officer. Relieved he gets out of his car laughing "I almost got jammed up. Glad you here." Not returning the laugh the officer says "Kevon was off limits. What were you thinking?"

Confused Prince responds "Kevon? Yeah, I heard what happened. Did you find the person responsible?" Walking closer to Prince, the officer angrily replies, "After all I did for you and this is what you do?"

Rejecting the accusations, Prince boldly interjects "Helped me? You better be thankful you still walking these streets. What you not gone do is sit in my face and accuse me of anything. You must have forgot who works for who."

Sarcastically shaking his head, the officer chuckles "You know what, you are making this easier than I planned." While walking toward the driver side of Princes vehicle, two additional police cars arrive.

The first police officer out of the car walks over and gives another officer a piece of paper. Stunned at the officer's dismissive reaction, Prince snarls "You have gone too far, I want a lawyer."

Giving the paper back to the officer he responds "officer can you walk this paper over to Prince and let him read it please?

The officer delivers the paper to Prince and watches as he reads it. He then asserts "You haven't been read your rights or put under arrest YET. What you are looking at is a search warrant. This gives us the right to search your vehicle. We have reason to believe the murder weapon that was used to kill Kevon is in this vehicle."

A big knot engulfs Princes' throat as he becomes speechless. He recalls Kasyn standing in front of the barber shop sweating. He rewinds when Kasyn said he was heading out to find the gun he used to kill Kevon. He also replays Kasyn and DJ shaking hands before Kasyn jogged away.

All these thoughts begin to weigh Prince down. He looks on as the officer opens his car door and reaches under the passenger seat seemingly assured of where to look. Ascending from the vehicle, the cop stands and raises his arm, holding a gun.

Dropping the gun into an evidence bag, the police officer looks toward Prince and mocks "This gun fits the description." Shaking his head in disappointment, the police officer continues "Well Prince, this is where you will be placed under arrest for the murder of Kevon. You will be read your rights and now you can make that call to your lawyer. You are going to need him."

Chapter 48

Concerned about DJ, Chasity peers out of her apartment window blinds. Suddenly she sees his car pull into the parking lot. Excited she bolts out of the apartment, meeting him before he can exit his vehicle. Without a word she jumps into his arms yelling "I love you. I love you. Thank God you are ok."

Returning her embrace a tear forms in his eye. Before separating, DJ wipes his eyes. Kissing him on the cheek Chasity notices the tear he is wiping away. Teasingly she whispers, "Is that a tear in your eye?"

Playfully poking her tummy, he jokes "Chill out. You know I don't cry." Pausing, he looks into her eyes continuing "thank you for being there for me. I had to send those texts in a hurry. The officer showed up and got the evidence. I am glad Fan was willing to help. It all worked out as planned."

Her mood turning gloomy Chasity asks, "What about Kasyn?" Hesitant, DJ looks up at her and replies "You know my brother once told me *'you can't be too clean! Being too clean can make you weak and sometimes you gotta get dirty to stay clean.'* When I heard it, I didn't know what the hell he was talking about."

Managing a slight smirk, DJ quips "Now I know what he meant. I was trying to do the right thing and be clean but that was not going to work. Doing the right thing made me weak and that's why they got me jammed up."

Seeing the confused reaction on her face, DJ asserts "Pickles thinks he got over, but I had to team up with him and get my hands dirty. I had to do that in order to take down Prince and stay clean."

Seeing the grin and look of comprehension on her face, DJ goes on "But trust me, I have a plan for Pickles. And I know with you on my side it will go as smooth as this plan did."

Smiling Chasity giggles "I told you I will always have your back and you know I'm a G." Smirking he jests "So you a G now huh?" Both laughing, DJ slowly grabs her hands and kisses them. Gazing at one another for a moment he leans in for a kiss. Not shying away, she returns the gesture.

Immersed into a passionate kiss they slowly separate and begin to feel guilty. Looking back toward the apartment DJ asks, "How is Fan?" Shrugging her shoulders, Chasity shakes her head in grief. Disappointed in her reaction, DJ goes on "I understand. Let's go and check on her."

Walking toward the apartment they engage in a warm embrace. Upon arrival, Chasity opens the door and allows DJ to enter as she follows him.

Locking the door after entering, DJ watches as Chasity walks into Fannah's room. Entering Fannah's room, Chasity find her curled on the bed. Seeking DJ's assistance to console her, Chasity peaks into the living room area where he is standing and gestures for him to come.

Hesitant, Demyre walks into the room and takes a seat next to Fannah. Chasity then jumps onto the bed and hugs her. Quietly sitting in the room, DJ breaks the silence "I know you really loved my brother."

Clearing his throat, Demyre continues "I know I am not in your shoes, but he is my brother, so I can relate to how hard it is to lose someone you love. And for you I'm sure it does not help to know that the person who killed the person you love was your dad."

Taking a deep breath, DJ continues "I know all of that is tough. I do want to thank you though. Thanks for contacting your grandmother and letting her know our situation. Chass sent her all the information and Prince will have to pay for everything."

In a somber tone, DJ goes on "I can't imagine the courage it took to do that. You volunteered to have your Grandmother indict her son. Fan, I had no clue how powerful your grandmother was and how many powerful people she knew. No one would have ever stood a chance against Prince without you or your grandmother."

Unresponsive to his comments, DJ continues "I know none of that makes up for the loss of Kevon. Maybe it even makes it worse. I just can't imagine what is going through your head right now Fan."

Hoping to cheer her up, DJ proceeds "Not to compare but if it makes you feel better, I lost everything. My scholarships were pulled. The friends I thought I had are all gone. I lost my brother, and because I worked with the cops to get my brother justice, I won't have any more respect in the hood."

Still embracing Fannah, Chasity gives him a puzzled look after listening to his comments. Choked up, Chasity remarks "What about me? You got me? Both of you have me."

Looking at them both, Chasity goes on "I didn't lose a brother or the love of my life, but I love you both. And when something hurts you all it hurts me too."

Shedding a tear, Chasity continues "DJ, Kevon was so happy you all made up. And Fan you know how happy he was with the love you all had for one another. He will be with us forever and he left happy."

Chocking up, Chasity goes on "We have to know he left happy. He left with love, He left respected and even though he didn't want it, Kevon had the power that others wanted. He still has it. He still has us, and we still have him.

Sinking into Chasity's arms after her remarks, Fannah begins to cry. Holding her close, Chasity says "Let it out. We are here for you." Continuing to cry they both console each other.

Laying in Chasity's arms for comfort, Fannah murmurs "I do love Kevon and you are right Chass. He left with love respect and power."

Pausing, Fannah continues to cry "He also left a baby." Shocked and not sure if they heard her correctly, Demyre and Chasity gaze at Fannah in astonishment. With tears rolling down her face, Fan squeezes Chasity and cries "I'M PREGNANT!"

ACKNOWLEDGMENTS

This book is dedicated to the memory of my first-born daughter, LaJasmine M. Jackson. My inspiration for life and my push in getting this novel complete.

I thank God for my other daughters, Simone Jackson, and Kendall Jackson. The loves of my life. You give every day of my life a purpose.

Thanking all my Marine Corps family, my IOTA Phi Theta family, my Jackson family and also my Pine Bluff, AR; Ardmore, OK and Plain Dealing, LA friends and family.

To Lucille, Markee, Sherdena, Drezavious, Dale Jr., Dezmond, Drenasha, Logan, Kasyn, Lulani, Ayden, Jasmir and Tara. Thanks for being my foundation and pushing me across the finish line. RIP Pops, Anderson BossMane Jackson.

Born in Pine Bluff, Arkansas, raised in Ardmore, Oklahoma and Plain Dealing, Louisiana. Nothing came easy. I was not afforded the opportunity to be raised in ideal living environments. However, I pushed forward to serve as a testament that no matter how meek your upbringings, your environment doesn't dictate your outcome. You can overcome your circumstances.

I push forward not for myself but because of my desire to help others strive to be better. Better than their surroundings, better than their environment and better than the low ceiling others may place on you.

SPECIAL THANKS TO

Rudi Hartono / Rudi_design: Cover Designer

Adil Khasanov / Munjarat / Instagram @munj_art: Logo Designer

Joe Simpson / Onvoyp, LLC: WebSite Designer

L. McGill / Leo Legacy Photography: Photographer

Simone Jackson: Audio Book Narrator

Dezmond J. Jackson: Book Cover Model

LaJasmine M. Jackson: Book Cover Model

Tee Marine: Social Media Consultant

T. Denae: Editing Assistant / Merchandising / Advertising:

A thank you to everyone who has assisted, advised, and supported me over the years in the completion of this project.

Made in the USA
Columbia, SC
11 September 2021

45194349R00198